MW01136678

STAY UP TO DATE

Join the conversation and get updates on new and upcoming releases in the Facebook group called "JN Chaney's Renegade Readers." This is a hotspot where readers come together and share their lives and interests, discuss the series, and speak directly to J.N. Chaney and his co-authors.

https://www.facebook.com/groups/jnchaneyreaders/

He also post updates, official art, and other awesome stuff on his website and you can also follow him on Instagram, Facebook, and Twitter.

For email updates about new releases, as well as exclusive promotions, visit his website and sign up for the VIP mailing list. Head there now to receive a free copy of *The Other Side of Nowhere*.

Stay Up To Date

https://www.jnchaney.com/the-messenger-subscribe

Enjoying the series? Help others discover *The Messenger* series by leaving a review on Amazon.

THE SILENT FLEET

BOOK 4 IN THE MESSENGER SERIES

J.N. CHANEY

TERRY MAGGERT

CONTENTS

THE MESSENGER UNIVERSE KEY TERMS

The Messenger: The chosen pilot of the Archetype.

Archetype: A massive weapon system designed for both space battle, close combat, and planetary defense. Humanoid in shape, the Archetype is controlled by a pilot and the Sentinel, an artificial intelligence designed to work with an organic humanoid nervous systems. The Archetype is equipped with offensive weaponry beyond anything known to current galactic standards, and has the ability to self-repair, travel in unSpace, and link with other weapons systems to fight in a combined arms operation.

Blobs: Amorphous alien race, famed for being traders. They manufacture nothing and are known as difficult employers.

Clan Shirna: A vicious, hierarchical tribe of reptilian beings whose territory is in and around the **Globe of Suns** and the **Pasture**. Clan Shirna is wired at the genetic level to defend and protect their territory. Originally under the control of Nathis, they are space-based, with a powerful navy and the collective will to fight to the last soldier if necessary.

Couriers: Independent starship pilots who deliver goods—legal, illegal, and everything in between—to customers. They find their jobs on a centralized posting system (See: **Needs Slate**) that is galaxy-wide, ranked by danger and pay, and constantly changing. Couriers supply their own craft, unless they're part of a Shipping Conglom. Couriers are often ex-military or a product of hard worlds.

Fade: A modification to the engine. It is a cutting edge shielding device that rotates through millions of subspace frequencies per second, rendering most scans ineffective. If the Fade is set to insertion, then the ship will translate into unSpace, where it can go faster than light. The Fade is rare, borderline illegal, and highly expensive. It works best on smaller masses, so Courier ships are optimal for installation of the Fade. One drawback is the echo left behind in regular space, an issue that other cloaking systems do not have. By using echoes as pathway markers, it is possible to track and destroy ships using the Fade.

Golden: A transhumanist race of beings who are attempting to scour the galaxy of intelligent life. The Golden were once engaged in warfare with the **Unseen**. They are said to return every 200,000 years to enact a cycle of galactic genocide, wiping out all technologically advanced civilizations before disappearing back from which they came. They destroyed their creators at some unknown point in the distant past and are remaking themselves with each revolution of their eternal, cyclical war.

Globe of Suns: A star cluster located in the far arm of the Milky Way Galaxy. It is an astronomical outlier. Dense with stars, it's a hotbed of Unseen tech, warfare, and Clan Shirna activity. Highly dangerous, both as an obstacle and combat area.

Kingsport: Located in the Dark Between, these are planetoid sized bases made of material that is resistant to detection, light-absorbing, and heavily armored. Oval in shape, the Kingsport is naval base and medical facility in one, intended as a deep space sleep/recovery facility for more than a thousand Unseen. The Kingsports maintain complete silence and do not communicate with other facilities, regardless of how dire the current military situation.

Lens: Unseen tech; a weapon capable of sending stars into premature collapse at considerable distance. The Lens is not unique—the Unseen left many of them behind in the Pasture, indicating that they were willing to destroy stars in their fight with the Golden.

Ribbon: Unseen tech that imparts a visual history of their engineering, left behind as a kind of beacon for spacefaring races.

Sentinel: A machine intelligence designed by the Unseen, the Sentinel is a specific intellect within the Archetype. It meshes with the human nervous system, indicating some anticipation of spaceborne humans on the part of the Unseen. Sentinel is both combat system and advisor, and it has the ability to impart historical data when necessary to the fight at hand.

Shadow Nebula: A massive nebula possibly resulting from simultaneous star explosions. The Shadow Nebula may be a lingering effect from the use of a Lens, but it is unknown at this time.

Unseen: An extinct and ancient race who were among the progenitors of all advanced technology in the Milky Way, and possibly beyond. In appearance, they were slender, canine, and bipedal, with the forward-facing eyes of a predator. Their history is long and murky, but their engineering skills are nothing short of godlike. They commanded gravity, materials, space, and the ability to use all of these sciences in tandem to hold the Golden at bay during the last great war. The Unseen knew about humans, although their plans for humanity have since been lost to time.

unSpace: Neither space nor an alternate reality, this is the mathematically generated location used to span massive distances between points in the galaxy. There are several ways to penetrate unSpace, but only two are known to humans.

Pasture: Unseen tech in the form of an artificial Oort Cloud; a comet field of enormous size and complexity. Held in place by Unseen engineering, the Pasture is a repository for hidden items left by the Unseen. The Pasture remains stable despite having thousands of objects, a feat which is a demonstration of Unseen technical skills. The Lens and Archetype are just two of the items left behind for the next chapter in galactic warfare.

Prelate: In Clan Shirna, the Prelate is both military commander and morale officer, imbued with religious authority over all events concerning defense of their holy territory.

1

THE *SLIPWING* WRENCHED through a hard-lateral acceleration, burning her fusion drive at full power, trying to shove herself out of the path of the oncoming missiles. Dash could only grit his teeth and wait, desperately hoping that the maneuver would be enough—that the *Slipwing's* acceleration could outpace that of the onrushing salvo.

But it wasn't going to work.

The missiles had no crews or sensitive components to protect; they were just drives, guidance packages and warheads, launched on a one-way trip. They could afford to accelerate much harder than their target could, pulling g's that would overwhelm any inertial dampening system. They easily slid inside the *Slipwing's* possible maneuver envelope.

At the last moment, there was a change of tactics. The *Slip-wing's* drive went dark and she spun, using thrusters only, to face the looming missile barrage. Her particle cannons opened up, blasting three of the projectiles to clouds of scrap, but she couldn't track, acquire, and change targets quickly enough. The remaining two missiles both slammed into her, detonating with terrific plasma explosions. Dash groaned as the searing energy ripped through her shields and left a smashed, glowing hulk. A second later, her own fusion containment failed, and the *Slipwing* momentarily outshone the distant star.

"Dammit," Amy snapped. "I was so *close*."

"Hate to say it, Amy, but no, you weren't," Dash replied. "You were dead the moment you tried to outburn those missiles. You should have turned into them and started shooting as soon as they came in range."

Dash drifted the Archetype back toward the very much intact *Slipwing*, the simulated missile attack replaying across the heads-up display. Amy had come a long way in her piloting, but she had a long way to go. Still, they had no choice. Someone had to be able to pilot the *Slipwing*, since Leira was soon to have her own version of the Archetype to fly, a smaller mech called the Swift. Custodian said the Forge only needed a few hundred more kilograms of Dark Metal to complete it, which was the main reason they were out here—testing a new device the Forge's AI had cooked up with Conover, that could more reliably detect Dark Metal at a distance. Dash figured it offered a good opportunity to get Amy some more flight time in the *Slipwing*. She clearly needed much, much more, especially if she was ever going to take the ship into combat.

"I thought I could outburn those missiles, though," Amy said.

"It worked last time, and these were the same types of missiles, right? At least, that's what the scans told me."

"I programmed more uncertainty into the scans," Dash replied. "To screw with you. You can't just go by the data. You have to be able to go by…let's call it the *feel* of the situation."

"The feel. Really."

"Yes, really."

"And what, exactly, is the *feel* supposed to be?"

Dash rolled the Archetype to face the *Slipwing* as they both drove through space. As he did, he tried to formulate a way of describing it—the *feel*. But it was tough to come up with anything. It was instinct. It was intuition. It was something that came from a pilot's gut. It included cues from hard data scrolling across the cockpit displays, sure. But it also included sounds and vibrations in the ship's structure, as well as known behaviors from enemy ships and missiles. Dash even used the natural world—gravity, celestial bodies, and the effects of their eternal dance—in configuring how he reacted to life in space.

But how to put that in words?

As the silence dragged on, Dash decided how to explain such a nebulous concept to Amy, but before he could, Leira piped up. She was aboard the *Slipwing*, but under firm orders to only observe, for later critique.

"Let me give it a try," she said. "Amy, remember back when you and I were working together, doing maintenance on a…I think it was a freighter, from the Algaran Collective. Its fusion drive was stuck at eighty-odd percent efficiency, and no one could figure out why."

"Yeah, I remember that," Amy replied.

Dash was intrigued. "What was the problem?"

"Oh, it turned out to be an issue with the way the system was drawing fuel from the deuterium tanks," Amy said. "Whoever fabricated them screwed up, making them all slightly skewed off the right geometry. The pumps couldn't draw the fuel out of them quite right, so they couldn't feed it to the engine properly."

"Exactly," Leira said. "And out of everyone who tried to work the problem—which included a couple of pretty experienced engineers—you were the only one to think of looking upstream of the engine, instead of just focusing on tweaking the engine itself. Why?"

"Uh…because it seemed obvious?"

"To you. Not to anyone else. Did you do a detailed fuel flow analysis? Use a bunch of analytical gear, run a pile of tests and simulations?"

Amy frowned. "No."

"Then what made you think the tanks were the wrong shape?" Leira asked.

"I just…figured that was probably the trouble."

"And there you go. That's the *feel*." Her smile was pure grudging admiration.

"Oh."

Dash made an impressed face toward the heads-up at Leira's terrific explanation, but before he could reinsert himself into the conversation, another voice cut him off.

"I get the sense that Leira did a good job of explaining the concept you were trying to communicate to Amy, by means of a related anecdote," Sentinel commented.

"Yeah, she did. Better than I would have, that's for sure."

"Unfortunately, such a personal anecdote is of little value to an outside observer, who might seek to understand what you mean by the *feel*," Sentinel went on.

Dash smiled. Sentinel had lately become keenly interested in things like intuition and instinct and, yes, the *feel* of things. The AI that ran the Archetype was supremely intelligent but, as Dash had come to learn, simply didn't have the means of treating problems as anything other than a set of data to be input, run through a series of calculations, then output as the optimum and most efficient actions. That was great for things like complicated navigational tasks or managing the stability of the many systems that were incorporated into the Archetype. But it also made her somewhat predictable, a trait shared by other AI's he'd encountered, such as Custodian, or the various constructs of the Golden.

But Sentinel wanted to learn. She'd made it clear to Dash that coming to understand how he came to do the things he did was important to her. He wanted to help her but, just as he'd balked at explaining the *feel* of things to Amy, he couldn't quite figure out how to communicate it to Sentinel, either.

"Well, you've got your own bunch of personal anecdotes with me," Dash said.

"True. However, despite attempting to connect them through unified threads of understanding and reasoning, they remain isolated, each unique. I can discern no problem-solving or decision-making process that is common to all of them."

"Are you saying I'm random?"

"I am saying you are unpredictable." Sentinel paused, then said, "Which, I must admit, can appear to be random to an observer."

"Yeah, but it's not random."

"You do it because of your *feel* for the situation."

"Exactly. It's all about…" Once more, he struggled for an explanation; once more, all he could come up with was trailing off into a lame, "…uh…the *feel*. Sorry, there's no better word."

"This conversation has returned to its beginning," Sentinel concluded.

"Yeah, I know. Okay, look. It's like this—"

"The detector's online," Conover said over the comm. "We're ready to launch it."

"All right, folks, practice time is over," Dash said, a little relieved he could take some time to think about how to respond to Sentinel—because she seemed genuinely interested, and genuine interest deserved a measured answer. "It's time to do what we came out here to do."

The Archetype and the *Slipwing* both cruised just a few million klicks away from the Forge, still well within the star system Dash had come to think of as Forgeville. The *Slipwing* would launch a missile, modified by having its warhead replaced with the experimental Dark Metal detector. Dash had already seeded a small piece of Dark Metal among some nearby asteroids so they could run a control test.

"So, as I understand it, you and Custodian have come up

with some way of using neutrinos to detect Dark Matter, right?" Leira said, letting the comm carry her voice to Dash.

"That's right," Conover replied. "A neutrino can pass through a million miles of lead without slowing down, so normal matter is basically transparent to them. Dark Metal, though, somehow stops neutrinos dead. So that's what our detector does. It looks for what are basically shadows in the neutrino field. Those shadows have to be Dark Metal…or, at least, something opaque to neutrinos, but Dark Metal seems to be the only thing we know about that is."

"So, since neutrinos pass through matter without interacting with it, how does your detector even, well, detect them, in the first place?" Amy asked.

"Ah, well, that's where Custodian came in. See, it turns out neutrinos do interact with things at the quantum level. It's those interactions we can detect. I can explain the math if you want."

"Okay, whoa there, Conover," Dash said, holding up a hand. "This could be a great discussion over some of Freya's plumato hooch back on the Forge. Right now, let's just fire this thing up and see if it works out here in the field."

"Right, of course. Any time you're ready, Leira."

"Missile away," Leira said.

Dash tracked the missile as it zipped away from the *Slipwing*. It immediately started along a corkscrewing spiral trajectory designed to let it scan as much of the starfield as possible. Conover had explained that the detector could only see a narrow angle of space at any one time, so figuring out a course that would let it scan through a full sphere, using only the fuel it could carry, had been a much bigger challenge than it had first appeared.

If this didn't work, they'd try an even lazier, lower-g course. They could even have the thing sit in place and rotate around, using the inertia of spinning flywheels, or else some weird Unseen tech. In any case, if they could get this detector working, they could use it to scan old battlefields or abandoned Golden outposts to quickly locate and recover scrap Dark Metal.

"Got a hit," Conover said. Dash had to smile at the smug satisfaction in his voice.

"That was quick," Dash replied. "Good work."

"Yeah—except the hit isn't from that piece of Dark Metal you seeded out here, Dash. It's coming from a moon orbiting that brown dwarf."

Dash narrowed his eyes at the detector's data that was being repeated on the Archetype's heads-up. "Huh. So it is. Sentinel, any ideas?"

"You did engage the Golden Harbinger in combat in the vicinity of the brown dwarf. Perhaps it is a remnant of that."

"It might also be something the Golden put there," Leira said. "Maybe something that's spying on us."

"That'd be a definite upside," Amy put in. "Gives us a way of detecting any sneaky crap the Golden try to pull on us."

"Only one way to find out," Dash replied. "Let's recover Conover's detector then go find out whatever the hell this is."

DASH CUT the power to the Archetype's drive and let it drift, the brown dwarf a wall blotting out half the starfield. Whatever had triggered Conover's detector was somewhere ahead, trailing a small moon only a few hundred kilometers across. Ironically, Conover's device was the only thing that could actually sense it; radiation from the brown dwarf, a gas giant so large it hovered on the edge of collapsing under its own gravitation and igniting as a star, simply washed all other signatures away.

"How far ahead of me now?" Dash asked.

"About a thousand klicks," Conover replied. "If you just keep closing on that moon, you should eventually see it."

Dash stared intently, his nerves on alert. They'd recovered the detector, then redeployed it in a higher orbit where it could keep the source of neutrinos in sight. It helped that the detector also saw the Archetype, its Dark Metal components casting their own, unique shadow. What he didn't like was that the *Slipwing* had to come in a lot closer than he wanted. They'd never anticipated taking this prototype Dark Metal detector into a situation that might be a threat—not on its inaugural run, anyway. So it used only a simple comm system to send its telemetry back to the *Slipwing*, and in the electromagnetic hurricane raging around the brown dwarf, that meant it had to stay close to the ship and the receiver apparatus Conover had rigged up for it.

"Leira, make sure you stay as far away from all this as you can."

"We will, promise. Oh, and I'm not flying. Amy is."

Dash opened his mouth, then closed it with an effort. He'd have much preferred Leira being at the controls, but this was, he had to admit, good practice for Amy—and Leira wasn't far away from the helm. "Okay, I'm going to close in. And if I yell for you to run?"

"We'll come flying in to join you as fast as we can," Amy said.

"What? No, wait. I don't want you—"

Amy's laughter cut him off. "I'm just screwing with you, Dash. I'm all in on this. No mistakes."

Dash exhaled, if slowly. They knew their stuff, which meant they knew the *Slipwing*—even with her drive and weapons upgraded by Amy and Custodian—was still no match for Golden tech. Taking a breath, he resumed closing on the target.

At two hundred klicks, he could see it: a small, black shape silhouetted against the deep, ruddy glow of the brown dwarf. At a hundred, the Archetype's scanners could finally resolve it through the soup of radiation and electromagnetic noise emanating from the wannabe star.

"That's a Golden missile," Dash said.

"That is correct," Sentinel replied. "It matches the configuration of missiles fired by the Harbinger when you were fighting it."

"Yeah, I remember, believe me." The Harbinger, a powerful mech sent by the Golden to attack the Forge, had fired a multitude of these things at him and the Archetype. They'd destroyed most of them, but they'd also taken a few hits.

There was only the missile before them left from that fight. It had either malfunctioned when the Harbinger fired it, or it had some more sinister reason for just lurking in orbit around the brown dwarf.

Either way, Dash kept himself poised, ready to instantly react, in case the missile came to life and attacked the Archetype, or the *Slipwing*, or did…anything else, really. Ideally, the thing was dead, and he could just recover it; it contained hundreds of kilograms of Dark Metal they could most definitely use as feedstock for the Forge.

If it was dead.

At twenty klicks, Dash stopped relative to the missile again, eyeing it warily. He could see and scan it clearly, which meant it could just as easily see and scan him. It just hung there, though, about five hundred klicks behind the brown dwarf's small, rocky moon. The moon itself was probably an asteroid captured by the wannabe star's prodigious gravitation; the missile was likely the same, powered down and effectively dead, caught in the gravity well the same way and now another, tiny moon of the brown dwarf.

"Okay," Dash said. "This is just *way* too easy."

"I am detecting no power signatures or other emissions from the missile," Sentinel said. "It does, indeed, appear to be dead."

"I know. Like I said, too easy."

"That is your sense of the feel of the situation?"

Despite his tense suspicion, Dash couldn't help smiling. "Yeah, it is, actually. Something about this just feels…off."

"Off?"

"Not right. Like, we're not getting the whole picture, here."

"You suspect a trap, in spite of the available data, which suggests this missile is entirely inoperative."

"Yup, I do."

"Interesting."

Dash thought about saying more, but a conversation about something possibly being a trap, while in close proximity to said something, seemed like a reckless distraction. Instead, he resumed closing on the missile.

He eased the Archetype to within five klicks of it. Sentinel had raised and boosted the big mech's protective shield, but even so, a detonation at this range could do serious damage. Still, he wanted to recover it, and its precious Dark Metal, so he needed to get closer still—literally close enough for the Archetype to reach out and grab it.

"Okay, we need to disable that thing's warhead," he said. "Any suggestions?"

"Unfortunately, even at this extremely close range, it is not possible to develop a firing solution that will ensure only one, particular part of the missile is affected. The Archetype's weapons were not designed with that degree of precise discrimination in mind."

"So, that's a no."

"That is correct. I would note, however, that destroying the missile will still allow you to reclaim at least some of the Dark Metal from the debris."

Dash thought back to long and tedious spells in the Archetype, doing nothing but tracking and recovering debris in the aftermath of battles with the Golden—a kilogram of Dark Metal here, a few hundred grams more there. It was a colossal time sink; they'd eventually decided it would be more efficient to just keep using the Archetype to harvest Dark Metal from the crashed Golden ship they'd found near Port Hannah, on the planet named Gulch. That took the Archetype away from the Forge for a few days at a time, though, and the Golden could return and attack the station at any moment. Speeding the whole process up to gather the Dark Metal feedstock the Forge needed was the reason Conover and Custodian had developed their new detector in the first place.

Time. There just wasn't enough of it.

"No," he finally said. "I want to grab this missile more or less intact, not turn it into a million little pieces of scrap flying in every direction. It should give us enough Dark Metal to pretty much finish off the Swift and get Leira deployed in it." He sighed. "So, let's just get this done."

He eased the Archetype toward the missile.

"Dash, are you sure you want to do this?" Leira asked.

"To answer that, I don't want to," he replied, his eyes locked on the heads-up. "But I'm going to, because it has to be done."

One klick.

"Sentinel, if that thing detonates now—?"

"Damage to the Archetype would likely be severe, but not catastrophic," Sentinel replied.

"Well, that's something, at least."

Hundreds of meters. A hundred.

Close enough to touch.

Still, the missile just hung there, a silent, ominous shape a few meters away.

"Messenger, I have a concern," Sentinel said.

Dash's stomach tied itself into an even tighter knot as he studied the missile. "Just one?"

"It strikes me that this could be a subterfuge on the part of the Golden," Sentinel went on. "Perhaps their intent is that, believing it to be entirely inert, we take this missile intact, hoping that we will take it aboard the Forge, whereupon it will detonate and do maximum damage."

Dash gave a quick nod. "That's possible, yeah." He glanced at the heads-up. The missile's systems were still showing as fully powered down. There were no emissions, and not even any heat being given off; the missile showed the same temperature as the surrounding space.

"However, the Golden would presumably know that we might suspect that, and would attempt to disarm the missile first," Sentinel said. "They could further reason that we would attempt to do so with a view to keeping it as intact as possible."

Dash pulled his gaze away from the missile, suddenly intrigued. "Go on."

"Therefore, the missile will continue to appear entirely inoperative. However, once we are engaged in disarming it, detonation will occur. This will set a precedent of doubt for all future stray Golden weapons, as well as causing injury or death to everyone investigating."

"What are you basing this on? Do you have any data saying this is what they're up to?"

"I do not. This is merely speculation. At best, it is an extrapolation from previous behavior we've seen the Golden exhibit—albeit, an admittedly tenuous one."

Despite the razor-edged tension, Dash couldn't help smiling. "So, you have a *feeling* this might be their nasty little plan?"

"I am not sure. It simply occurs to me as a potentially trouble-some possibility."

Dash's smile became an involuntary laugh. "Well, congratula-tions, Sentinel. Next to your occasional snarkiness, you've just done the most human thing I've seen from you yet—you've managed to start *worrying* about something."

"I am not sure this is desirable. There is an effectively infinite number of possible outcomes that are not based on available facts and data about any given situation. Considering them all would be an enormous waste of time and effort."

"So, don't consider them all. Just consider the ones that really stick out—like you just did."

"Stick out?"

Still chuckling, Dash shook his head. "You know, I'd be happy to help you explore this growing humanity of yours, but now isn't the time."

"I agree. Moreover, raising the possibility of this Golden subterfuge is not the same as finding a solution to it."

"Ah, but there you're wrong."

"What do you mean?"

"Well, if the Golden really are playing us, then we need to play them right back."

"How?"

"Like this," Dash said, suddenly reaching out and grabbing the missile with the Archetype's massive hands. Straining, he twisted it, until the forwardmost quarter of it containing the warhead ripped free. He flung that piece toward the nearby moon; at the same time, he decelerated the Archetype, hard, so it and the rest of the missile abruptly plunged toward the brown dwarf. Before he lost the warhead in the stew of radiation and emissions from the wannabe star, he targeted it with the dark-lance and blasted it to tiny fragments.

"That was unexpected," Sentinel said.

"And that was the point," Dash replied.

"Dash, you're falling toward that brown dwarf pretty fast," Leira said, worry tightening her voice. "Is everything okay?"

Gripping the remnant of the missile in both of the Archetype's hands, he accelerated, raising his orbit again. "Yup, we're fine. I was just teaching Sentinel a lesson about feelings."

"I see," she replied, in a way that said she really didn't. Dash just smiled as his stomach began unknotting itself.

"Let's talk about it back at the Forge," he said. "Custodian is going to want this Dark Metal—and, after holding a freakin' Golden missile in front of my face, I could use a glass or four of some of that plumato wine."

2

DASH SIPPED plumato wine from a flask and watched as Custodian sized up the remains of the missile he'd brought back to the Forge. Articulated robotic arms lifted and turned it, while sensor clusters scrutinized it closely.

"How can you stand to drink that stuff?" Viktor asked. "It's much too sweet."

"I like things that are sweet," he replied, though in truth the wine *was* a touch sweet.

Leira grabbed the flask from his hand. "You've had enough."

"I've had a sip," Dash said, then ran his tongue over his teeth. "Maybe two. Enough to realize we need to brew beer as well, anyway."

"But it's powerful stuff," Leira shot back. "What if the Golden attack right now while you're two sips into, well, I'm not going to say a buzz, but you know."

"First, I am not altered by two large, albeit sweet sips of wine. Second, I do some of my best fighting while I'm two sips in. I mean, barroom brawls happen in bars, right?"

"This isn't a barroom brawl, it's a battle to save all sentient life in the galactic arm, remember?"

"Yes, dear."

Leira stuck out her tongue at Dash, but Custodian cut in as they both dissolved into grins.

"If I may interrupt your charming but absolutely pointless dialogue, I can say with confidence that the Forge now has access to sufficient Dark Metal to complete the Swift."

"Perfect," Dash said. "How long until it's finished and ready to launch?"

Another set of articulated arms appeared from the multitude hanging above them, grabbing the missile and carrying it toward the central forge for disassembly and smelting into components for the new mech. "It will take several days to complete the Swift, then another day to power it up and run thorough tests."

"That gives you another few days to get to know your new friend—Tyler, or whatever he's called," Viktor said to Leira.

"Tybalt," Leira replied. "And—yesss."

Tybalt was the name assigned to the AI that would operate the Swift, analogous to Sentinel and Custodian. Tybalt had apparently been retrieved from data storage and activated, so he and Leira could start getting to know one another. They hadn't actually Melded, yet; that would happen once the Swift was completed and operational.

"You do not sound impressed, my lady," a new voice said, its tone stiff and formal. "I could take that as somewhat insulting."

"You take most things as being somewhat insulting, Tybalt," Leira replied. "And I've told you, I'm not *my lady*. I'm Leira. Just Leira. *My lady* makes me sound like some character in a play."

"As I have noted, it is a term of deepest respect for humans of your gender."

"From a thousand years ago, sure." She gave Dash an exasperated glance. "Did you have to go through this with Sentinel?"

Dash seized on Leira's distraction to snatch back the flask. "Nope. Sentinel never called me *my lady*, not even once."

Viktor actually chuckled at that, earning him a look from Leira. "Don't encourage him."

"I would point out that a formal title is appropriate for one chosen to pilot such a magnificent construct as the Swift," Tybalt said. "That is why your companion who pilots the Archetype is known as the Messenger."

"Even though I prefer Dash, though Messenger works," Dash said, swallowing plumato wine. He winced as he did. Viktor was right, actually; it got cloying after a while. He stoppered the flask and put it down. "Don't worry, you'll soon get used to being called *my lady*."

"I don't want to get used to it," Leira snapped back. "Look, Tybalt, here's my first order. I want you to call me Leira, got it?"

"I will accept that as a placeholder until we can agree on a title suitable for your status."

Leira looked at Dash. "Didn't I just say it was an order?"

"You don't really order these AI's around," Dash replied. "You have to treat them more like—partners."

"Partners. Great."

"Dash," a new voice cut in. "Do you have a moment?"

"Go ahead, Kai." Dash hadn't heard much from the monk who, along with his order, tended to work quietly away in the background of the Forge. They had a relatively deep under-standing of the language and culture of the Unseen, gained from two centuries of laborious study of the alien race's complex hidden beneath the city of Featherport, on the planet called Shylock. Even the knowledge Dash had gained through his Meld with the Archetype hadn't given him the degree of awareness of the Unseen possessed by Kai and his fellow monks.

That made the fact that they'd obtained it from nothing more than long, hard work all the more remarkable. It also made them perfect for teasing out whatever new information they could from the data archives of the Forge.

"We have prepared a summary of our findings so far regarding the Unseen," Kay said. "If you would care to join us in the third lounge, we'd be more than happy to present them to you."

"Sounds good," Dash replied. "Leira, how about you stay here and keep getting to know your new best friend. Viktor, care to join me?"

"Hey, I'd like to sit in on whatever new things Kai's learned about the Unseen, too," Leira said.

Dash opened his mouth, but Tybalt spoke up first. "You will have ample opportunity for that, my—rather, Leira. I will ensure that you are fully briefed regarding whatever you need to know. In the meantime, Custodian and I have developed a simulator for the Swift to allow you to begin getting accustomed to its employment. Worry not, I shall guide you through every aspect of the process and not leave your virtual side in the meantime."

Leira gave Dash a desperate look and mouthed, *Help me!* Dash just chuckled, put his arm around Viktor, and led him away. As he did, he said, in a deliberate stage whisper, "Let's leave these two alone for some quality time."

Dash could *feel* Leira's glare on the back of his neck like the heat of a fusion drive.

———

DASH STEPPED into the third lounge, so named because it was, quite literally, the third of the lounge facilities to which they'd been introduced by Custodian when they first toured the Forge. At least, it certainly seemed to be a lounge, with reasonably comfortable furniture and an expansive view of the nearby gas giant through deck-to-ceiling viewports. Whether the Unseen actually used it in a way they'd have recognized as lounge-like wasn't clear, but Dash did rather like the idea of the mysterious aliens sitting about the place, chatting away about the latest gossip and drinking their own version of plumato wine. At the very least, it humanized them in his mind, making them seem a little less distant and enigmatic.

"Kai, what have you got for us?" Dash asked, moving to a seat near the monk, Viktor sitting beside him.

Kai had been joined by two of his *brethren*, as he called the others of his Order of the Unseen. The fact his entire order consisted of eight people didn't seem to be an issue, nor did it seem to hold them back; despite their small size, the order had made huge strides filling gaps in their knowledge of the Unseen. So far, none of this new information had been especially profound. However, just as imagining the Unseen lounging around drinking and gossiping helped make them seem more real, and less ancient ghosts, these little bits and pieces the monks had gleaned about them gave them a nuance and texture that brought them a little more to life.

Kai offered a shrug. "We've discerned a number of new facts about the Unseen. Brother Cannus has been particularly focused on their social order and has some new insights to offer." He gestured at one of his companions, who smiled and activated a small holographic viewer. It showed a three-dimensional star map, depicting about half of the galactic arm.

"The Unseen appear to have developed a very egalitarian society," Cannus began. "With little distinction between those who were leaders, and those who were led…"

As Dash and Viktor listened, Cannus went on to describe various aspects of the Unseen social order—for instance, how leadership was determined by functional expertise, so that in a situation requiring detailed knowledge of astrogation, one Unseen well versed in the subject would be in charge; then, if things changed so that now it was, say, a good understanding of planetary evolution that was needed, another suitable Unseen would step up as the leader.

Dash found it all very interesting—particularly since it suggested that the Unseen either had virtually no egos or were somehow able to simply put them aside in favor of whatever most benefited the group. By the time Cannus was done, it struck Dash that while it would all probably fascinate a whole generation of xeno-cultural researchers, it didn't seem to offer anything to obviously assist in their fight against the Golden.

It was a good theory, and great history, but they needed an edge.

Viktor seemed to be thinking the same thing. "This is all very interesting, but to be frank, I'm not sure how we can use this information in any substantive way." He gave an apologetic shrug. "That's not to belittle the work you've put into this, but…"

"But how does this help us now?" Dash finished.

"It doesn't," Kai replied flatly.

Dash blinked at that. "Oh. Okay then."

"What's the point of it?" Kai said, then shook his head. "There is none—or, rather, none that's of any obvious, immediate use. I don't think the effort was wasted, by any means—"

"No, of course not," Dash said, giving Cannus the most encouraging smile he could. "We're definitely not saying that."

"However, we recognize that such abstract information as this is probably better left to study after the Enemy of All Life has been defeated and we have the luxury of such academic pursuits," Kai said. "And that, Dash, brings me to the point we really wished to discuss with you."

"And what would that be?"

"I have spoken at length to Custodian, and we agree that,

while the resources of the Forge are formidable, they are not limitless."

"It would be more correct to say that we do not know what the limits to those information resources are," Custodian said, speaking up. "It is possible that large stores of information remain inaccessible."

"Which means that we need to keep doing whatever we need to do to power this station up," Viktor said. "If we can get it working at a hundred percent, then we should have access to everything, right?"

"That is true," Custodian replied. "However, we do not know what *everything* includes. It may be a complete and comprehensive suite of knowledge about the Creators and everything they knew."

"Or it may not," Kai said. "We literally don't know what we don't know."

Dash nodded. Despite the lingering taste of the plumato wine, he got what they were saying. The Forge might hold everything they needed—or it might not. But it wouldn't be possible to know until they'd got it fully operational, by which time it might be too late to fill in crucial gaps. The maddening penchant for the Unseen to compartmentalize the crap out of their information raised its ugly head yet again. Dash glanced around the lounge, wishing he had one of the Unseen here right now, at whom he could shout, "Just open the gates. Stop it with the enigmas and half answers and hidden tech and give us what we need to defeat these Golden bastards."

Dash winced, realizing he'd actually balled up his fists in frustration. He made himself relax before Kai thought it was about him and his monks, and said, "So what are you suggesting, Kai?"

"One of the things we learned about the Unseen from the archived data back on Shylock was that they maintained a redundant information store. We didn't learn that until just a year or so before you arrived, so we'd been making plans to investigate it, but never actually did."

"From the description Kai has given of this facility, it would appear to be a major node in the Creator's information network," Custodian said. "It likely houses a substantial store of data, which you could almost certainly access more quickly than the time it will probably take to finish powering up the Forge."

"Where is this facility?" Viktor asked.

"On a planet called Orsino, orbiting a much larger companion planet called Brahe." Kai tapped at the little holo-projector, highlighting a particular star system. "If the information we need is anywhere, Dash, it's there."

Dash leaned back in the chair. "Okay, then. I'm sold. Kai, you'd better pack your bags, because it looks like we're going on a little trip."

3

LEIRA'S ATTENTION snapped back to the Swift's heads-up as a warning chimed, announcing another missile launch from the Golden ship. She immediately flung herself hard to one side, smiling as the mech's powerful drive smoothly accelerated them in response to her body's movements. It was, she thought, less like the barroom brawl analogy Dash liked to use to describe fighting aboard the mech, and more like dancing.

Not that she'd ever been much of a dancer. Opportunities to hit the dance floor just didn't come up very often when you were a courier jammed into some creaky little ship and trying desperately to stay ahead of your schedule. This, however, was nothing like that. There was no lag as a balky engine powered up in response to a hasty control input, no thrum of vibration, no teeth-rattling harmonics from a stressed-out fusion core. There was just movement. Leira moved, and the Swift moved with her —fluid, dynamic, powerful. Seamless.

She watched the missiles racing in, tracking their progress as they conformed their trajectories to match, and then intersect her path and position. She noticed a growing spread between the trio of missiles now streaking toward her; they were attempting to hem her in, arranging themselves so that no matter which way she tried to dodge, she'd inevitably have to face a hit from at least one of them.

The Golden missiles learned fast. Her smile fading, Leira eased off her hard-lateral acceleration, selected one of the missiles, and deliberately arced her way toward it. Sure enough, the other missiles changed their courses slightly, just in case she tried some hard, last-second maneuver like she had last time.

I know they're going to try to trap me. And they know that I know that. But I know that they know that I know that.

Time stretched as the missiles continued their unerring flight, and Leira felt her breath catch as combat unfolded with her in the center.

Holy crap, she thought. That might be one of the worst things about tangling with these Golden weapons. Unlike the conventional missiles she'd had to face as a courier, which had rudimentary AI at best, each of the Golden projectiles might as well have its own pilot on board—a pilot who was at least as smart as her, or perhaps even smarter.

She drove on, directly toward the oncoming missile she'd chosen to confront. The others now angled again, converging on her; as soon as they became a threat she wasn't comfortable having to confront, she threw herself to one side again as hard as she could. All of the missiles accelerated to compensate, just like she knew they would.

...I know that they know that I know...

Seconds from closure, she flung herself back toward her original course, guaranteeing that, at these velocities, one missile would score a direct hit, while the other two would miss by a gaping margin.

Perfect.

She prepped to fire the dark-lance, destroy the most immediately threatening missile, then swing hard about and try to pick off the other two before they could reverse course, and she'd have lots of time to do that—

Fire the dark-lance.

The Swift's arms and hands and fingers flexed as she reached for the firing controls.

Except there weren't any.

Shit.

The dark-lance, she *had* to fire the dark-lance—

Too late.

The missile slammed into the Swift and detonated. The heads-up immediately faded, the starfield beyond it vanishing.

Leira ripped off the VR headset and threw it aside. "Damn it!"

"All of your actions were adequate," Tybalt said. "Until, of course, they were not."

Leira stalked across the compartment she'd been using as a makeshift VR; the space suited her as a place to train with

Tybalt. She'd removed everything except a table, which held some nutrient bars and two flasks—one of water, and one of Freya's plumato wine. The latter was intended as a sort of celebratory treat for herself for when she finally mastered the control of the Swift. Although mastered had become a bar seemingly far higher than she could reach. She was aiming for competence and hoping for more.

And she still hadn't touched the wine.

"Leira," Tybalt said. "I assume you are frustrated—"

"Damn right I am," she snapped, pouring water. "I keep doing that, reaching for physical controls that aren't there."

"That is because it is unnecessary—"

"I know that."

"Then do not do it."

She took a sip of water. As soon as it hit her tongue, she realized just how parched she was and gulped down half of it. Dash had told her flying a mech could be quite a workout, and her desiccated mouth and dripping sweat confirmed it was. But that wasn't the problem.

"Look, this is overwhelming. It's every sense, all at once.

"It seems that way because every one of your human senses is being challenged. This is not a punitive event, Leira. It is necessary."

"You make it sound so…so simple," she said. "Doesn't seem like Dash had this much trouble when he started flying the Archetype."

"Ah, yes. Ego. Sentinel and Custodian have been clear that it is an unfortunate attribute of organic species in general, and your species in particular."

She paused with the glass just short of her lips, then lowered it again. "What do you mean?"

"Your ego is your sense of self-worth or self-esteem."

"Yes."

"Essentially, it is the value you place upon yourself."

"I know what ego is," she said, eyes narrowed. "And that's not the issue. It's my performance."

"You are evaluating yourself in the context of another individual's achievements. In this case, the Messenger."

"I am not." Leira stopped and frowned. "Am I?"

"Yes, you are, which is strange and inefficient. Your performance with respect to the Messenger is not an issue. Your performance with respect to the Golden, however—"

"Yeah, yeah, I get it." She sighed, crossed her arms, and glanced up at the ceiling. "Am I going to have you inside my head from now on? Because of this Meld thing?"

The prospect of the snooty AI—because the word *snooty* absolutely nailed Tybalt's stiff and always slightly disapproving behavior —being co-resident in her own mind made Leira decidedly uncomfortable. When the searing pain of the "interface" had faded and she had the tech required to allow her to Meld with the Swift and Tybalt implanted, she'd been intrigued, even a little excited. Now, though, it seemed she'd need to share her headspace with the AI, at least to an extent. The fact that he was something of an asshole hadn't occurred to her as a pitfall. Sentinel sure didn't seem as…well, snooty.

"Which is because Sentinel was created for the express purpose of waiting to Meld with the Messenger and, therefore, had to be somewhat generic in terms of her personality," Tybalt said. "I, on the other hand, am more distinctly tailored to accommodate your particular way of thinking."

"Okay," Leira said. "First of all, I get the whole Meld thing when it comes to piloting the Swift, or understanding Unseen or Golden tech and history and such things. But I'm really not comfortable with you being able to just…I don't know, read my mind any time you want."

"Leira, I—"

"And second, what do you mean you're tailored to my way of thinking?" she went on, deliberately cutting Tybalt off. "What's that supposed to mean? What, exactly, is my way of thinking?"

"To clarify," Tybalt said, "I am not truly capable of knowing all of your thoughts—even if I was inclined to know them, which I am not. Frankly, the majority of your thought processes are irrational, to the point of being bizarre."

"Hey!"

"For instance, your preoccupation with the mechanical aspects of your species' reproduction is especially puzzling."

"Okay, whoa! Stop right there! I am not preoccupied with— ah, *that*."

"Every time you observe one of the males of your species, a portion of your mind evaluates them according to a variety of criteria, including age, physical characteristics, bodily odors—"

"Stop…right there." Leira put her hands on her hips, then

adjusted them, and then crossed and uncrossed her arms. Twice. "I do not do that."

"But you do. Of course, upon further consideration, it does seem that most of those thought processes are performed by your brain in an autonomous, subconscious manner." After a pause, Tybalt went on, "You are not even actually aware of them. Instead, they appear to happen automatically, as the basis of a biological imperative. Interesting." There was another pause. "I am curious then—of all of the male humans present on the Forge, with which one, or ones, would you most consciously like to engage in the act of reproduction?"

"You have got to be kidding me. Do you really expect me to answer that?"

"Of course. Why would you not? It would be interesting to compare your conscious and unconscious thought patterns regarding the matter."

"Look, Tybalt, there is no way…"

Her voice trailed off. Damn it, the AI had her intrigued now.

"What the hell am I *thinking*?" she muttered, shaking her head. "No. We are not going to discuss this, Tybalt. My concern is keeping you out of my thoughts in the *unlikely* event some random flash of, ah, biological memory flares up in my mind. Nothing more."

"You may choose to suspend the Meld whenever you wish."

"I—oh. Wait. Really?"

"Yes, really."

"How?"

"In the same way you would interact with the Swift—

including firing its weapons, a fact that still seems to elude you. You simply have to will that it be so."

"Will that it be so?"

"Indeed."

Leira tried to envision kicking Tybalt out of her mind. She got a nasty little thrill out of it but immediately wondered if it had worked, or if he could still read her mind, which made her wonder if she'd just invited him back in.

"Perhaps, Leira, we can agree that you will verbalize your desire to suspend the Meld, and that it will remain suspended until you verbalize your desire to restore it again," Tybalt said. "That will have to suffice until you have developed the mental discipline to do it the correct way."

"I finished school years ago," Leira said. "But this feels like I'm right back there, being lectured." She sighed. "Okay. Fine. Let's suspend the Meld. Get out of my head, Tybalt."

Silence.

"Are you still there?" she asked.

"I am. However, I can now only communicate with you by audible means, like this."

Leira narrowed her eyes at the ceiling. She pretty much had to take the AI at his word, didn't she?

What a huge, arrogant, condescending ass Tybalt was.

Her eyes flicked back up at the ceiling again, waiting for a reply.

"I realize that you are probably thinking all sorts of dire things about me," the AI said. "However, I am not currently capable of interacting with those thoughts."

Leira sighed again. "Fine." She walked over and retrieved the VR set from where she'd thrown it, but she hesitated before putting it back on her head.

"Tybalt, you said that you had been tailored to my thought processes. What does that mean, exactly?"

"Custodian and Sentinel analyzed your words and deeds as they have experienced them and then determined the personality to give me that was best suited to interacting with you."

"So they think I work best with a smug, full-of-himself know-it-all?"

As soon as she voiced it, she realized that she had, in a way, just described Dash—hadn't she?

"My personality is designed to challenge you, to provoke you into following productive lines of thought, and to point out shortcomings and deficiencies in your intent. Would you really rather I just accede to your every whim?"

Leira opened her mouth, meaning to say, Yeah, kind of. But she didn't, because Tybalt was actually right. She didn't need an AI for that—at least, not one more complicated than the simple virtual assistants that took care of basic ship functions for the *Slipwing*.

She put the VR set on. "Okay, Tybalt, you can come back into my mind. Now, let's try this simulation again."

As the cockpit of the Swift popped into existence around her, it struck Leira that having Tybalt looking over her shoulder, ready to assist her as another Golden attack on the Forge materialized, wasn't entirely terrible.

LEIRA PUT the VR set down on the table, grabbed the flask containing the plumato wine, and poured herself a glass.

"I earned this," she said, licking her lips.

"You are rewarding yourself for a performance that was, at best, adequate?"

She sniffed, said, "Damned right I am," and took a swig.

The door slid open, admitting Dash, Viktor, and Kai.

"Hey, Leira," Dash said. "How goes the sim training?"

"There," Tybalt said. "You are currently experiencing the unconscious evaluation I described, with particular emphasis, I might add, on the Messenger's—"

"Get out of my head, Tybalt!"

Dash gave her a puzzled look. "What was that all about?"

"Oh. Tybalt noticed that I tend to evaluate everyone when I see them…you know, critically. Because I'm too…critical. Judgmental. That sort of thing."

As she spoke, Leira felt herself turning a shade redder. She braced herself for the AI to go on speaking, and was ready to cut him off again if he did, before he said something truly embarrassing. But Tybalt held his virtual tongue.

"I see," Dash said. He paused a moment, then shrugged. "Anyway, I just wanted to let you know that we're leaving the Forge for a while. Kai has a line on an Unseen data repository that might give us a whole lot of answers to stuff well before we might manage to unlock it all here, on the Forge."

"Okay, but the Swift isn't ready yet," Leira said. "Custodian said it would be another couple of days before it's ready to fly."

"I know."

She put down the plumato wine and picked up the last nutrient bar. She'd eaten the others, satisfying the ravenous hunger that seemed to come from the vigorous, full-body work-outs flying the Swift seemed to require. "Well, it'll be nice to have one last crack at flying the *Slipwing*."

"Yeah, about that," Dash said. "You're not coming this time. You need to stay here and keep working with Tybalt, get yourself as ready to pilot the Swift as you can."

Leira had the bar unwrapped, but she lowered it without taking a bite. "What? Who's going to fly the *Slipwing* then?"

"Amy will."

"Dash, she's not ready."

"And she never will be if we keep letting you fly her, Leira. Just like you won't be ready to fly the Swift."

"But—"

"Dash is right, Leira," Viktor said. "We need to start thinking bigger picture. Your place is here, looking after the Forge and working with Tybalt."

"I understand your desire to get to grips with the Enemy of All Life, and I applaud it," Kai said. "But this really is the best course of action."

Leira snapped out a frustrated growl and bit into the nutrient bar. "This sucks," she said through a mouthful of what tasted like sweetened wax—not exactly a treat, but for some reason, she really liked the damned things. "I feel like I'm being sidelined."

"Hardly sidelined, Leira," Viktor said. "More like your role has changed. We need you ready to pilot the Swift."

She chomped into the nutrient bar. "M'guess."

"That said, if you continue consuming nutrient bars at the current rate, it will be necessary to revise the configuration of the cradle interface aboard the Swift to accommodate your revised girth," Tybalt added.

Leira gaped at the ceiling. "Did you just call me fat?"

"No, I am saying that you will potentially become so, given your intake of calories."

"Custodian, I have a question," Leira said, swallowing.

"Proceed," Custodian replied.

"Can you melt Tybalt back into slag and start over? I don't like this model."

"Tybalt seems to be functioning normally. That would, therefore, be a wasteful use of the resources of the Forge."

She turned her glare on Dash. "How come you don't have to put up with this sort of crap from Sentinel?"

Dash, who was clearly trying very hard not to laugh, shrugged. "Sentinel and I have an understanding."

"We do?" Sentinel asked. "And what is the nature of this understanding we have?"

"That I'm the boss."

"Ah."

"Ah? That's it?"

Leira smirked. "Maybe you don't have quite the understanding you thought you did."

"Yeah, well, at least Sentinel and I don't seem to need couples counseling the way you and Tybalt do."

Leira shrugged but somehow suddenly felt protective of her AI, no matter how snooty he might be. "It's just early days. We'll get along just fine."

"At least Sentinel doesn't think I'm, ahh...thick." Dash held his hands up, grinning.

Leira put her hands on her hips, but Viktor interposed himself. "Before we find you two taking this outside and settling it like mechs, how about we sort out the details of our trip to Orsino, and that Unseen data archive, hmm?"

"Close call. It's unseemly for us to fight like—well, like the couriers we are," Dash said, laughing.

"Agreed. Wouldn't want to sully our image," Leira said, but she gave Dash the stink eye just for good measure.

Viktor rolled his eyes at Kai. "Maybe we should just leave them both behind and let the *grown ups*"—he shot both Dash and Leira a bemused glare— "get the job done."

Kai grinned. "Indeed. Perhaps we should just lock them both in this room and not let them out until they make up."

"We're at peace, gentlemen," Leira said, looking at the half-eaten nutrient bar. Sighing, she wrapped it back up and tossed it on the table.

As they left to find the others and start working out the details of their upcoming trip, Dash leaned close to Leira. "By the way, what was Tybalt talking about when he mentioned your unconscious evaluation? With particular emphasis on my...what, exactly?"

Leira smiled sweetly back at him. "Your ego. Apparently, it's the biggest part of you—by far."

4

As soon as the Archetype dropped out of unSpace, Dash scanned the system ahead. He immediately located the obvious binary planets of Orsino and Brahe, along with another dozen or so rocky bodies, all much smaller. Strangely, he found only one gas giant—a dim, cold world far from the star, on the very edge of the system. Conversely, starward of the binary pair, a massive asteroid field whirled around the star, a chaotic swirl of rocks that would render navigation through the innermost part of the system almost impossible.

What he *didn't* see was any evidence of Golden activity. That didn't mean there was none, of course, but at least there weren't flotillas of ships or drones, or threats like the Harbinger, the mech that attacked the Forge. But the Archetype did sense Dark Metal on the moon, Orsino, and somewhere else. Now that *was* odd. Dark Metal signatures were generally pretty specific once the stuff had been detected. This particular return shimmered and wobbled across the heads-up like Dark Metal that just couldn't decide where it wanted to be. It skittered across only a few degrees of view, but that still represented a volume of space big enough to hold millions, maybe tens of millions of ships, but with no two ever being in visual distance of one another.

With a flicker on the heads-up, another ship fell out of unSpace. It was the *Slipwing*, right on time. They'd agreed that, when approaching a new system, the Archetype would lead and reconnoitre, raising the alarm if the system wasn't safe. Absent any such alarm, the *Slipwing* would follow, but stay in the netherworld sandwiched between real space and unSpace using the system called the Fade. No one had balked at the caution, though. If they were going to land in a pile of crap, better for the Archetype to lead the way.

"Okay, guys," Dash said. "I'm still reading nothing except some Dark Metal on Orsino, and some more somewhere else in the system. Can't seem to resolve the second one very well. Conover, what's your spiffy new Dark Metal-o-tron getting?"

Conover's sensor array was good—and might even be a little better at resolving Dark Metal at short ranges than the Archetype was. At this distance, though, Dash could imagine Conover just shaking his head.

"Pretty much the same. Which is weird. This second signature"—Conover paused as he studied and tweaked his detector—"isn't behaving right. It's like something containing Dark Metal is constantly jumping around the inner system."

"Yeah, among all those rocks close into the star," Dash said.

"Well, let's keep a close eye on that and head in-system. Amy, stay well behind me, in case whatever Conover's weird signal is turns out to be something nasty."

"Got it, Dash!" Amy replied, the enthusiasm in her voice making Dash smile. The novelty of flying the *Slipwing* had worn off Dash long ago, but Amy's delight around piloting her was undiminished. He assumed it would eventually fade—probably. When it came to Amy, everything seemed fun and exciting, always.

What a way to view the world, with such unjaded glee. Dash found it easier to understand an ancient and bitter alien war than Amy's constant grin.

The Archetype leading the way, they started in-system, Orsino dead ahead.

"There are power emissions down there," Conover said, as the Archetype and the *Slipwing* slid into orbit around Orsino. "Solid returns, too. Something's pretty active on the surface, all in one small area."

"Yeah, I see that," Dash said. "Now, let me guess—they're coming from right where we want to go, aren't they? Kai?"

"Based on the data stores about this place back on Shylock, yes, they are. The Unseen archives are in the same place these power emissions are coming from."

"Of course they are. They couldn't be on the other side of the planet for once, could they."

"Dash," Viktor said. "I've been searching the colony registry, but it's not showing any settlement here. What I did find, though, on the Needs Slate, was a job listed by something called the New Vistas Mining Co-Op. They were looking to contract cargo ships for deliveries to and from here."

"*Were* looking?"

"The listing expired a couple of months ago."

"Okay, so we've got some miners down there," Dash said.

"Or some of their equipment still generating power, anyway," Viktor replied.

"They wouldn't just leave a bunch of perfectly good stuff behind, would they?" Amy asked.

"If it would cost them more to recover and transport it than to just buy new stuff for their other mining operations, then they would, sure," Viktor said. "These little frontier mining companies usually run on the edge of bankruptcy as it is—until they either strike it rich, or go belly-up entirely, that is."

"And if they're mining illegally, they might just abandon their stuff anyway," Dash said. "If they think they're about to get caught."

In theory, mining permits throughout the galactic arm were administered by the bloated bureaucracy known as the Unified Planetary Directorate. All inhabited planets, colonies, and stations were supposedly signatories to it, agreeing to allow the UPD to administer not just mining and other resource extraction, but also astrogation conventions, interplanetary trade, and myriad other things for which regulation and standardization was simply a really good idea. In practice, though, the UPD was a creaky, grossly inefficient, and hugely corrupt institution mostly concerned with making those overseeing it rich.

Frankly, Dash didn't care if this was an illegal mining setup. All he wanted to ensure was that they didn't get in the way of what they'd come here to do. Unfortunately, illegal miners could be fiercely—even violently—protective of their shady operations. So what was needed here was a show of force to convince the miners not to interfere.

"So what's the plan here, Dash?" Viktor asked.

"I'm going to take the Archetype down and flex some alien muscle at them—convince them right up front that they don't want to screw with us, but also that we don't want to screw with them. The classic 'we come in peace.' Sort of."

"Are you sure that's a good idea?"

"No, of course not. But we don't have time to screw around with this. And, if tiptoeing around Port Hannah when we went to find that crashed Golden ship on Gulch taught us anything, I think it's that, one way or another, the dust clouds are going to part and let the truth show through anyway."

"That's a good point, yes."

"Okay, then. Amy, put the *Slipwing* into a high orbit and wait for my signal to come down."

"Or to run like hell?" she said, chuckling.

"Yeah, or to run like hell," Dash replied. "No matter what, we live to fight another day."

DASH LANDED the Archetype just a few hundred meters from the power emissions, which turned out to be a cluster of prefabs. They squatted atop a relatively dry piece of high ground surrounded by gloomy, noisome swamps. The Archetype actually sank to its ankles as it set down, giving Dash a momentary flash of fear that it would get stuck or even topple over. And neither of those things would do much to instill fear in whoever these people were.

But the mech's feet finally either touched bottom, or simply compressed the slimy muck enough so that it could hold its weight. Right away, Dash could tell the place wasn't abandoned; light flared atop tall poles, illuminating not just the buildings and the metal-mesh walkways connecting them, but also spilling across the surrounding swamp. A drill sat among the buildings, whirring away as it chewed into the bedrock, probably to collect core samples of what would hopefully turn out to be valuable ore.

Dash waited.

As the minutes dragged by, he was beginning to wonder if having giant mechs come drifting out of the sky was no big deal around here, such a commonplace thing that no one found it all that interesting. But movement caught his attention, resolving into a small group of four figures approaching the Archetype from among the nearest buildings. The shapes appeared human, even at a distance. They picked their way cautiously toward the Archetype, their weapons—three slug-rifles and a thermal carbine—at the ready. They stopped about fifty meters away, then one of them stepped forward. Dash saw a sturdy, hard-faced woman, probably in her mid-thirties, with close-cropped hair and a missing hand, now replaced by a sophisticated prosthetic.

She stopped. "Hello?"

Dash smiled. The woman was doing her best to come across as tough, no nonsense, and unimpressed, but the querulous tone in her voice hinted at just how unnerved she was by the abrupt appearance of the Archetype.

"Hello," Dash said, Sentinel broadcasting him from the Archetype's external speakers. "How goes it?"

The figures behind the woman winced, one of them ducking. The woman herself managed to at least keep up the pretense of not being utterly terrified.

"It goes okay—" she started, then shook her head. "Wait. No, it doesn't go okay at all. Who the hell are you? And what the hell is this thing?"

"This is the Archetype," Dash said. "It's a mech built tens of thousands of years ago by an alien race. You've probably heard of them. They're called the Unseen."

She gaped, then shook her head again. "The Unseen? They're just a legend."

"Yeah, that's what I thought, too," Dash said. "Turns out they're not. Anyway, this thing, the Archetype, was theirs. Now it's mine. It's built to fight a war against another alien race called the Golden, who are bent on wiping out all sentient life in the galactic arm. That war is heating up again, and that's why we're here. There's something we need to help us, and it happens to be located really close to your mining operation here."

"Just hang on a second," the woman said.

"Actually, how about I just dismount from this thing and tell you guys the whole story," Dash cut in. "You can ask as many questions as you want when I'm done."

"So you're human?"

"Yup. My name's Newton Sawyer, but my friends call me Dash. And you are?"

The woman laughed, but there was no humor in it, just amazement. "Dash. Well, okay, Dash, my name is Harolyn deBruce, and I'm the project manager here."

"Nice to meet you, Harolyn," he said. And then, because he couldn't resist, he stretched out the Archetype's hand.

Harolyn's eyes widened as the massive hand approached her, stopping a few meters away. Then, to her credit, she shrugged, slogged a few paces through the swamp, and put her own hand, the prosthetic one, on the very tip of one of the massive mechanical fingers.

"Fair enough," she said. "Welcome to Orsino, Dash."

Dash laughed. He was probably going to like this woman.

DASH WRINKLED his nose at the pervasive reek of drill lubricant. It seemed to permeate every nook and cranny of the small outpost, including the compartment Harolyn called "the board room." It was really just a space with a table, a few chairs, and a plethora of maps, drill data, and ore reserve calculations tacked to every available surface. He made himself ignore the oily stink, though, and concentrate on the proceedings. The *Slipwing* had touched down on a rough landing pad a couple hundred meters away from the outpost and connected to it by another string of mesh walkways. Now Amy, Conover, Kai, and Viktor were jammed into the board room with him, leaving barely enough space for Harolyn and her operations manager, a thin, intense older man named Preston.

Harolyn leaned back as Dash finished telling her his story, a dramatically abbreviated recounting of everything he and his friends had experienced so far. He didn't try to conceal anything, only leaving out things he considered unimportant in the interest of saving time. Deception, like they'd tried at Port Hannah, just didn't seem worth the effort, the time, or the distrust it would ultimately engender. Besides, it was time, Dash thought, to start waking people up to the threat humanity was facing.

"Well, that's quite a tale, Dash," Harolyn said. "I'm sure you'd understand why my inclination is to label it bullshit and just move on. But, well, I can't really ignore that big mech thing of yours out there, the Ark...er—"

"Archetype."

"Right. The Archetype." She put her prosthetic hand on the table with a metallic click. The Archetype's scanners had already registered it as surprisingly sophisticated tech; Harolyn saw Dash noticing it and smiled.

"Lost my hand in a drill accident a few years back, on...oh, crap, I can't even remember the name of the planet now. Anyway, decided to go all out on a replacement. Cost me a fortune, but it's one of those things it just doesn't seem worth skimping on, you know?"

"I can imagine," Dash replied. "Having the best tech available is critical."

"Which is why you're here, I gather," Preston said, his eyes narrowed at Dash. "There's supposedly something here that you need for this war of yours."

"It's not *our* war," Viktor said. "It's everybody's war."

Preston leaned forward. "Actually, I believe you. I took a look at that Archetype. It's got components and contains materials I can't even begin to identify."

"And if Preston believes it, then so do I." Harolyn flexed her prosthetic fingers. "Now, of course I want to run and hide somewhere on some out of the way place where these Golden aren't likely to come looking for me—"

"Won't make any difference," Conover cut in. "The tech these two races have, there isn't anywhere they couldn't eventually find you."

"Well, aren't you the little ray of starshine," Harolyn replied. "Anyway, it might make me want to do that, but I think it might be better for all of us just to help you out however I can. So, Dash, what is it you need from us?"

"Somewhere near here there's a facility that belonged to the Unseen. It's a—" He glanced at Kai. "A library, I guess."

"A data archive," the monk said, nodding. "A large facility. As far as we know, anyway. Probably very secure, and also probably well hidden."

Preston turned to Harolyn. "The Pillar," he said, and she nodded.

Dash raised his eyebrows. "The Pillar?"

Preston stood then wormed his way around Dash and the others, stopping near one of the geological plans on the wall. He pointed at a circular blank spot amid a multitude of data points. "The Pillar. It's literally that—a cylinder of rock smack in the middle of our western survey grid that we can't sample, can't drill, can't seem to affect at all." He moved to another chart, this one a cross-section built up from drill core results and remote geophysical readings. This time, he traced his finger along a straight, vertical path empty of data, extending downward from the surface. "We've tried every drill bit we can think of. We've tried explosives, even shaped charges. Nothing even scratches it."

"Yeah, that sounds like Unseen tech," Amy said. "No matter how sophisticated you think it is, it's a little more sophisticated than that."

"We can't even get any data about it from geophysics," Harolyn said. "Magnetic, electromagnetic, conductivity, resistivity, gravimetric—every survey we could think of, and it just shows up on every output as a place where we *can't* get data." She gave Preston a bemused glance. "We assumed it was something natural. Weird, sure, but natural. We were actually going to let the UPD geological survey know about it, maybe find out it was some new type of rock or mineral and it'd be named after us." She smiled. "Harolynite. Has a nice ring to it."

"I prefer Prestonite," Preston said.

Harolyn chuckled, but it quickly faded back into a grave look. "Have to admit, alien tech wasn't very high on the list of things we thought it could be."

"Well, that's got to be it," Dash said, glancing at Kai, who nodded.

"The Unseen facilities on Shylock were similar. Though, they just didn't show up on planetary surveys at all. We believe they were being deliberately concealed," Kai said.

"Unlike this one, it seems," Viktor said, his eyes on the cross-section and the blank stripe of the so-called Pillar. "This one seems to just be entirely impervious."

"Makes sense for a secure data archive," Conover said. "Whether you hide it or not, you'd want it to be secure, right?"

Dash rubbed his eyes. "So, we have to dig to get to this thing? I mean, you guys haven't actually started mining and excavating yet, right?"

"No," Harolyn said. "We're still in the exploration stage of the project. We've got some promising results, but it ain't ore yet. We don't have to dig to get to the Pillar, though—your archive, that is, if that's what it is."

Dash frowned. "What do you mean?"

"What I mean is that the damned thing sticks about fifty meters out of the ground, like a tower. No idea how deep it goes."

"So that doesn't really rule out digging," Viktor said.

"Or having to climb it," Conover added.

Dash stood. "Only one way to find out. Harolyn, can you spare us a guide?"

"Oh, hell, I'll take you myself. No way I'm missing out on this!"

DASH FROWNED as murky water slowly rose up the waterproof boots Harolyn had procured for them. Away from the mining operation itself, the ground seemed to get less and less solid—more a gelatinous muck than actual soil, into which you'd slowly sink if you stood in one place for too long. He extracted one foot, then another, with loud and somewhat disgusting slurping sounds, moved a few paces, and immediately started sinking again.

"Is there a bottom to this swamp somewhere?" he asked.

Harolyn grinned. "Bedrock's about eighty meters below us here. Nothing but water and organic mud sitting on top of it." Her grin broadened. "So you don't have to worry, that's as deep as you're going to sink."

"Good to know," Dash said, shading his eyes against the midday glare of the sun and peering up at the Pillar towering over them.

It rose fifty meters for sure, and probably a little more. He could have mistaken it for a steep-sided hill, rising only a little higher than some of the trees towering around them—things like colossal ferns, growing from the swamp in discrete clusters as far as he could see in every direction. Apparently, their entangled roots made each of these clusters the only thing resembling solid ground for kilometers around; Harolyn's people used them as natural platforms for their drills and other equipment. As soon as you stepped away from them, though, you were right back in the sucking muck.

It all stank, too—an acrid, sulfurous reek edging toward outright decaying corpse. And there were clouds of nasty little bugs, things like flying caterpillars that tried boring into flesh by using their multitude of legs like the teeth of tiny chainsaws. Dash flicked one off his face, tugged his feet out of the muck again, and found a new place to stand.

"It's going to take us forever to figure out exactly what's underneath that mess," Viktor said, and Dash nodded.

Foliage, apparently ecstatic at actually finding something to grow on, had rooted in even the tiniest hint of soil caught in cracks and fissures on the Pillar's surface. That was why it could be mistaken for a hill—bushes, grassy fronds, vines, and even trees festooned the thing, burying it under a pile of lush greenery. They'd hacked their way through it in a few places, revealing what looked like nothing but blank, dun-grey stone. So Viktor was right. They could spend days, maybe weeks, worming their way through all the greenery, trying to find some clue as to exactly what the archive was and how to access it.

"We don't have time for this," Amy said, chewing her lip.

Dash turned to Kai. "Do you have any ideas about this? Do you remember reading anything that might help us here?"

"I'm sorry, Dash, I don't. The records on Shylock were clear that this facility existed, but they didn't really offer any other details."

Conover looked at Dash. "I take it that there's nothing you can tell about this from your Meld. Frustrating."

Conover had been pulling his own feet out of the swamp, and one popped free without a boot. He wobbled on one leg and windmilled his arms, then he snapped out a curse and planted his bootless foot back in the muck. When he lifted it again, his sock was black and dripping brownish water.

Harolyn chuckled. "Now you see why I told you to make sure those boots were strapped up good and tight."

While Amy helped Conover recover his boot, Dash sighed in frustration. "To answer your question about the Sentinel, no. It just looks like a big hunk of rock covered by plants. Didn't even get a flicker when I tried touching it."

Dash grimaced, yanked his feet out of the gooey sludge slowly drawing him down, and found a new spot where he could start sinking again. "Anyway, it looks like this might have just been a big waste of time. Whatever is inside that thing is just going to have to stay there, at least for now."

"I believe I can offer some assistance," Sentinel said.

"I'm listening. Please continue," Dash said, waving grandly.

They'd left the Archetype where Dash had landed it, since the ground around Harolyn's mining operation proved stable enough to support its weight—and also to provide immediate protection to the miners, in case they managed to rouse something danger-ous. Dash exchanged a hopeful glance with Kai, then said, "Go ahead. Anything would be a hundred percent better than what we have right now."

"The archive, which you refer to as the Pillar, is impervious to any scan. It is composed of a Dark Metal alloy, composited with a ceramic-like material"

"Understood, but let's skip ahead to the part where you give us a solution," Dash said.

"The only anomaly is from the top of the structure. There is a weak power emanation from there, barely detectable, even at this relatively close proximity."

They all craned their heads upward, at the top of the matted pile of foliage.

"So up there, huh?" Amy said. Dash caught a hint of nervous quaver in her voice.

"Amy, are you okay with heights?" he asked.

She grinned, but he could tell it was forced. "Absolutely. As long as I don't have to experience them, that is."

"Amy, you've worked in space most of your adult life," Viktor said. "You've been literally hundreds of kilometers up, working on ships in orbit."

"Hey, hundreds of kilometers, no problem." She looked up at the Pillar and swallowed. "Fifty meters? Yeah, that shit's scary."

Conover opened his mouth to say something, then winced and said, "Crap."

Dash looked at him. "What? Don't tell me you're no good with heights, either."

"No, it's not that. I've got water and…whatever's in the water inside my boot now. Got it squelching between my toes." He grimaced again. "Yuck." He turned to Amy and gave her the warmest smile he could muster. "Anyway, if you don't want to make the climb it's no big deal."

"Oh, no," she said. "I'll make the climb. I mean, it would be pretty silly to be able to fight nasty alien robots but wimp out at facing heights, right? I just need a few minutes to work up to it, okay?"

Harolyn reached for her comm. "We've got climbing gear back at the camp. I'll get a crew to bring it out here."

"Why not just have the Archetype lift us up to the top, Dash?" Kai asked.

For the umpteenth time, Dash dragged his feet out of the swamp before they sank too deep. "With our luck, it'd get stuck in this crap and then wreck the archive getting back out again." He nodded to Harolyn, who began rattling orders into her comm.

Conover waved at her, getting her attention. "While they're at it, could you have them bring along a dry pair of socks, too?"

———

As IT TURNED OUT, Amy didn't have to confront her fear of heights. At least, not this time. Sentinel described the top of the Pillar, if all the sprouting, dangling vegetation were removed, as being only three meters across. After discussion, Dash decided that he and Kai would make the climb, while the others worked safety lines and supported from the ground.

Viktor had climbing experience from his younger days, and had even scaled a mountain or two. "There was one climb on… hell, I don't think the planet even had a name, just a number," he said, sorting through ropes and pitons. "Low gravity, too. It made climbing this one peak called the Spike a lot easier. But the low gravity meant the mountains could get a lot higher, and this one actually stuck above the atmosphere."

Dash smiled and nodded as Viktor went on with his story, which was both interesting and engaging. But his mind was really focused ahead and upward. So far, every Unseen outpost they'd encountered had either posed some kind of threat or been far more complicated than they'd anticipated. This one, Dash sensed, would be no different.

Harolyn's people had brought a portable, floating platform aboard the hover buggy they'd used to reach them, finally giving them a solid surface upon which to stand—and change into dry socks, in Conover's case. They'd also brought along a pair of drones, which were able to fasten lines to the top of the Pillar. Once they were rigged up, Dash and Kai started their ascent.

Their gear, combined with the handholds and footholds the vegetation provided, made the climb less laborious, but it still proved hard and sometimes dangerous work.

Dash picked his way carefully, stopping to loosen his foot from a loop in the rope.

"Are you alright?" Kai asked.

"Fine. Just aware of our height. And gravity."

"These are good qualities in the Messenger," Kai said, smiling up at him.

"Let's just make sure I'm not the Traveler."

"How would that become your name?" Kai asked.

"By falling," Dash said.

They proceeded with care, in good, if cautious humor. Dash's lines got fouled twice, requiring Kai to climb up to him and help him work free. By the time they reached the top, they were both soaked in sweat, smeared with sap, bruised, scratched and covered in itchy little wounds from the saw-bugs, as the miners called them.

Dash levered himself past a massive fern and clambered over the rocky lip at the summit of the Pillar. Turning, he helped Kai up beside him, then they both took a few moments to just drink water and rest.

"Quite the view," Kai said, looking out.

"Just swamp," Dash said. "I'm sensing a theme on this world."

Indeed, framed by his own splayed feet as he sat in the damp moss and rested, Dash could see nothing but flat swamp, punctured by clumps of fern-like trees out to the horizon. It was one of the most dreary, desolate landscapes he'd ever seen.

Kai shrugged. "This part of it certainly is nothing but primal swamp." He patted the ground beside him. "Hard to believe that when the Unseen constructed this it was entirely beneath the ground."

Dash nodded. Harolyn and Preston had explained how the part of the Pillar now extending from the bedrock almost a hundred and fifty meters below them had been exposed by erosion over the past two hundred thousand years. Even to Dash, who knew little about geology and rocks beyond the fact that you had to avoid smashing into them while flying a ship, thought that seemed unusually fast.

Apparently, it had something to do with the chemistry of the bedrock and the air and water on top of them; the rock hadn't been eroded away by the steady chew of the elements, as much as it had been dissolved away by the relatively acidic water of the growing swamps. He wondered if the whole planet would someday just be a ball of acidic mud, then decided it didn't matter. He had a war to fight first.

Dash shook himself out of his reverie. They only had a few hours of daylight left, so they needed to do what they came here to do: get inside the archive and climb back down before it got dark. Otherwise, they'd be spending the night up here, because Viktor had already declared climbing in the darkness too dangerous.

"Okay, Sentinel, where exactly is this power signature you're detecting?" Dash asked.

"I can only resolve it to an approximately two-meter circle."

Dash and Kai looked around at the top of the Pillar, which was covered in moss, long and sharp blades of some sort of grass, a few bushes, and who knew how much mud. "That's most of the top of the thing," Dash said.

"I'm afraid I can't resolve it any more clearly than that."

They'd brought a portable scanner with them and tried to use it, but its returns weren't much better than Sentinel's.

Dash groaned and lowered himself to his hands and knees. "I guess we dig and see what we can find then." He clawed at the moss, pulling it aside, then scraping away handfuls of the black mud exposed by his efforts. Kai did likewise, the two of them trying to be methodical by digging a rough grid of small pits. Fortunately, there was less than half a meter of wet, organic soil to excavate; unfortunately, it was dense, heavy, and clung to them like grease. By the time he'd started on his fourth pit, Dash felt like he'd run a long-distance relay. He wiped sweat from his forehead with his forearm and looked at Kai.

"Who'd have thought saving the universe could be such a grubby job?"

"And tedious," Kai said, then he tossed aside a handful of mud with a wet plop. "Actually, Dash, I think I've found what we're looking for."

Dash crawled to join him. Sure enough, what Kai had exposed wasn't rock. It was something flat and metallic.

"That looks like a hatch," Dash said. "See, this little indentation here seems to be where you grab it."

"It seems rather small," Kai replied, as they both began pulling away moss and mud.

By the time they'd fully exposed it, Dash had to agree. The hatch was only about a quarter of a meter square, far too small to allow anyone human-sized to enter. He reached for the handle, but hesitated, then looked at Kai.

"Care to do the honors? This is your history as much as my duty."

Kai gave a *why not* shrug, grabbed the handle, and opened the hatch. It swung open without a sound, revealing a keypad—nine square, illuminated touch-pads, each bearing a symbol Dash knew were numeric characters.

"Don't suppose you know the key code we're supposed to enter, do you?" Dash asked.

Kai shook his head. "No. If there was anything like the recorded one on Shylock, we never found it."

"Okay. Sentinel, please tell me you can offer some insight here."

"Actually, I can."

Dash raised his eyebrows. "Really? Outstanding." He'd been expecting a no, followed by some laborious, convoluted way of finding out the correct code.

"Yes. Anticipating such a security feature, I have been analyzing the available data, along with similar situations recorded in the archives to which I have access, as well as our own experiences."

Dash gave Kai an impatient glance and made a *hurry up* gesture with his hand. "Yeah, okay. And?"

"And, the Creators employ a complex mathematical equation to encode information in the environment of each outpost. That equation can, therefore, be solved by extracting that information and using it—"

"Sentinel, this is all very interesting, and I'd love to hear all about it on the way back to the Forge. Right now, though, do you know the code we need to input into this thing?"

"Very well," Sentinel said. Dash could swear she sounded a little petulant, like she resented not being allowed to explain her findings. The twelve percent personality in her was beginning to make itself known. *Twelve point five*, Dash corrected himself.

She recited the digits of the code that she'd calculated to be the correct ones, and Kai input them.

Nothing seemed to happen.

Well, Dash thought, at least I'm going to get to tell Sentinel she was wrong about something.

But the moss suddenly shifted, and then slowly began to rise.

Dash and Kai were forced back toward the edge of the Pillar's top as a large hatch slowly swung open. It took an agonizingly long time, but eventually Dash and Kai were left staring into a dark opening, down into which a narrow set of stairs spiraled and disappeared.

Dash looked at Kai. "Well, that doesn't look too ominous, does it?"

5

THEY DECIDED to bring Conover up to go inside the Pillar with
them, reasoning his unique tech-sight might come in handy. Dash
also invited Harolyn to join them, but she declined—apparently
not being much better with heights than Amy was—so Preston
climbed up instead.

By the time they reached the top, they were down to just over
an hour of daylight. Dash decided to proceed anyway, reasoning
that if anything went wrong, they could also have the Archetype
perform a quick extraction of the four of them, even in the dark.
It was, he thought, a risk worth taking, rather than losing the
night and waiting until the next day to enter the archive.

Dash led the way, walking a short distance down the stairs,
then doing a comm check with Viktor, who was still on the
floating platform at the base of the Pillar. "Loud and clear,
Dash," was Viktor's reply, meaning the comm repeater they'd set

up at the top of the stairs was working. Dash hoped it would *keep* working as they descended, since the Pillar itself was as opaque to comm signals as it was to apparently everything else.

"Everyone ready?" Dash asked, looking back up the stairs.

Kai nodded, followed by Conover and Preston, then they began to descend. Dash took a last look at the late-day sky then carried on down the stairs, their steady, right-hand twist soon taking him out of the spill of daylight. He switched on a lamp, lighting the way. One hand rested on the grip of a slug-pistol, a much-improved version Ragsdale, ex-soldier and their security liaison from Port Hannah, had worked out with Custodian back on the Forge. This version not only had better range and accuracy, but it could fire multiple kinds of rounds—regular slugs, explosive anti-personnel, and an armor-piercing round that should be able to penetrate the armored carapace of the Golden bots they'd encountered so far. All were housed in a compact drum magazine, and the ammo type could be changed before each shot. Dash kept it set to regular slugs for now. The Clan Shirna plasma pistol hung on his other hip, but it would be suicidal to start firing blasts of incandescent, ionized gas in the cramped little stairway, so he kept his hand well away from it.

As they wound down inside the Pillar, forever turning right, Preston said, "This is amazing. We had absolutely no idea what this Pillar was."

"Is it going to get in the way of your mining operations?" Conover asked.

"Don't know. We're not even sure if there are going to *be* any mining operations here yet."

"You seem to have done an awful lot of work, and invested a lot of time and resources, in something that might not pay off," Kai said.

Preston laughed. "You just perfectly described mining, my friend. For every one of these jobs that leads to a profitable mine, there are probably a hundred more that don't."

"So what happens if you don't find—what exactly is it you're looking for here, anyway?" Kai asked.

"Thorium, mainly for fusion initiators. We've got some promising results, but promising results are a long way from credits in the bank."

Dash held up a hand and stopped. "Sorry, guys, I hate to interrupt, but there's something lit up ahead of us. Eyes forward now."

They fell silent as Dash cautiously resumed his descent, approaching a panel illuminated with a soft, pastel blue glow. It was set into the wall beside a landing on the stairs. Studying, Dash could make out more characters.

"Looks like an actual data repository of some sort," he said.

Kai nodded and pointed at a particular symbol. "We've seen that same character marking empty data ports on the Forge."

"Conover, what do you see?" Dash called back. "Does this lead into a room or something?"

"No. There's no space behind that wall."

"Uh, how could there be?" Preston asked. "This whole Pillar's not much bigger in diameter than this stairway."

Dash gave a grim laugh. "A place being bigger on the inside

than the outside wouldn't surprise me at all when that place was built by the Unseen."

"There is a small compartment there, though," Conover went on. "Right behind that panel."

Dash glanced at Kai, shrugged, and touched the glowing panel. It flashed once, turned from blue to yellow, then slid silently aside. Inside a small space that was, sure enough, right behind it, was a small crystalline slab about the size of Dash's palm.

He reached for it, ready to snatch his hand back. But nothing happened, and he was able to extract it from the little compartment. As soon as he did, the light turned a pinkish color and the panel slid closed again.

Dash held the object, which he presumed was some sort of data storage device, up so the others could see it. Kai pointed at a grooved strip along one edge of it.

"That also matches the empty receptacles at the Forge. It would appear that this is meant to be plugged into one of them."

Dash nodded. "Well, that's a good sign. Let's keep going down and see what else we can find."

BY THE TIME they reached the bottom, they'd retrieved seven more of the data modules. All looked outwardly identical, but Conover said there were slight differences among them, minor variations in the way their crystalline structure had been composited. He also described a weak but steady emanation of radio-frequency energy from the Pillar, which got stronger as they went deeper. Sentinel analyzed it and declared it was frequency-modulated, which meant it was carrying data.

"It appears to be encrypted," she said over the comm. "And this time, I am aware of no corresponding encryption key. Without that, all I can do is record it so that it can, perhaps, be unencrypted at some point in the future."

"That'll have to do, I guess," Dash said, then turned to the others. "So this place isn't just storing data in these modules, but it's...what, broadcasting it, too?"

Conover and Kai shrugged. Preston just held up his hands in a helpless gesture.

"Perhaps the answer is beyond that door," Kai said, gesturing ahead.

The stairs ended at a door. This time, there were no lit panels or keypads, just an indentation in the middle of it. It resembled a small, four-fingered hand. Dash put his own hand next to it, and the indented handprint looked like that of a young child, in comparison to his.

He thought back to the one time he'd seen what seemed to be the Unseen themselves in a data playback shortly after he'd first hooked up with the Archetype. He remembered vaguely canine-like creatures, probably a good head shorter than the average human. This indentation would probably fit their hands perfectly.

"That's an Unseen handprint," he said.

Kai pushed in beside him and gave it a reverent look. "So this is what their hands would have looked like? Amazing..."

"You mean that in all the time you studied them, you never saw any images or recordings of the Unseen?"

"They seemed to be most reluctant to record themselves," the monk replied. "It was a striking omission from their otherwise comprehensive archives." Kai looked at him. "Why? Have you seen them, Messenger?"

Dash shrugged. "Think so. They kind of looked like—"

He was going to say *dogs* but realized how mundane that might sound and didn't want to deflate Kai's opinion of the beings he'd revered all of his life. So he stopped and shook his head, instead.

"Now that's weird. I can't remember how they looked. It's like the memory is, I don't know, just *gone*."

Kai gave a sage nod. "The Unseen obviously had good reason to guard their appearance. It certainly isn't my place to question their wisdom."

Okay, Dash thought, let's go with that, and not the fact that this mysterious alien race, who created all of this almost magical tech, looked a little like something that might like ear-scratches and belly rubs.

"Regardless, let's see if we can get this open," Dash said.

He placed his hand in the indentation, or tried to, but it wouldn't properly fit, of course. Squeezing his hand into it as best he could had no effect. Kai tried the same, just in case the door might somehow recognize him because of his connection to the facility hidden on Shylock, but that did nothing either.

"Conover, anything?" Dash asked.

"Sorry, Dash. I can't see past this door. It's the same way I couldn't see inside this Pillar in the first place. Whatever it's made of, it really is totally opaque."

They looked around for keypads or other data inputs but found none.

Eventually, Dash gave a resigned shrug. "I guess this is as far down as we go"

Kai nodded. "Whatever the Unseen have placed behind this door, it obviously isn't intended for our eyes."

"Which, of course, just makes me just want to know what it is all the more," Dash said, shooting the door a final glare before starting back up the stairs.

DASH TOOK a long swig from the water bottle but let the cool liquid just linger in his parched mouth a bit before swallowing it. The climb back down—which, despite Viktor's fussing over the comm, they'd managed to finish just as darkness fell—had seemed even more gritty and laborious than the climb up. Now, they all rested on the floating platform, bathed in illumination from banks of work lights glaring from the nearby swamp buggy, as well those mounted on the platform itself.

Harolyn knelt beside Dash, who'd sat down in one corner of the platform, giving his aching arms and legs a break. She waved a hand in front of her face. "Whew! Not that you smell great, but some of that sap you got on you really stinks!"

Dash gave a tired smile. "Believe it or not, it's worse when it first hits the air and is still fresh. This has actually faded quite a bit."

She chuckled. "We'll get you a shower as soon as we get back." Her face quickly went serious. "So I gather you found what you were looking for?"

Dash shrugged. "We found something. Some data modules that look like they'll plug into the systems back on the Forge."

"And now we've got a genuine alien outpost or library, or whatever it is, right on our doorstep, huh? And one with a closed door inside it that you couldn't get open." Her eyes narrowed. "Have to admit, Dash, that makes me a little nervous."

"Just a little nervous? If I were you, I'd probably be pretty freaked out about all this right now."

"You're not making me feel any better."

"I'm not trying to." Harolyn opened her mouth, but Dash raised a hand and sat up. "I'm not just trying to be an asshole for the sake of it, either. I've just decided that we've danced around the reality of what's going on for long enough."

"Your war."

"*Our* war. It's *our* war, Harolyn. Like it or not, the Golden aren't giving anyone a choice about it. If we can't stop them, then their plan is to exterminate everyone, everywhere."

She ran a hand through her brush-cut hair. "Holy crap. Not sure what else to say about that."

"How about, we'd like to help?"

Harolyn shot Dash a surprised frown. "Us? You mean our crew here? Why? What good could we possibly do, a bunch of geologists and engineers?"

"Hey, I'm a courier, basically a freelance delivery guy—or at least I *was*. So was Leira, back on the Forge. Viktor and Amy are both spaceship engineers, but more from just doing the job than any formal training. Conover's a kid."

"You said you weren't going to call me that anymore," Conover cut in, glaring up from applying first aid gel to a nasty scrape on his arm from the climb.

"As in, you're young," Dash said, before looking back to Harolyn. "Super bright, and he's got augmented eyes that can see tech and how it works, but he's still a teenager. Kai's a monk. We've got an ex-soldier, Ragsdale, back on the Forge, along with the only actual scientist type of the bunch of us—Freya, and she's a botanist." Dash shrugged again. "So we're a pretty motley crew. If you were going to assemble a group of people to save the universe from an ancient alien threat, would we be your first picks?"

Harolyn smiled and shook her head. "No, probably not."

"You'd be bringing us a lot of expertise, actually. Geology, geophysics, mining—"

"Sure, but do you need those sorts of skills, really?"

"Who knows? I can think of a few times it would have been handy to have had a geologist around. Like when we were trying to figure out how to get into, and then back out of, a crashed and buried Golden ship. Besides, you guys are tough and resourceful and used to living in shitty places like this one."

"And we end up in a lot of shitty places," Conover added.

"Well, new mineral finds don't happen much where all the

people are," Harolyn replied. "You kind of have to focus your attention out on the fringes, where everyone *isn't*."

She rocked back on her haunches then ran a hand through her hair again. "I don't know, Dash. I mean, I hear what you're saying, but maybe we'd be more use just doing what we do. A war takes materials, right? And materials have to be made or found. A thorium deposit could be pretty valuable right about now."

Dash frowned, about to hit her with the unpleasant truth, that only things like the Archetype, the tech of the Unseen, were going to be able to stand against the Golden…that another hundred thorium deposits wouldn't be of anywhere near as much use as another few hundred kilograms of Dark Metal.

Before he could speak, though, Preston knelt beside her, a mini data-pad in his hand. "Yeah, before you get too excited about new thorium deposits, you'd better look at this." He handed the data-pad to Harolyn, who scanned it then swept a thumb across the screen, scrolling through whatever information it held. As she did, her face creased in a deeper and deeper frown. Finally, she said, "Shit."

"What is it?" Dash asked.

"Collated results from the latest round of drilling," she replied, handing the data-pad back to Preston with a glum nod. "Turns out those promising thorium results we got are cut off by a fault in the rock just a hundred meters below the top of the deposit. The rest of it is gone, carried off to who-knows-where by movement along the fault over the past billion years or so."

"So that's a problem, I guess."

"A fatal one for this project, yeah. The value of the thorium that's left, and that we can still get at, won't even come close to covering the cost of mining it." She gave Dash a narrow-eyed look. "Timing's pretty convenient. You ask us to join your cause right before our project completely tanks. If it wouldn't have been accompanied by a massive earthquake, part of me would wonder if your alien friends had anything to do with it."

"Yeah, no, the Unseen are pretty powerful, but——"

But they could harness the power of black holes and blow up stars with a device you could stick in your pocket. Now it was Dash's eyes that narrowed. "Sentinel, you *didn't* have anything to do with this, did you?"

"Are you asking if I was somehow able to alter the geology of this planet to suit your agenda of recruiting others to assist in the war against the Golden?"

"Yeah, I guess I am."

"I am flattered that you would assign such capabilities to me. As Harolyn observed, moving such a volume of rock even a short distance would have resulted in a catastrophic earthquake. You presumably would have felt that."

"That wasn't exactly a no."

"No, I did no such thing," Sentinel said with finality.

Yeah, sure, Dash thought, but again, your "Creators" could blow up stars. But he just let it go. He doubted that Sentinel really cared much whether Harolyn and her people joined the cause or not, as long as they retrieved the Unseen data from the archive here.

Dash, though, *did* care. The more smart people he could get helping him, the better. He looked back at Harolyn and said, "Well, then? Sounds like you're done here, right?"

"But fight a war against aliens, Dash?"

"You'd be asking our people to basically just give up their livelihoods," Preston said. "Some of them have families who count on them earning a living."

Kai, who'd been sitting nearby and tending to a deep scratch on his neck, bristled. "If the Enemy of All Life prevails, then livelihoods will mean nothing," he said, an indignant edge in his voice.

Dash raised his hand again. "Kai, you're right. But Preston is, too. We can't expect them to drop every obligation and help us." He gave Harolyn and Preston an earnest look. "We can ensure your people are taken care of."

A bit of Harolyn's discouraged air faded. "How?"

"Well, most of this alien tech we've had revealed to us should probably never get into the hands of anyone, ever. But there are a few things we could get into—let's say enterprising hands."

"Dash, are you sure you want to do that?" Viktor asked, his tone one of wary concern.

Dash nodded. "I am. Ideally, we'll fight and win this war, and the vast majority of the galactic arm will never even know it happened. If that happens, everyone on our side—me and you included—will still have lives to live, families to raise and bills to pay. If that means selling off a bit of Unseen tech to raise some credits, then yeah, I'm okay with that."

Harolyn nodded. "Okay, then. I'll call a team meeting tomorrow morning and we'll work this out." She glanced at

Preston. "No reason to hang around this miserable swamp if it's not going to pay off, right?"

Preston glanced back at the looming shape of the Pillar, now just a sprawling pile of deeper shadow beyond the glare of the work lights. "Agreed. Especially with that thing sitting there. When I thought it was just a column of strange rock, that was one thing. But an alien library?" He gave a thin smile. "Not sure I'd be able to sleep with both eyes closed after this, if you know what I mean."

"Oh, I do indeed," Dash said, leaning his head back against the railing around the platform. "I haven't done that in a long time."

6

"This is quite the little armada we've got coming together, here," Dash said, scanning the Archetype's heads-up.

Now, besides the mech and the *Slipwing*, they also had the *Rockhound*, a light but sturdy freighter owned by Harolyn. Having the *Rockhound* available would be good; the fact that Harolyn's entire crew had decided to throw their lot in with Dash in the struggle against the Golden, was better. It had only taken them a day to strip down their operation on Orsino, load all of their equipment into the *Rockhound*—with room to spare—and lift into orbit, where they prepared to depart for the Forge in company of the Archetype and the *Slipwing*.

"Okay, is everybody ready to break orbit?" Dash said.

"Ready here," Amy answered.

"You know, I still have trouble believing everything you've told us about the Unseen and these Golden." Harolyn paused then gave a *huh* sound of amazement. "Anyway, seeing that Archetype up here in space, I guess it's really all true, isn't it?"

"Unfortunately, it's all very true," Dash replied.

"Okay, then. We're ready to depart, Dash. Just give the word."

"Okay, let's get this party started."

"Messenger," Sentinel said. "Before you begin your return to the Forge, I would alert you to new readings regarding the second, indeterminate Dark Metal signature we detected upon arriving in this system."

Dash frowned at the heads-up. He'd almost forgotten about that. Sure enough, the second signal glowed on the display. It had shrunk, though, to a more constrained and distinct return from—

"From Brahe?" Dash said. "The big planet Orsino orbits? It's that close?"

"It is not coming from Brahe itself," Sentinel said. "Rather, it is coming from something apparently orbiting on the far side of it, relative to Orsino. Brahe is an ice giant, a large planet with substantial gravitation. It would appear that the Dark Metal signature is being refracted around it by some form of gravitational lensing."

"So there's something containing Dark Metal on the far side of it, and we're seeing"—Dash hunted for a word— "Echoes. We're seeing echoes of it on this side of the planet, because they're being bent around it."

"Surprisingly, that's essentially correct."

"What do you mean, surprisingly?"

"You have not previously demonstrated a particularly keen grasp of astrophysical phenomena."

"I *am* a spaceship pilot, you know. And a pretty damned good one, if I do say so myself."

"Now that is more typical of your character," Sentinel said.

"What is?"

"Boundless self-confidence. You are actually quite accomplished at it."

"Sentinel, dear. Before you really hurt my feelings, how about we figure out what's causing this gravity lens-Dark Metal thing?"

"Dash," Conover said over the comm. "I've cranked up the gain and narrowed the focus on our new detector as much as I can. Whatever is on the other side of Brahe contains a lot of Dark Metal. Like, thousands of kilograms of it. Maybe tens of thousands, or even more."

"Crap."

"What? With that much Dark Metal, we could restock the Forge."

"And end up facing something terrifying," Dash retorted. "That crashed Golden ship on Gulch had at least that much Dark Metal built into it. Imagine running into that thing intact and fully operational in space."

After a moment of silence, Conover said, "Crap."

"Okay, new plan," Dash said. "Harolyn, you've got the data for a course back to the Forge loaded into your nav, right?"

"We do."

"Okay, you break orbit and head there now. Translate into

unSpace as soon as you can. The sooner you're out of this system, the better."

"This sounds serious. And bad."

"It might be. But that's the problem. We don't know. I'm going to find out. Amy, you bring the *Slipwing* up behind me, but at my word, or even just the first sign of trouble, you rocket yourself out of here and get back to the Forge, too. I'll cover your retreat, if it comes to that."

"Dash," Harolyn said. "Are you saying there might be something lethal in this system, where we've been working away in blissful ignorance for weeks now?"

"Yeah, that's exactly what I'm saying. That Unseen archive in the Pillar, that was threatening to cost Preston some sleepless nights? Well, it might barely rate being called an *interesting tidbit*, compared to what might be lurking on the other side of that planet."

The *Rockhound's* fusion drive immediately lit, and she lifted out of orbit. "Don't need to tell us twice," Harolyn said. "You take care of yourself, Dash. I'm expecting you to give me a personal tour of this Forge thing."

"I'll keep that in mind," Dash replied, launching the Archetype toward Brahe, the *Slipwing* falling in behind.

"So just what the hell *is* that thing?" Viktor asked.

The only answer was the faint carrier hiss of the tight-beam comm laser connecting the *Slipwing* and the Archetype as they settled into a synchronous orbit over Brahe. Sentinel had designed the orbit to allow them to *just* see over the limb of the big, bluish planet, at whatever lurked on its far side.

Whatever turned out to be something cylindrical and ominously dark, at least a kilometer long, with a massive umbrella-like structure protruding from one end. A number of much smaller objects clustered around the other end. Whatever it was, it wasn't of conventional manufacture, which meant it had to be alien.

"Don't suppose it's some sort of Unseen tech, is it?" Dash asked Sentinel.

"There is nothing matching this in the archives. At least nothing in the archives to which I currently have access."

"Dash, we're using the *Slipwing's* telescope to take a closer look at this thing," Conover said. "Since we don't want to use any active scans. Those objects clustered around the end of that big cylinder look like much bigger versions of the Golden drones that attacked the Forge."

"You sure?"

"Oh, yes. Believe me, Amy and I spent enough time up close and personal to one of them that I'll never forget what they look like."

"Have to agree, Dash," Amy said. "That's exactly what they look like. Which kind of takes away any doubts."

"Hold on," Viktor said. "Something's happening. Take a look."

Dash zoomed in on the Archetype's visual imagery. Sure enough, one of the objects—which, now that Dash gave them a close look, did resemble the Golden drones that had assaulted the Forge ahead of the attack by the Harbinger—had detached from the cylindrical station. At least, Dash had come to think of it as a station, although he really had no idea what its purpose might be. Likewise, he'd named the smaller objects mega-drones, but they might actually be full-fledged ships in their own right, perhaps even with crews.

Dash inhaled sharply. *These might be actual Golden.*

The mega-drone that had detached abruptly accelerated away. Dash braced himself, ready to react if it came after them, but it sailed off in a completely different direction, obviously on some inscrutable mission of its own.

"I wonder where it's going," he said. He was just musing out loud, but Sentinel answered.

"There is a strong signal being generated by the large antenna. It's directional." Through the Meld, Dash knew she meant the big, umbrella-shaped construct on the end of the cylinder. "It is a conventional radio transmission, but it is being injected into an unSpace portal being generated several kilometers ahead of the antenna."

Dash studied the heads-up. Sure enough, a gravitational distortion registered where Sentinel described it. "So they're producing a signal and transmitting it through unSpace to somewhere. Can you tell where?"

"Other than a very general direction for the transmission, no. Neither can I decipher it, as it is encrypted."

"That smaller ship it just launched seems to be heading in that direction, too," Conover said.

"Yeah, I see that," Dash replied. "So this is all very interesting, but what's the point of it? What is this facility for?"

"And why are they using relatively primitive radio transmissions and injecting them into unSpace?" Viktor added. "All Golden comms we've seen so far have used some sort of unSpace carrier directly, at least as far as I can remember."

"Maybe this is an older setup," Conover suggested.

"Or maybe it's because of whoever, or whatever, they're sending the signal *to*," Amy said.

There was silence as they all chewed on that. She had a good point, Dash thought. Clan Shirna had been a Golden ally—actually, a puppet, destined for extermination as much as anyone else, but they'd been rendered blind to that by greed. Their technology had been conventional, on par with that of things like the *Slipwing*. It stood to reason that the Golden had similar minions out there, didn't it?

"Well, it looks like we haven't been detected yet," Dash finally said. "So let's hang around here a bit longer, learn as much as we can, and then head back to the Forge. Sentinel, can you record whatever that thing is transmitting?"

"I already am. I would note that, since we are only detecting spillover from the transmission, the signal is relatively poor quality and the data is of questionable completeness."

"Doesn't matter. We'll take whatever we can get." Dash shook his head. "Hard to believe that Harolyn and her people were working right nearby and had no idea this thing was here."

A new voice came on. It took Dash a moment to realize it was Kai, because the monk rarely spoke over the comm.

"Isn't that odd, actually?" he asked. "That Harolyn's people didn't know about this facility of the Enemy so close by?"

"What are you getting at?" Dash asked.

"Well, this facility, whatever its purpose, is located on almost exactly the opposite side of Brahe, the larger planet, from its moon, Orsino. And Orsino is where Harolyn and her colleagues were based. It almost seems like the Enemy deliberately sought to avoid detection, doesn't it?"

"By keeping Brahe between them and Orsino."

"Yes. What reason would they have to avoid Orsino otherwise? Were it uninhabited, it would just be another uninteresting celestial body, wouldn't it?"

"Maybe it's because they have to keep the antenna aligned for their signal?" Amy said.

"They're not in a synchronous orbit, though," Viktor replied. "They're orbiting around Brahe at exactly the same rate as Orsino, as though they want to keep out of sight of the moon, like Kai says. So if their signal is meant to go in one particular direction, then it will be eclipsed for a chunk of each orbit by the planet."

"Kai's right," Dash said. "They're trying to keep all of this secret. When they detected the *Rockhound* first arriving in this system, they must have reconfigured things so this would forever sit on the other side of Brahe. And because Harolyn and her miners had no way to detect Dark Metal—"

"They were blissfully unaware," Viktor said.

"Why wouldn't the Golden have just destroyed the *Rockhound* when it first showed up?" Amy asked.

"Because that might have brought more ships looking to find out what happened," Viktor replied.

Amy's brow furrowed. "Okay, but what if they'd actually found a mine on Orsino and started—"

"Hey, guys," Dash put in. "This is all good stuff. But I think we might want to talk about it as we get the hell out of here."

"What are you talking about, Dash?"

"Check your scanners. Something big just dropped out of unSpace."

Dash watched as the sudden, powerful scanner return began accelerating, heading in-system fast. Sentinel brought it into view then zoomed in.

"That is one hell of a big ship," Dash said.

It was a huge, angular vessel, almost as large as the biggest of the Clan Shirna battlecruisers. It had an entirely unfamiliar design, though. Even Sentinel couldn't identify it.

Dash saw Amy spin the *Slipwing* and light her fusion drive, powering her away from the planet. As soon as she did, potent scanner emissions erupted from the big ship, bathing Brahe and the space around it. An instant later, four smaller vessels launched from the huge vessel and began streaking toward them.

"They're using fusion drives," Dash said. "At least they look like fusion drives."

"They are. However, the properties of their plasma exhaust show them to be advanced forms of that technology. Considerably more advanced than the drive of the *Slipwing*."

"Why does my ship always get used as the benchmark for tech that's better than it?"

"Because you are presumably most familiar with it, so it gives you an immediate point of reference."

Dash wanted to push back at that but didn't bother and just launched the Archetype in the *Slipwing's* wake. The mystery ship and its smaller spawn powered after them at full thrust, but they had too much of a head start. The *Slipwing* reached translation distance from the system first and vanished into unSpace. Dash was about to follow, but Sentinel spoke first.

"We are receiving a powerful broad-band transmission from the unknown vessel," she said.

"Let's hear it."

The voice that rang in Dash's ears sounded human but underlain by a strange, almost mechanical timbre.

"Submit to the Bright and be elevated."

Dash scowled at the distant ship, muttered, "Not today, whoever you are," and flung the Archetype into unSpace after the *Slipwing*.

7

DASH LANDED the Archetype in the Forge's docking bay, settling it onto its feet in the slightly hunched posture that seemed to suit its particular center of gravity. It gave the mech, even at rest, an air of brooding menace, like it was about to explode into action. His attention this time, though, was on the other people already in the bay, watching them as the Archetype settled into place. Viktor, Amy, and the others from the *Slipwing* barely spared it a glance and were instead milling about near the *Slipwing*, gesturing in animated conversation. Leira and Ragsdale had joined them. But the bay also held the *Rockhound*, Harolyn's ship, making the place seem packed tight in a way it never had been before. And those standing near the freighter's lowered egress ramp weren't gesturing or speaking, they were just staring—no, gaping—at the Archetype as it arrived.

It did him good to see so many people here. The place didn't feel quite so desolate. Dash gave a thin smile to Harolyn and her crew, though. "Probably had pretty much the same expression on my face when I first came aboard the Forge."

"If anything, you exhibited an even more stunned attitude," Sentinel replied.

"First of all, I was not stunned. And second—you were watching?"

"You are the Messenger. I am specifically designed to understand and accommodate your particular idiosyncrasies."

Dash paused as he unlimbered himself from the cradle. Idiosyncrasies? He wondered what exactly Sentinel considered his *idiosyncrasies*. Dash considered just asking but decided that it could be one of those conversations that went on for a while in the manner of a teacher he'd disliked some years ago. If there was one thing these Unseen AIs seemed to lack, it was tact. Being almost brutally to the point might be efficient, but it sometimes stung. What made it worse was the fact that the AI's themselves seemed entirely impervious to criticism, so it always ended up pretty one-sided.

Dash dismounted from the Archetype and walked to join Harolyn and the dozen or so geologists, engineers, metallurgists, and other tech types standing with her. They simply gaped around at the docking bay, wide-eyed, their expressions caught somewhere between awe, fear, and sheer scientific wonder.

"Wait until you get the full tour," Dash said, grinning at their stunned amazement. "Custodian, please make sure our new guests have appropriate access to the rest of the Forge."

"Understood," the AI replied.

Ragsdale caught Dash's eye and nodded. Ever the security officer, he'd already made this point with Dash—anyone who came aboard the Forge would be given *appropriate* access. Custodian knew this meant access to hab and medical sections, but no access to critical areas, like the engine room, control center, or the fabrication facilities themselves.

"Based on what you've told me about those Clan Shirna bastards you had to deal with, it sounds like the Golden are actively trying to recruit agents elsewhere," Ragsdale had said. "That means we shouldn't trust anyone, at least until they've proven themselves to us."

Dash couldn't argue with that. After all, they'd met Harolyn and her team in a star system containing a secretive Golden facility of unknown purpose, about whose existence they were wholly unaware. And they'd been conducting a mining operation in close proximity to a hidden Unseen outpost. If Dash let himself get paranoid, he could easily imagine that Harolyn and her people were working for the Golden, trying to get access to the Unseen archive.

For now, though, he just kept a friendly smile on his face. It was made easier by the fact that he didn't *really* think Harolyn was a Golden spy.

Of course, isn't that exactly how a spy would want it?

Harolyn shook her head at Dash. "This is...I mean, it's—" She just stopped, shrugged, and shook her head again.

"Who's Custodian?" Preston asked. "An Unseen? Are there actually Unseen here?"

"Nope, no Unseen here on the Forge," Dash said. "At least

none that we've found in the parts of it that are currently accessible, anyway. A few sections aren't powered up yet."

"Why not?"

"Don't need them powered up," Dash said, again tickled by a glimmer of suspicion. The Golden would probably love to know what parts of the Forge were working, and which weren't, wouldn't they?

"All the important stuff is up and running at full capacity, though," he went on. "Anyway, as for Custodian, he's the custodian of this place. He's the AI who runs the Forge."

"So you mean to say that all of this huge station is run by a single AI?" Harolyn asked.

"More or less. Anyway, let's get you guys settled into your quarters, and then we can start filling you in on what's going on. From there, we can work with you to decide how you can help us out the most."

"Yeah, sounds good," Harolyn said. "Just let me pick my jaw up off the floor here, and then we're all yours."

Dash laughed, moved to join Leira and the others, and asked Kai to have his monks help Harolyn's crew get settled in. In the meantime, he suggested to the rest of them that they all meet in the lounge they'd taken to calling their War Room to discuss what they'd learned and, more importantly, what their next steps were.

As they dispersed, Dash paused and watched two of Kai's monks leading Harolyn and her people out of the docking bay. He was glad for more allies but couldn't silence Ragsdale's ominous words that were still ringing in his ears.

...we shouldn't trust anyone, at least until they've proven themselves to us.

Were any of Harolyn's crew actually Golden agents? No, probably not.

But that was the trouble. *Probably not* wasn't the same as *no*.

"So who exactly are the Bright?" Viktor asked.

They'd reassembled in the War Room—everyone, that is, except for Harolyn's people and the monks helping them get settled into quarters and giving them a tour of the parts of the Forge they most immediately needed to know. Dash had given Leira, Ragsdale, and Freya a brief recap of what had happened in the Brahe system, ending with the sinister mystery of the huge ship that had appeared and issued that cryptic message, *Submit to the Bright and be elevated.*

"No idea who, or what, the Bright are," Dash said. "You all saw the same thing I did. Big ship, launched smaller ships, told us to submit and be elevated, whatever that means. Ominous at best."

"Kind of reminds me of how Nathis used to talk," Leira said. "All inscrutable and holier-than-you-are."

Dash nodded. Nathis, one of the leaders of Clan Shirna, had outwardly seemed to be your typical, fanatical religious nutcase. Dash could well imagine him saying something like *submit and be elevated.* As it turned out, Nathis had actually been a corrupt and greedy pawn of the Golden, motivated by the all-too-familiar drive to gather power and wealth, rather than any actual religious belief. The Bright might very well be the same.

"So you're thinking that the Bright are just another version of Clan Shirna?" he asked Leira.

She shrugged. "Like you said, all we know is what we know. But it would fit, right? The Golden manipulating some race or other, so they come across all about enlightenment and purity and being elevated."

"Maybe the Bright *are* Clan Shirna, just rebranded," Dash said.

"That ship was entirely different from anything we saw Clan Shirna use, though," Conover replied. "Unless, of course, they already had it mostly built when we encountered them and just put it into service. But the tech seemed entirely different from what we saw Clan Shirna using."

Viktor rubbed his chin with a rasp of stubble. "I have to agree with Conover. Who or whatever these Bright are, they just seemed...I don't know, different from Clan Shirna. They had a different feel to them."

"There's that feel thing again," Amy said, grinning.

"You have to admit, cuz, *feeling* things is a big part of how we ordinary mortals operate," Leira said.

"I think it's actually our competitive advantage against the Golden," Dash said. "We can do things they don't expect. Of course, they do learn pretty fast—I saw that when I was fighting the Harbinger. Got some moves in that it didn't anticipate. But when I tried them again, it was more ready for them. It adapted. And quickly."

"Which means we should save our newest and most unexpected stuff for when it really counts," Viktor said.

Dash nodded. "And that, I guess, brings us to the current question—where we go next given our lack of information."

There was a pause, the question hanging in the silence.

Conover finally broke it. "I think we need to know more about what the Golden are up to in the Brahe system. It makes me nervous knowing that big facility, whatever it is, is there. Why? What's it for? Who is it transmitting to? And what are those things that look like big drones for?"

"All excellent questions," Viktor said. "As to the questions, we can go back to who or what the hell are the Bright, and what's their role in all of this?"

"It's too bad we couldn't have hung around that system longer," Amy said. "Maybe we could have figured out what was going on...what the Golden were up to." She gave a resigned shrug. "They'll probably be watching over that system pretty closely now."

"Will they? Or will they assume that's what we'll think, so we won't go back there?"

They all turned to the speaker who, it turned out, was Freya.

She looked around at the stares directed her way. A skilled botanist, her main contributions to meetings in the War Room were updates on their food supply which, thanks to her particular talents, along with some stolen Golden technology, was burgeoning. She rarely spoke up about operational matters, though.

In answer to the unspoken questions, she said, "Well, you just made the point about being unpredictable, right? So, if you think the Golden are going to be trying to keep that system locked down now, and they expect you to think that, then they probably won't be expecting you to go back there any time soon, right?"

Dash looked at Freya, then exchanged glances with the others. Finally, he said, "Yes, Freya. That's *exactly* what we're going to do."

Freya sat up, looking uncomfortable. "Oh. Well, I was just thinking out loud. I mean, the Golden really might be expecting you, so they probably have a bunch of nasty things keeping an eye on that system now.

"Oh, they might very well, sure," Dash replied. "But you know what? Who cares? So far, we've been meeting the Golden on their terms. We've basically been waiting for them to come at the Forge so we can fight them off. It's time to take a bit of the initiative here and strike back at them."

"So what are you proposing, Dash?" Viktor asked.

"Well, I'm saying I take the Archetype back to the Brahe system and get some hard information about what's going on there."

Viktor rubbed his chin again. "You once asked me to play the devil's advocate and point out the things that could go wrong with any plans we make. I'm not even sure where to really start with this one."

"I have to agree, Dash," Leira said. "I'm hardly the most cautious person around, and even I'm thinking this might be a really risky idea—*too* risky, in fact."

"On the other hand, it's hard to win a war by strictly playing it safe," Ragsdale added. "From what you've told me, you really have been spending your time reacting to the Golden. If we'd done that aboard that crashed ship, instead of taking the initiative and going after those Golden weapons in their armory—and credit where due, that was Dash's idea—I highly doubt we would have made it out of there."

"I'm with Ragsdale on this," Amy said. "Not knowing what the Golden are doing in that system, what all that stuff is for—"

"And what the Bright are," Conover put in.

"Yeah, and that," Amy went on. "I don't know, it makes me really nervous."

Dash nodded. "Me too. So I think we need to make this our priority. We need to know what's up. To do that, we need to get back to Brahe and figure out what the Golden are doing there."

"If I may," Kai said. "Perhaps there are answers in some of the archive data we brought back from Orsino. The Enemy's purposes there might be related to whatever is contained in those records."

"Now that's a good point. Kai, can you and your brethren get to work digging through that stuff and see what you can find out? Anything about Orsino and Brahe would be useful, but—really, anything at all that could help us out."

"I'll help with that," Conover said, looking at Kai and nodding.

"Absolutely," Kai replied. "We'll begin this task immediately."

"And I am going to take some time here to rest and get cleaned up," Dash said. "Then I'll take the Archetype back to Brahe. All I need now is a plan for what to do when I get there. Leira, Viktor, along with Amy, Ragsdale, and Freya—all meet back here in a couple hours to finalize how this is going to work. Be ready to work. I recommend food and caffeine, but I want you at your best."

Since they were in agreement, everyone started to stand, but Ragsdale said, "There's one other thing I think we need to talk about. Not to put too fine a point on it, but we need to talk about our new arrivals," Ragsdale said.

"You mean Harolyn and her people?" Amy asked.

Ragsdale nodded. "Dash and I have talked about this before, briefly. We figured that if and when we recruited more people to help with the war effort here, we probably shouldn't just give them the run of the Forge. We arranged with Custodian to give them access immediately to non-critical parts of the place, with the understanding we might eventually trust them enough to let them have more freedom—get them involved in more sensitive operations."

"Makes sense," Viktor said.

Leira nodded. "We know the Golden use agents. Look at Clan Shirna."

"Hell, the Unseen are using human agents," Dash said. "That's basically what we are."

"Yes," Ragsdale said. "And now that we have our first group of new recruits, as it were, we need to decide what happens next. Do we screen them? How? And how do they prove themselves trustworthy?"

A long silence followed. Dash saw everyone looking uncertain, and realized that, for once, they really had no answers. He gave a small nod and grinned, filling the moment with his own confidence because he knew they needed it.

"We're going to figure this out," Dash said. "Or we might as well stop trying to get more people on-side with what we're doing. I have a path, but I need you all with me, and not halfway."

"I'm with Dash. We can't afford to do this on our own, even with the tools we have," Leira replied. "If we try to fight this war by ourselves, just us in this room, then…" She trailed off into a shrug.

"Yeah," Dash said. "Exactly." He turned to Ragsdale. "This is a job for you. Come up with some way we can satisfy ourselves that we're not letting Golden spies and saboteurs into our happy little family here?"

Ragsdale gave a curt nod. "Will do."

"Okay, then," Dash said. "Let's reconvene here in two hours and figure out how we're going back to Brahe."

DASH BROUGHT the Archetype out of unSpace on the far side of Brahe's star from the planet, counting on the hurricane of energy pouring off it to obscure his approach into the system. Before heading in-system, he studied the heads-up, looking for any telltale signs that they might have triggered Golden defenses.

"There is nothing to indicate we have been detected," Sentinel announced. "I am sensing no emissions of any type that are not from a natural source."

"So far, so good then," Dash said, and aimed the Archetype straight for the star.

This was the easy part. Once he rounded the star and came into view of Brahe, things would get more complicated. Even then, the star—a very hot, blue, type B—was active enough that by keeping it directly behind the Archetype with respect to the planet, they should remain obscured until they were ready to move on the Golden's orbiting…whatever it was.

The real wild card was the massive ship belonging to the Bright, whatever *that* was. Dash had made finding it, if it remained in the system, an absolute priority. Without using any active scanning systems and just relying on whatever the Archetype's passive sensors could detect, he'd hamstrung their ability to reliably locate even something as big as that ship had been. It wasn't anywhere obvious, but that didn't offer a lot of comfort.

"I hate this part," Dash said.

"You hate which part, of what?" Sentinel asked.

"Just waiting while we deliberately head into trouble. It's nerve-wracking *and* tedious, both at the same time. That's not a good combination."

Time passed, and the star looming ahead slowly swelled, filling the heads-up. Dash could see loops and whorls of gases leaping off its roiling surface, then falling back, each the size of a hundred planets. Finally, as the Archetype's hull temperature began to creep up, he eased the mech into a tight orbit, gaining velocity from the star's immense gravitational pull. The Archetype had no shortage of power despite being down a few cores from it's top limit —but stealing momentum from the star meant not having to use the drive, and that meant one less thing to give them away.

"Brahe is now in sight," Sentinel said.

Dash nodded. The planet itself was invisible, of course, but a symbolic icon on the heads-up showed it rising over the surface of the star in the distance. Dash adjusted their course again, now aiming the Archetype on a trajectory that would take it directly there.

"Still no sign of any other ships?" he asked.

"I am now detecting spillover radio emissions from the Golden construct orbiting Brahe, similar to those I recorded previously. Other than that, I am not sensing anything out of the ordinary."

Dash frowned. "So where the hell are the Bright?"

"I cannot answer that other than to say not currently here."

"Then I have to assume they're hiding."

"That is possible. However, there are no gravitational anomalies to suggest such a large ship that is cloaked in some fashion. Nor are there any Dark Metal signatures other than the ones we already know about. Moreover, if it is using the cover of a planet or other body, as we did with this system's star, then it is unlikely to be close enough to affect your intended actions here."

"Unless it's hidden on the other side of Brahe—you know, hidden by the planet directly ahead of us."

"That is possible, but I would then pose the question, why? That would only be a useful tactic against the particular course of action we are now following."

Sentinel had a point, Dash thought. If the Bright knew their plan, then it would be a clever strategy. Stealth and surprise could go a long way toward changing the outcome of a battle, especially one in space where most combat ended in the complete destruction of a ship. Nothing was as unforgiving as the hard vacuum of space.

Dash let his gaze linger on the deep black stretching before him, then snapped himself alert. Space wasn't just dangerous. It was unknowable. "Amy, you ready?"

Amy spoke up "I am. You're doing the grab, but I'm ready to assist."

"Countermeasures are in place per your plan, Messenger. I will silence the drone after you secure it. I would remind you to use the star for maximum stealth until the moment of contact."

"Authorizing you for autopilot while under approach to the star. I'll keep weps under my thumb at all times," Dash said.

"Understood."

"I am ready with countermeasures as well," Tybalt added.

"Weps are hot if needed. Return path to Forge already plotted after the grab," Leira said. "Between Tybalt and me, it's all covered."

"Stay out of the corona and come in hard behind me. Keep your delta V within reason; that dwarf's gravity well packs a punch," Dash told Leira.

"Will do. We're ready. Just like we planned," Leira said.

"That's what I'm afraid of. Beginning burn now," Dash said. They were committed. It was bold—bordering on reckless—but it also offered a good compromise between quick, simple, and effective. It also had an aggressive, striking-back-at-the-Golden flavor to it.

And it *felt* right.

"We are nearly clear of the inner-system debris field," Sentinel said.

Dash scanned the heads-up. The cloud of asteroids and other debris filling much of the inner system, the bulk of it falling behind. The hunks of rock, most not much bigger than the Archetype itself, formed an especially thick field, being as close together as only a few thousand kilometers. That sounded like a lot, but considering the velocities of the bodies, their unpredictable trajectories, and the enormous amount of speed the Archetype had stolen from its sling-shot around the star, reaction time for maneuvers still came down to seconds. The piloting would have challenged even Dash, but Sentinel handled it pretty much as a background task.

"Okay," Dash said. "Time to speed things up." He drove the Archetype forward, running the drive up to full power. The only hint of the mech's vast acceleration was a brief, tiny vibration deep in its Dark Metal bones.

"No indication yet that we have been detected," Sentinel reported.

Dash nodded. They were far enough from the star now that their approach should be obvious to any Golden sensors that might happen to look this way. Still, he gritted his teeth and focused, eyes ahead as the target hove into sight.

Crap. They'd discussed all the things that could wrong with this, but it had seemed either all so academic, or just stuff they couldn't really do much about. Now, every one of those potential disasters, minor to catastrophic, played through his mind like some horrifying vid.

"The Golden station is now in visual range," Sentinel said, zooming in the heads-up. The long, dark cylinder of the station stood out starkly against the bright blue backdrop of Brahe's icy atmosphere. Dash aimed himself straight at it, ignoring the mounting sense of impending disaster. He checked and confirmed that the Archetype's shields were fully powered up, the weapons all charged and standing by.

"Target acquired," he said to Sentinel, picking out a drone. Just as he did, another detached itself from the station and set off on a course he had the AI note and record.

Minutes passed, the station swelling in the heads-up, forcing Sentinel to step the zoom back down in increments. Dash blinked away sweat.

"Stand-by for capture," Sentinel said.

"Augment my senses." Dash turned his head slightly, eyes twitching in anticipation of a reality beyond what anyone would consider normal.

"Will do so," Sentinel said, taking the cue to assist.

Dash forced himself to relax, letting the Meld start guiding his actions. By itself, his own physiology simply wouldn't be up to the precise timing this would require. Grabbing his target drone at such a high velocity required actions within a window of a few thousandths of a second. At the last instant, he closed his eyes, letting the Meld itself be his sole interface with the universe outside.

He reached out and snatched the drone, ripping it free of the station.

Dash had expected and prepared for most of what happened next, but not all.

The sudden addition of mass to the Archetype, all of it off its centerline of flight, slammed its center of gravity to one side. They'd expected this, and Sentinel compensated with the Archetype's drive, even as she began hacking into the drone's systems to disable them.

Dash fired the distortion cannon at a point between the Golden station and the planet. Then he fired it again. And again. Each time, the Archetype had to drive even harder to overcome the sudden yank toward the momentary, artificial gravity well the weapon created.

The station, far more massive, was barely affected at all. But barely affected was enough to change its orbit a fraction, meaning it would eventually spiral into Brahe's icy atmosphere. It also knocked its massive antenna out of alignment. Dash fired the dark-lance, slamming shadowy pulses into the station's massive structure, ripping chunks out of it as glowing clouds of atomic dust began to spread, silent havoc in the dark around them. The station returned fire—and this was the part that had been setting Dash's teeth on edge. They'd had no idea how heavily armed it might be, so the Archetype risked having to escape a torrent of deadly fire worthy of a battlecruiser.

Only a handful of weapons actually opened up, though, and most of them seemed configured for point defense. Blasts of energy raked the Archetype, flaring against its shields. A few, apparently fired through unSpace, actually detonated inside the shield envelope, but the mech weathered the damage and raced quickly out of range.

Well, that hunch had played out at least, Dash thought. Whatever this station was all about, it apparently wasn't primarily battle. Its hidden, elusive nature had hinted at a dual purpose but there'd been no way to know for sure—not without getting up close and personal like this, anyway. It briefly made Dash consider trying to just destroy the damned thing now, while he was here—

Them with a flash of plasma, the drone, which Sentinel still sought to shut down, fired up its drive.

The Archetype immediately spun, hard, the starfield becoming a dizzying whirl of luminous streaks in the heads-up. Dash fought back with the Archetype's drive, desperately trying to compensate. Their outward trajectory was the one that would take the mech to a safe translation distance in the least possible time, but the drone's off-center thrust flung them thru a spiraling path entirely in the wrong direction. Worse, it kept them in range of the station's weapons. Even point-defense systems could be a problem if they were able to fire on the Archetype long enough.

"Sentinel, shut that damned thing down!"

"I am working on it."

The starfield had become a blur. Dash had no idea where they were headed now—into space, back toward the star, into Brahe's atmosphere, or even into a collision with the station itself. He just couldn't react to the drone's wild blasts of thrust fast enough. In the meantime, blast after blast crashed into the Archetype, ripping at its armor, hitting Dash like hard body blows.

"Sentinel!"

"I am proceeding as quickly as I can."

Dash shook his head. This wasn't going to work. He'd have to release the drone and just get the hell out of here, before—

"Done," Sentinel said. "The drone is now inert."

Dash applied hard thrust, finally stabilizing the Archetype. More shots slammed home, but he was finally able to resume a fast course away from the station, toward the nearest translation point.

"Okay," he said. "That was no fun at all."

"I wasn't aware that enjoyment was a measure of success in our struggle against the Golden. In the future, I will try to ensure our operations are more…fun."

Dash blinked, then managed a weak smile. "You do that."

"Incidentally, while neutralizing the drone's systems, I learned several things you will find of interest."

Back to business, Dash thought. "Such as?"

"These drones are not configured for combat. Rather, they appear to be intended to locate and harvest Dark Metal."

"Okay, that explains why it wasn't armed. It also means that the Golden are looking for the same stuff we are. Which isn't really surprising."

"Moreover, based on information contained in this drone, this station has only recently been activated," Sentinel said. "It appears to have been triggered by the receipt of a signal approximately four months ago."

Dash narrowed his eyes in thought then decided to play a hunch. "If you correct that for the best possible transmission time from the Forge, what date would you get?"

A precise date and time came to him through the Meld, one that made Dash nod.

"There we go. I think we can figure out the activation time for every Golden system in the galactic arm," he said. "And it's been right in front of us all this time. It was the signal sent by the Harbinger right before we fought it." He took a breath and sighed. "So there it is. The official start of the war, thanks to the Harbinger."

8

DASH LANDED the Archetype back on the Forge amid excited chatter. It wasn't so much about his success and recovery of the Golden mining drone, though. Rather, Kai had found something in the data they'd recovered from Orsino—something big.

"You have to see this, Dash," Conover said, as Dash dismounted from the Archetype. "It's pretty amazing."

The drone was already stashed in another docking bay in a remote part of the Forge, just in case it harbored any nasty surprises. Following that, Dash had hoped to be able to shower, have something to eat, and slump into some down time, but it appeared that wasn't going to be the case. He gave Conover an *after you* gesture and followed him back to the War Room. Kai, Leira, and Viktor were already there.

"So I hear you guys have found something that won't wait," Dash said.

Kai nodded vigorously. "The Unseen, in their wisdom, have given us what could be a decisive boon."

Dash nodded back and plunked himself down in a chair. Even sweaty and tired, he enjoyed being away from the Archetype's cradle. "Alright, well, don't keep me in suspense. Show me what you've got."

"Custodian," Kai said. "Please show Dash the data we have been discussing."

In answer, a translucent image popped into existence in the middle of the War Room. It depicted a dozen or so ships Dash didn't recognize, orbiting a binary star system he couldn't place.

He turned to Kai. "Okay, what I am I looking at exactly?"

"It's called the Silent Fleet."

"Ominous. What's it mean?"

"It is an inert fleet of Unseen ships orbiting a binary star system known only by its catalog number," Kai replied. "The closest approximation of their name, in our language, is *Shrike*. There are twelve of them, along with another four smaller support craft."

As Kai spoke, the specifics of the star system's location, details of what information was available about it, and anything Custodian could draw from his available data sources regarding the ships came to Dash over the Meld. He sat back as the information settled in and said, "Huh."

"They're warships, Dash," Leira said. "All the size of conventional destroyers, and all armed with Unseen weaponry."

"Yeah, I get that." Dash paused, and then said, "Huh," again.

"You don't seem very impressed," Viktor said.

Dash shook his head. "No, it's not that. I mean, I am, but —" He shook his head. "This is a game changer. A fleet that size, all using Unseen tech. Shit, we could probably take over the whole galactic arm with that kind of power if we wanted to."

Leira narrowed her eyes at him. "But?"

"But, unless those ships are all entirely automated, how do we crew them? Custodian, *are* they entirely automated?"

"No," the AI replied. "Each is intended to operate with a crew complement of twenty personnel. However, by slaving the ships together so they operate in a networked fashion, each can be crewed by as few as five."

"Yeah, that's still sixty people minimum that we need." Dash looked at Leira and Viktor. "You haven't happened to see sixty people hanging around the Forge, looking for something to do, have you?"

"There's Harolyn's people," Leira replied.

Dash ran a hand through his sweaty hair. "That's twelve, and only one of them is even flight qualified." He rubbed his face in frustration. "Look, don't get me wrong—this is fantastic. This Silent Fleet could be the difference between not losing this war and winning it. But where the hell are we going to find enough people who are even remotely qualified to crew it? Especially since, if Ragsdale were here, he'd be warning us about more Golden agents—and rightly so."

Kai gave Dash an uncomfortable look. "You are quite right, of course. Which is why I hate to make things even more complicated."

"More complicated how?" Dash asked, mentally bracing himself.

"After you returned to the Forge, but before you got here to the War Room, Custodian and Tybalt apparently reviewed data that Sentinel collected while you were snatching the drone from the Enemy's station." The monk shrugged. "Perhaps they should explain."

Sentinel spoke up. "As you will recall, Messenger, shortly before retrieving the mining drone, we saw another drone depart the station."

"I remember, yes. So what?"

"That drone's trajectory will take it through star systems that could include the binary system where the Silent Fleet is located."

"Shit. So the Golden know about this fleet."

"Not necessarily," Kai said. "If they did, would they only send a mining drone?"

"Possibly, but I don't believe in coincidence. Not with a race like the Golden," Dash said.

"Fifty-fifty," Leira said. Dash just stared at her, and she shrugged. "Hey, it either happens or it doesn't."

"I don't think that's how odds work."

"Of course not, I was just—just trying to lighten the mood," Leira said, spreading her hands in apology.

Dash turned back to the image of the fleet, as though it might offer some sort of answer. This was, he thought, probably the most aggravating thing to have happened so far. It was even more aggravating than the glorified scavenger hunt for power cores for the Archetype and the Forge. He simmered with frustration at finding a powerful fleet and seeing it remain inert, all while the enemy was closing in. Probably.

"Actually, the Golden likely don't know about this Silent Fleet," Viktor said. "And yes, that drone may very well stumble on it. But look at it this way, Dash. Drones have been departing on different trajectories from that station orbiting Brahe for months now. Maybe instead of thinking how unlucky it is that there's one heading in that direction, we should consider ourselves lucky that they haven't discovered it before now."

"Custodian," Dash said. "Can you give any estimate on how long it might take that drone to get close enough to the Silent Fleet to discover it? What the absolute minimum time would be, anyway?"

"There are a number of assumptions involved. For instance, assuming it will translate out of unSpace in every intervening star system to scan for Dark Metal, and that the scanning technology it uses is similar to our own, then the earliest it is likely to be able to detect the Silent Fleet is approximately three weeks."

Dash sat back again. *Three weeks.* By heading directly there from the Forge, at their best possible speed, it would take about three days.

"Okay, so that gives us about two and a half weeks to come up with a solution," Dash said. "Ideas?"

A lingering silence followed.

Kai finally broke it. "There is one source of possible help that, so far, we've been keeping at arm's length."

Dash nodded. "Harolyn."

"Her people may not be suited for crewing these vessels, but

I'm assuming that mining operations use ships, right? Is so, then they can fly."

Dash stood. "Kai, you're right, and it's time to pull the trigger. Yeah, they almost certainly would—which means it's time to trust them. We bring them into the fold, starting now."

———

"You don't really trust us, do you, Dash?" Harolyn said.

They'd met with the miner and her people in a lounge Custodian had given them access to. It didn't really differ much from the War Room, partially due to Ragsdale's natural, healthy state of mid-level paranoia. Dash sat across from Harolyn, with Leira and Viktor to one side and Ragsdale to the other. He didn't like the way it put them, and the miners, in opposition to each other, like adversaries facing off. Her question only underscored the problem.

"Harolyn, look—" he began.

But she cut him off. "It's okay. I think we all get it." She looked and gestured around at her people. Their responses were all over the map, but Harolyn gave them all a hard stare. She was getting her point across without making a sound. "You don't know us from a hole in the ground—miner's joke, by the way—and worry we might not be everything we seem."

"We could even say the same about you," Preston added.

"That would be a fair point," Leira replied. "Except for, you know, the giant space station and everything."

"Oh, it's not that we don't believe in all the alien super-tech,"

Preston said. "Because, well"—he gestured around— "it's more that since there seem to be at least two sides to this apparent war, you could be on either one of them."

"You're absolutely right," Ragsdale said. "We want to see all life in the galactic arm exterminated, but the key to doing that is a dozen mining techs we picked up on some random planet—"

"Okay," Preston cut in, bristling. "There's no need to—"

"Time out," Dash said, raising his hands. "This kind of division serves no one—except the Golden. Period. We don't have the time and I don't have the inclination to engage in a civil war of any size. Not now, not ever."

"Dash is right," Harolyn said. "It's pretty obvious there's something going on here that's...well, *big* barely even begins to describe it. I mean, giant space station, right?" She smiled at Leira, but it quickly faded as she turned back to Dash. "But it is true that neither of us are one hundred percent sure about the other. We get why you've obviously locked us out of all the important parts of this station. I'd have done the same if I were you."

Dash gave her a grateful nod. That someone used to working in the rough-and-tumble of the fringe worlds had a diplomatic touch wasn't surprising. He could tell there was hard alloy under the soft words, though.

I really do like this woman, he thought.

"But, we are going to have to figure out a way to start trusting one another, Dash," Harolyn said. "Otherwise, me and my gang here might as well pack up and head back out to look for ore."

"You're right. And we might have a way of doing just that," Dash replied.

Harolyn nodded. "We're all ears."

"What we really need is more ships," Dash said. "We do have yours now, the *Rockhound*, which is handy."

Harolyn scowled. "She's a refurbished class C freighter with no armor to speak of and a single particle cannon that's offline half the time. If you're counting on her to be much help, then you guys must be more desperate than you look."

Dash grinned. "No, no—she won't be of any help fighting, we know that. That's why I said she'd be handy. She can do cargo runs, move people around, that sort of thing."

"In fact, we have a supply of a material called Dark Metal sitting on a planet called Gulch," Viktor added. "That's where Ragsdale here is from. We've only been able to retrieve a small amount of it, because we can't carry much with just the *Slipwing*."

"And the Archetype has more important uses than lugging cargo," Leira said.

"Anyway, we actually do have some ships available—a fleet of Unseen ships parked in orbit around a binary star," Dash said. "Trouble is, we *don't* have anyone to crew them."

Harolyn looked doubtful. "I'm not sure we can help much with that. Aside from Kenton over there who flies the *Rockhound*, none of us know much about crewing ships, much less flying them."

"I served aboard a freighter," one of the drill techs said. "Had to give it up because I tend to get space-sick, though."

"That's fine," Dash said. "We're not suggesting you guys

would be crewing these ships. In fact, using the *Rockhound* to bring back Dark Metal from Gulch isn't a bad idea." He glanced from Harolyn to Ragsdale. "It *would* be a good use of your crew here, since it's basically a mining operation, digging stuff out of a crashed ship."

Ragsdale nodded. "It would, yeah."

Dash turned back to Harolyn. "What we're hoping is that you've got some contacts, people you know that could make good crews. Leira and I were both couriers, but we've been out of the business for a while now, saving the universe."

"And we were both more the loner types, anyway," Leira said.

"I'm hoping that you might know more people, Harolyn," Dash said. "Ideally, people used to space, who already work as ships' crews."

"Even better if they know how to fight," Ragsdale added.

Harolyn just stared.

Dash started to deflate. Harolyn's blank expression said it all. Well, at least they could still have her excavate and retrieve Dark Metal from the crashed Golden ship on Gulch.

Harolyn leaned back in her chair and started to laugh.

Dash gave her a puzzled look. "Did I say something funny?"

"Oh, no," she said, still chuckling. "It's not that. It's more that you asked exactly the right question."

"What do you mean?"

Harolyn sat forward again, her eyes bright. "What I mean is that I know exactly the people you need to talk to. They'd be almost perfect for what you need."

DASH SCOWLED at the display Harolyn had called up—data retrieved from the *Rockhound* and now shown by Custodian in the War Room. He'd decided that they had to make that first gesture of trust, and inviting Harolyn into their planning sanctum seemed a good start.

But this—

He looked at Harolyn. "Seriously? Pirates?"

"They're skilled spaceship crews because, well, they kind of have to be. Good in a fight for the same reason."

"Sure, but—pirates? Really?"

"Hey," Harolyn said. "I'm not going to pretend they'll be easy or cheap to recruit. But the Gentle Friends are some of the best damned pilots and crews I've ever worked with."

Leira gave a derisive sniff. "The Gentle Friends?"

Harolyn leaned closer to her. "Yeah, about that," she said in a stage-whisper. "They're not really very gentle, or all that friendly."

"Probably because they're freakin' pirates," Dash said. His own experience with pirates consisted of worrying about them and, on a few occasions, avoiding them. Of all the people Harolyn would count among her contacts—Dash shook it off. He needed warm bodies more than an internal moral debate.

"How did you even get hooked up with these so-called Gentle Friends?" Viktor asked.

"Pirating is just something they do," Harolyn replied. "They'll happily take credits to fly legitimate jobs, too. And, I have to admit, of all the ships I've ever contracted or chartered, theirs are probably the most reliable and best run."

"I guess when you're a pirate you kind of have to be good at what you do," Leira said.

Dash narrowed his eyes at the display. *Pirates*. His instinct was to pass and try to find someone else to recruit. Someone, at least, that hadn't been pirates, but he was well past the luxury of choosing willing partners for a galactic war.

But the more he thought about it, the more the idea actually appealed to him. He'd considered trying to go the military route, but getting them involved, especially so early on in the war, could complicate things a lot. For one, he couldn't imagine military types being all that keen on following a down-and-out ex-courier, even if he was the Messenger. Moreover, the military would make everything—well, military, which meant rigid discipline and inflexible protocols. He'd never been one for discipline or protocols of any type. Sure, the war might very well eventually involve military forces, but for now—

"Pirates," he said, rubbing his chin and staring at the display.

"Dash," Ragsdale said. "You're not seriously considering this, are you?"

"Actually, I am." Dash raised a hand as Ragsdale's expression soured. "I know, there are a lot of good reasons to not go to a bunch of pirates for help. But, if we want crews for the Silent Fleet that are skilled, aggressive, and used to being pretty independent, then I'm giving them the keys to the castle. I know who they are. I know *what* they were, and trust me when I say they'll leave that life behind, because their only other option will make me their enemy. They don't want that."

Ragsdale grabbed Dash's elbow and pulled him to one side. "Are you seriously planning to put the sort of weaponry and other tech we're likely to find on an Unseen ship into the hands of *pirates*?"

"What's the bigger problem here?" Dash asked. "Some pirates getting their hands on some super-weapons, or the destruction of all life in the galactic arm?"

"Well, yeah, I see...I mean, sure, when you..." Ragsdale stopped and let out a frustrated sigh. "Yes, I get your point. But it's a terrible risk, Dash."

Dash shrugged. "Ever since I was *promoted* to Messenger, terrible risks seem to be all I take, and to be candid—I'm kind of addicted to the rush. If it's a simple task, I'd rather take a nap."

Ragsdale sighed again then shrugged. "Fine. This is going to be a security nightmare, though."

"You don't say."

They returned to the group. "So these Gentle Friends hang out in this system—um, Rayet-Carinae?" Dash asked, gesturing at the display.

Harolyn nodded, but Ragsdale just shook his head. "According to this, Rayet-Carinae is a heavily developed system."

"Where else would pirates hang out?" Leira asked. "I mean, they need something to pirate, right?"

"Sure, but with as much development and traffic as this shows, how are they able to keep operating? How are there not all kinds of security forces clamping down on them?"

Dash looked at Harolyn, who shrugged. "Hey, they're good at what they do. Doesn't hurt that there's a massive asteroid belt in the system that makes it almost impossible to find anyone who doesn't want to be found."

"Well, folks," Dash said, turning to the others. "Looks like the next port of call on our happy little cruise is Rayet-Carinae."

Leira grinned. "You sure know how to show a girl a good time, Dash."

"Hey, don't say I never take you anywhere."

9

Dash put his hands on his hips and said, "Okay, that's damned impressive."

The Swift, finally completed, stood in a docking bay alone, framed against the starfield beyond the force-field. It generally resembled the Archetype but was a little smaller. The mech made up for it by being slender and sleek, making it look as though it was moving fast even when standing still. It still packed a hefty punch, too, being armed with a dark-lance, missiles, and a clever weapon called a nova gun.

Like the point-defense systems that had engaged the Archetype from the station orbiting Brahe, the nova gun translated its shots, powerful blasts of raw plasma, through unSpace—or, more accurately, the Dark Between, although the actual distinction was a little lost on everyone but Sentinel and Custodian. It could bypass shields with its attacks, letting it punch well above its weight. But it lacked the Archetype's distortion cannon, and also the big force-sword. Dash understood omission; close-in combat wasn't what the new mech was designed for.

"I have to admit, I'm more than a little nervous," Leira said. "I mean, I've done a lot of flying in simulations, but this is…" She looked at Dash and shrugged. "It's real. It's actual, Unseen tech, and I'm supposed to climb aboard and fly it."

"Have to admit that hovering on the brink of a really nasty, lonely death gave me a lot of incentive to get past all the awe and wonder about the Archetype when I first found it," Dash said.

Viktor grinned at Leira. "Now, imagine if someone had told you six months ago that you'd be standing here now."

Leira glanced at him, shook her head, and said, "Exactly."

"Well, if you want to get yourself strapped in, I'll go fire up the Archetype and help you out on your maiden voyage," Dash said.

"It's also a mission," Leira replied. "You sure we can't spend a day or two here letting me get used to flying this thing?"

"When it comes to these mechs, it seems like on-the-job training is the only sort you get." Dash turned serious and added, "We really do need to get those ships of the Silent Fleet crewed up, and we don't have much time to do it."

"Yeah, yeah, I know." She sighed and started toward the mech. "You ready for this, Tybalt?"

The Swift's AI responded in its particular fussy way. "I am indeed, and I'm only waiting on you."

Leira gave Dash a backward look, one tight with uneasy anticipation. He wished he could think of something to say that would help, but the only things that came to him would probably come across as trite, even silly. So he just waved then turned and headed for the Archetype, Viktor at his side.

They'd decided to keep the Archetype and the Swift in separate docking bays, in different parts of the Forge; that way, if one bay was somehow compromised or blocked, they wouldn't lose the use of both mechs. Fortunately, Dash and Viktor were able to make most of the trip via a fast elevator. They arrived in the Archetype's bay to find Amy supervising last-minute preparations for the *Slipwing*. She'd pilot it, with Viktor, Conover, Kai, and Harolyn as passengers. They'd also decided to bring along a few of her crew, including the erstwhile pilot of the *Rockhound*. Harolyn had suggested that, if they were going to make a pitch to the Gentle Friends for an alliance, they might as well try to get a ship that she and her crew could use as well—something more capable than the *Rockhound* in a fight.

"You guys all set?" Dash asked, pausing on his way to the Archetype.

Amy nodded. "Pretty much. Just checking a few last-minute things." She frowned and pointed up at the flank of the *Slipwing*, which was looming over them. "Did you know there's a coolant leak in the starboard-side thruster array?"

"Um...yeah, I did."

"And you never got it fixed?"

Dash shrugged. "Forgot all about it, actually. Just seemed easier to keep the system topped-off."

Amy scowled. "Pilots. They're a ship's worst enemy."

"Might I remind you that you're a pilot now, my dear?"

"I'm an engineer, who also *happens* to be a pilot. Big difference."

Dash grinned. "Whatever you need to tell yourself."

Amy stuck out her tongue at him, turning his grin into a laugh.

As Amy herded the last stragglers aboard the *Slipwing* and started to prep her for launch, Dash made his way to the Archetype then boarded and settled into the cradle.

"Amy, you ready to fly?"

"I'll follow you out," she replied.

"Roger that." He scanned the heads-up, then said, "Okay, Sentinel, let's get powered up and on our way."

"Switching Archetype systems from stand-by to active."

Dash felt the big mech come to life, both through the Meld, and in his hands and feet where they were locked into the cradle. Just like that, the Archetype was once more an extension of him —he was it, and it was him. Lifting off, he turned and slid smoothly through the force-field, into space. Amy eased the *Slipwing* out behind him.

"Leira, how about you?" Dash said.

No answer.

Dash frowned and scanned the heads-up again. There, the Swift traveled on a straight course, heading directly away from the Forge.

And directly toward the nearby gas giant.

"Uh, Leira? Any particular reason you want to visit that planet right now?"

Still no answer.

A hard knot formed in Dash's stomach. Had something gone wrong? Had the Swift suffered some catastrophic failure on its first flight?

He reoriented the Archetype and prepared to accelerate after the other mech, to recover it if necessary, or at least rescue Leira.

"—totally impossible!" she said, her voice slamming through Dash's head.

"Holy crap, Leira, what's going on?"

"It's Tybalt! He's insisting that he should pilot us away from the Forge. But I'm the one supposed to be piloting."

"Which you will do," Tybalt put in. "As soon as you are ready for it—as I have said twice prior to this."

"I can fly this thing just fine," Leira snapped.

"You have only piloted the Swift in simulations," Tybalt replied. "Until the Meld is fully established, it would be irresponsible, even reckless, to allow you full control of its systems in actual flight."

"So get the damned Meld *fully established*!"

"Once we are sufficiently clear of the Forge—"

"Damn it, Tybalt!"

Dash shook his head and cut in, saying, "Okay, you two, break it up. Leira, I hate to say it, but Tybalt has a point."

"Are you taking his side?" she asked, her voice ominously quiet.

"Yeah, I am. But before you bite my head off, just listen for a second. You are going to be piloting one of the single most advanced and destructive machines in existence. Tybalt—"

"Is a pain in the ass!"

"Yeah, maybe he is. But he's also an AI specifically designed by the Unseen to run their tech. Right now, *he's* the expert. You understand?"

There was silence. Finally, she said, "I suppose."

Dash ignored her resistant tone, knowing that a singular experience like piloting a mech could rattle anyone.

"If he thinks you should finalize the Meld away from the station, then, well, you should listen to him. For now," Dash added. "Ultimately, you'll be the boss. But make sure you're actually ready to *be* the boss first."

"Surprisingly wise words," Tybalt said.

Dash curled his lip. "Why surprisingly?"

"I was merely stating—"

"Remember that I'm on your side right now, Tybalt. Don't make me regret it."

This time, Leira chuckled. "See, it's not just me. He really is a pain in the ass, isn't he?"

"All of these AI's are," Dash said. "Anyway, Tybalt, we need to get underway as soon as we can, so whenever you can finalize that Meld—"

"We should be sufficiently clear of the Forge shortly."

Dash shook his head. It was bad enough that he was facing negotiating with a bunch of pirates; now, he had to mediate between Leira and her own AI.

"Messenger, I have a question for you," Sentinel said.

"Go ahead."

"In what way, exactly, have I been a *pain in the ass*?"

Dash closed his eyes. *I don't need this. I really don't.*

L<small>EIRA SCREAMED.</small>

Dash's instinct was to race to her aid, but he held himself back. Tybalt had said that he was going to finalize the Meld with her—and Dash remembered the exquisite pain he felt when Sentinel had done it to him.

"Leira? You okay?"

"N—no!"

"Tybalt," Dash said. "Is Leira—?"

"Despite her protests, she is—"

"Screw you!"

"—quite well, yes," Tybalt said.

Dash waited, watching the Swift as it arced around, pulling away from the gas giant. The mech had been getting a little too close for comfort, and he'd been about to follow it in case Leira or Tybalt actually did need help. But at least one of them had control of the Swift, it seemed.

"Okay," Leira said, still gasping. "Okay. That was—"

"Stung a bit, huh?"

"Did you have to go through that?"

"I sure did," Dash said. "Mind you, I was kind of dying at the time, so searing pain was a good reminder I wasn't dead yet."

"Wow," Leira said. "That's...okay, I have to admit. That's...wow."

"The Meld, you mean?"

"Yeah, it's...wow."

"You said that already."

"I can see now what Tybalt meant. I really wasn't ready to fly this thing. Not until now, anyway."

Dash nodded. "Yeah. You're not flying the Swift. You're just…flying."

The Swift abruptly changed course and began speeding toward Dash. It accelerated at an impressive rate, even faster than the Archetype. Leira suddenly laughed and the Swift rolled, then somersaulted—and then did something like a little dance.

"Okay, now you're just screwing around," Dash said.

"Damned right I am," Leira replied. "I will never be able to sit in a g-couch and just fly an ordinary ship again."

"So, Leira," Tybalt said. "Have we established that my approach was the correct one?"

"If you knew this, then what was the point of all that simulator training?" Leira shot back. "Why didn't you just do this Meld thing right away?"

"The simulations were to ensure you had a basic understanding of the Swift's systems, functions, and capabilities, as well as its limitations. As for the Meld, it was not possible to finalize it until the Swift itself was fully operational."

"Fine," Leira said, her tone grudging. "You were right."

Somehow, Tybalt's silence still managed to ring with smugness.

"All right then," Dash said. "Now that that's done, let's get ourselves underway. Amy, haven't heard from you in a bit. Are you ready?"

When she answered, Dash couldn't make out her reply. He

thought at first that there was something wrong with comms but then realized she was laughing.

He couldn't help grinning. "Amy?"

"So help me, cuz, if this laughter is about me, I'll be punching you right in the nose—and I might just use the Swift's fist to do it." Leira snapped.

"Laughing about...you?" Amy said, her voice still hovering on the edge of collapsing back into hysterics. "About how you sounded back there? And Tybalt? And..."

The comm cut off momentarily. When it restored, Dash could almost hear Amy wiping her eyes. "Of course it wasn't about you, Leira. It was Kai. He just told me the most hilarious joke ever."

"Really?" Leira said. "How about sharing it then?"

"Oh, I could never tell it the way Kai can."

"Fine. Put him on."

"Oh, he's...lost his voice. All of a sudden, just lost it. Weird, huh?"

"All right, kids," Dash said. "Enough with the fun and games. Let's haul our collective butts to Rayet-Carinae and meet some pirates."

Ragsdale's voice sounded on the comm. "Dash? Now that you're all away, Custodian's going to activate all the Forge's defense systems. If you're coming back here with anyone new, make sure you or Leira is with them, or they might get kind of blown up."

"Roger that," Dash replied, watching as the Swift and the *Slipwing* closed in, settling into formation with him. "And since we've got some time, Leira, we might as well get you some prac-tice with your shiny new mech." He smiled. "Don't worry, I'll teach you everything I know."

"And once the Messenger has done that, I will teach you how to do it all *properly,*" Tybalt said.

Dash shook his head. Yup, these AI's really were a pain in the ass.

10

"Holy crap," Dash said. "That is a *lot* of planets."

There were, in fact, twenty-eight of them swinging around the yellow-white star called Rayet-Carinae. The two outermost were ice giants, similar to Brahe, but the rest were rocky worlds, all large enough to hang onto atmospheres of varying breathability. The Archetype's scanners returned life and artificial power signatures from all of them; some, based on atmospheric chemistry, were engaged in agriculture, while others hosted mining operations, and still others acted as trade and transport hubs for the others. The whole system had an air of bustling prosperity.

Except, that is, for the broad halo of asteroids that filled the space between the nineteenth and twentieth planets. Dash had seen it in the data about Rayet-Carinae back on the Forge, but seeing it portrayed on the Archetype's heads-up made him give a low whistle of surprise. It was, by far, the biggest and densest asteroid field he'd ever seen. "And that is one *hell* of an asteroid belt."

"I can see why these Gentle Friends would want to hang out here," Leira said. "Finding them in that mess of rocks would be almost impossible. But with all of this activity and traffic, how the hell do they manage to not get caught when they leave the cover of it?"

"Good point," Viktor said. "Most of the commercial traffic is star-ward of the belt. They'd have to come further in-system to get at it."

"I'll say it again, they're good at what they do," Harolyn replied.

Viktor sniffed. "By which you mean they're good at being ruthless, thieving thugs."

"Yeah, well, I'd suggest leaving that attitude aboard your ship when you meet these people," Harolyn shot back. "You're here to get their help, remember?"

Dash wanted to head off an argument, so he said, "Harolyn, I'm suspecting you had something to do with at least some of the mining operations we see in this system—and that's how you happen to know these people, am I right?"

"You got me. Yeah, we've set up three different mining ops here, and I spent some time managing two of them."

"So how did you even get to know them in the first place?" Leira asked. "I mean, from your perspective, they should have been the bad guys, preying on the legit work you were doing."

Harolyn didn't answer right away, but Dash did.

"I'll tell you how," he said. "She was paying them off. It was a protection racket. Isn't that right, Harolyn?"

"Yeah, you got me again. After a couple of shipments of helium-3 ore went missing, I got a message from them saying that they could make sure it didn't happen anymore."

"Let me guess, they were offering to escort your cargos," Dash said. "Probably at a little more than commercial rates, too."

"A lot more, actually. It was still worth it, though. It was the cost of—"

"Doing business. Yeah, I know. Seen it a hundred times in different systems." Dash shook his head. "Anyway, I'm assuming you got to know something about these Gentle Friends and their leader, who's name is…uh…" Harolyn had briefed them on this, but the name escaped him.

"Benzel," Harolyn said.

"Right. Benzel. And I'm willing to bet that he's not the most forgiving sort, is he?"

"He doesn't put up with shit, if that's what you mean."

Dash smiled. "Yeah, that sums it up nicely. So, I think that means we need to show him we don't put up with any shit, either."

"Dash, I'll say it again. I know you want to impress this guy, but I don't think trying to be all intimidating is a good approach."

Harolyn had already made this abundantly clear during their planning talks back on the Forge. She thought the Gentle Friends were dangerous enough people that they'd probably respond to any attempt to menace them with menace of their own. Her attitude made sense, given that she'd just given in and paid them off to avoid dealing with them. And Dash had considered doing that, too—just buying the services of the Gentle Friends, like hiring mercenaries.

The trouble was that mercenaries were only as loyal as the credits you paid them. They also tended to balk at being under any sort of command. Dash, Raglan, Leira, and the others had discussed it, and they came to the conclusion that the stakes were too high for anything but genuine commitment to the cause of fighting the Golden. So, while accruing wealth was certainly something they could offer the Gentle Friends as a perk of helping the cause, they also had to be crystal clear about being a part of something bigger, and absolutely devoted to whatever the plan might be.

That was especially true, Ragsdale had put in, given that they were planning on putting the staggeringly destructive power of Unseen tech into the hands of pirates.

"Harolyn, look, I get what you're saying. But we don't have time for a lot of negotiation, and we can't afford to bring anyone onboard who isn't willing to commit to our war. Period. We need to impress them, hard, and we need to do it first thing. My wishes won't be unclear in the slightest, and my will isn't flexible. Not now."

"Dash," Leira said. "Tybalt just pointed out there's something interesting happening on the star-ward rim of the asteroid field."

Dash studied the data Sentinel repeated on the Archetype's heads-up. Zooming in, he saw an asteroid about fifty klicks in diameter, upon which was anchored a transient mining ship. The big, bulky vessel was designed to poke around a prospective asteroid field like this one, finding bodies containing valuable ores, clamping itself onto them, and chewing the precious resources out of them. This one, an asteroid apparently named Nokumi, offered up a rich trove of helium-3 derived from the stellar wind continuously washing across its rocky surface. The mining ship had just topped off a bulk cargo carrier, which was now accelerating back into the system, its trajectory aimed at a chemical processing facility orbiting the nineteenth planet.

That wasn't the interesting part, though. What was were three small ships lurking among the asteroids on the edge of the field, obviously watching the mining operation and the space-lanes leading to and from it. They were stealthed, which probably meant the bulk carrier couldn't see them. Thanks to their Unseen tech, Dash and Leira could make them out easily as they worked themselves into position for a final, inexorable run at their quarry.

"Have to admit, these guys *are* pretty good," Dash said, casting a critical eye on the pirates' careful maneuvering.

"They are," Leira replied. "Looks like whoever's running that operation didn't pay to have their ships *escorted* through the asteroids."

Dash waited for Harolyn to respond, but she didn't, so he spoke up instead. "Okay, then. Here's a chance to break in the Swift, Leira. In a nice and gentle way, too, since we're not up against the Golden." He and Leira then had a quick discussion about tactics, with both Sentinel and Tybalt offering suggestions, observations, and—especially in Tybalt's case—a few criticisms. Once they'd finalized the plan, Dash said, "Amy, we're going in.

You just hang out here for now. And if you need help, for any reason—"

"Don't worry, I'll scream hysterically."

"Not my first choice, but it works. Eyes forward, everyone. This is our shot," Dash said.

Aiming themselves at the tiny world called Nokumi, Dash powered the Archetype into motion, with Leira and the Swift close behind.

***

Dash let the Archetype drift, the slight gravitation from the nearby asteroid he'd been using as cover nudging the mech slowly to one side. He corrected, keeping the three Gentle Friends' ships in view.

"Any second now, they're going to make their move," Leira said.

"Yup." He glanced at the icon portraying the Swift on the heads-up. It was adjacent to another asteroid a few hundred klicks away. "You ready?"

"Whenever you are."

Dash scanned the heads-up one more time, assuring himself that no other traffic might get caught up in what was about to happen. "Okay, then. As soon as they—"

"The targets are in motion," Sentinel said. "High acceleration, and almost directly conforming to the trajectories we anticipated."

"Right," Dash said. "Here we go!"

Dash accelerated the Archetype around the asteroid, then drove hard, straight for the bulk helium-3 carrier. A few seconds later, the Swift powered out from its hiding place and fell into place about a thousand kilometers away from, and slightly behind, the Archetype.

The carrier grew in the heads-up. So did the three pirate ships, which closed on the carrier relentlessly, approaching from three directions intended to give the big cargo ship no escape. Not that there was any chance of it outrunning its far more agile attackers, but pirates didn't like wasting time chasing things. After all, every minute that went by as they ran down a target was another minute something could go wrong, or some other party could intervene.

Which is just what was happening now.

Dash eyed his trajectory, making a slight correction with a burst of lateral acceleration. Leira conformed to his movements, he saw with some satisfaction; she'd obviously done a good job of learning how to maneuver the Swift. She also slid progressively in behind him. He wanted to keep the glare and electromagnetic racket of Rayet-Carinae directly astern of them both, using it to blind the Gentle Friends to their approach until it was too late to do anything about it. No doubt the pirates would be watching for this, but Dash knew all about the tech they'd likely be using. None of it would be able to discern the Unseen mechs against the backdrop of the star until they were—

About this close, actually. The nearest of the pirate ships turned and burned hard, reorienting itself toward them and bringing weapons to bear. The other two continued their attack run on the helium-3 carrier. Dash could see how their tactics were to play out; the closest ship would attempt to hold off whoever was coming to spoil their little party, while the others stopped and plundered the carrier. And if they couldn't be held off, then all three would scatter, using their no-doubt impressive acceleration to vanish back into the thick of the nearby asteroid belt. It was a sound plan, and would probably have worked fine against anything that wasn't two hundred-thousand-year-old alien tech.

Dash targeted the nearest ship with the dark-lance, carefully aiming it at the drive. A salvo of missiles erupted from the pirate, forcing Dash to take a moment to switch to the distortion cannon. He fired, the gravitational anomaly catching the missiles even as they began their attack burns, slamming most them together into a cloud of shattered debris. The pulse also yanked at the Gentle Friends' ship, pulling it fortuitously into a better orientation for Dash to target. He fired the dark-lance, a quick shot at low power as the pirate's drive went dark. "Perfect."

Leira now slid the Swift out from behind the Archetype. As one, she and Dash both fired at the remaining ships, each killing the drive of their respective targets. The helium-3 carrier burned as hard as it could, desperate to escape a battle that had ended as quickly as it began. Dash arced the Archetype away from the pirates, Leira close behind, swatting away a few sporadic missile shots with the dark-lance as he did. He finally brought the mech to a stop about ten thousand klicks away from their quarry.

Leira slowed and wheeled the Swift around, stopping a few kilometers away. "Okay, that was *amazing!*"

"I know, right? Of course, it gets quite a bit hairier when the targets belong to the Golden."

"Indeed, this was hardly a test of the Swift's capabilities," Tybalt said, "Or, for that matter, of yours, Leira."

"Just let me enjoy my moment, okay?"

"It would be remiss of me to allow you to consider this some major achievement—"

"Can you guys stop bickering on air?" Dash snapped. "We're not exactly done here yet."

Silence followed. Dash nodded and said, "Okay, Sentinel, let's see if our Gentle Friends out there are interested in talking."

"I am broadcasting a message now."

Dash waited.

Finally, Sentinel said, "We are receiving a reply." At the same time, a window opened on the heads-up, into which was painted the slightly grainy image of a dark-skinned woman with black stubble for hair, a silver ring dangling from her nose, and a truly amazing number of earrings. A defiant look hardened her face, but Dash could tell it was a façade over a mix of shock, fear, and awe.

"Okay," the woman snapped. "I don't know who the hell you are, but you might want to send some pictures back to your families so they've got something to remember you by."

Dash opened the channel to transmit back to her, smiling as he did. "Big words from someone sitting aboard a ship with a blown-out drive," he said.

"Oh, it's not me you need to worry about. I've let the Gentle Friends know all about you—"

"That is a falsehood," Sentinel said. "Your transmissions have been jammed, preventing you from making contact with any of your fellows."

To her credit, the woman's resolve slipped only a fraction. "Yeah, well, they'll find out about this. And when they do——"

"Please," Dash said. "I'd prefer we move past all the bravado and get down to business. Let's start with names. Mine's Dash. And you are…?"

The woman crossed her arms and Dash sighed. Was he really going to have to wait for her to work through all the bullet points in the *I'm going to be a stubborn asshole* playbook? But she finally said, "I'm Wei-Ping. I'm practically number two in the Gentle Friends, so once word of this gets back——"

"Yeah, I get it, terrible vengeance, we're doomed, all that stuff. So, with that out of the way—if you're just number two in the organization, then I want to talk to number one."

"About what?"

"About buying a ship."

"Buying a——" She stopped, then barked out a laugh. "You've got a funny way of doing business…it was Dash, right? What sort of name is Dash, anyway?"

"What sort of name is the Gentle Friends? You don't seem gentle or friendly."

A man with dark hair tied back in a ponytail and a face like a hatchet stepped into view and whispered something to Wei-Ping. While she listened, Dash watched her face, especially her eyes. They went briefly wide, then she clamped her air of bravado back in place.

"Okay, look—" she began, but Dash cut her off.

"Just found out your comms really have been jammed, haven't you?" he asked.

Wei-Ping hissed in frustration. "You did all this because you want to buy a ship? There are lots of other places you could do that."

"I didn't go to lots of other places," Dash said. "I came here. And I came with these." He waited as Sentinel transmitted clear images of both the Archetype and the Swift. "Not exactly what you'd call conventional, are they?"

Wei-Ping narrowed her eyes at something off to her right, presumably a display holding the image of the two mechs. "What the hell are those?"

"Something that you and all your Gentle Friends can't hope to take on."

Wei-Ping looked back. Now that it seemed Dash didn't intend to immediately destroy her, her face took on an appraising look, with a hint of cunning. "Okay, let's say I believe that. What's the point? You seem like someone who knows their way around hard vacuum. You could have just gotten word to us the way everyone else does."

"Yeah, but then I wouldn't have really gotten your attention, would I? I'd just be another guy in line wanting to do business with you. See, this way I've got your full attention. And, as soon as we stop jamming you, I expect to have Benzel's full attention, too."

"Oh, you got our attention all right," Wei-Ping said. "It's attention you're going to regret, though."

"Really? Back to this?" Dash aimed and fired the distortion cannon, the abrupt gravitational yank slamming Wei-Ping's ship hard to one side and knocking her partly out of the frame. When she recovered, he went on.

"Here's what's going to happen. You're going to get Benzel on this channel, and I'm going to talk to him."

Wei-Ping, whose bravado crumpled when something had pulled her ship aside, fought to recover her poise. "Okay. Fine. Stop jamming us and I'll get him on the line."

The window went blank.

"So did they manage to get comms through your jamming, Sentinel?" Dash asked.

"They did. They used a comm laser to establish a link with a remote relay located on an asteroid approximately fifty thousand kilometers away."

Dash nodded. He'd assumed the Gentle Friends would try something like that. He'd even hoped they'd try it. If they'd just rolled over and accepted their fate with no attempts at defiance, he'd have been awfully disappointed. Instead, they'd proven themselves both resolute and resourceful, two qualities they'd need if they were going to be of any use fighting the Golden.

Although that, Dash thought, was a far from certain yet.

"Dash," Leira said. "There are half a dozen ships underway in the asteroid belt, all converging here."

"I see them, yeah. Sentinel, how long until they're all in a position to come at us."

"Assuming they do not simply attack us piecemeal as they

arrive, and take sufficient time to position themselves for a coordinated assault, at least one hour."

Should be enough time, Dash thought. Wei-Ping would now play for time, trying to stall until her cohorts arrived to rescue her.

"All right," he said. "Her next move is going to be telling us that she can't get Benzel on the channel, she doesn't know where he is, blah, blah."

As though on cue, the window reopened on the heads-up. "I've tried raising Benzel, but he's——"

"Let me guess—he's not available right now."

He heard Leira chuckle.

"No, he's not," Wei-Ping replied. "You're going to have to wait."

Dash gave a theatrical sigh. "Benzel, let's cut out the bullshit, okay? I know you're monitoring this channel, I know you're probably aboard one of the ships that's coming to rescue poor Wei-Ping here——" He studied the heads-up. "Let's see, I'm guessing the ship coming at us from spinward, just about the ecliptic plane, because it's bigger than the others, which means you're probably compensating for a small——"

"Who the hell *are* you?" a new voice said, with a gruffness that was at least partly forced.

Sentinel opened a second window, this one revealing a stocky man, smoothly bald, with a neat, close-cut beard and an intricate tattoo that spilled from the middle of his forehead down the left side of his face.

"Benzel, I presume," Dash said, flashing a cheery smile.

"I'll ask again," Benzel shot back. "Who the hell are you?"

"My name's Dash—"

"Yeah, I got that already. Doesn't tell me who you are, though, or what the hell those bizarre ships of yours are."

"They're the reason I can see all of your ships approaching, despite what are probably the best stealth systems money can buy. They're also the reason you really want to order those same ships to hold back and not do anything stupid."

"Seems to me I've got the advantage of numbers here," Benzel said. "It's going to be fun taking those weird ships of yours apart and figuring out how they work. Oh, especially that seeing-through-stealth thing. That's going to be *really* handy."

"You done?"

"I—what?"

"Just wondering if you're done with the blustery bullshit."

"Look—"

"Yeah, I know, you're going to come and kick our asses." Dash grinned. "Except, you're really not. The only ass that'll be kicked is yours. I mean, we disabled three of your ships without even really trying," Dash said, pushing his gaze into Benzel's and letting his grin become a menacing leer. "Trust me, this is not a fight you want to try taking on."

Benzel locked his gaze on Dash. Dash let him. He had the advantage of not bluffing; the Archetype and the Swift definitely would make short work of any conceivable force the Gentle Friends could bring to bear on them. All Dash had to do was let that certainty show on his face. It was actually a novel situation. How many times had he pretended to be holding cards he wasn't, to sleaze his way out of trouble? Now, for once, he really *was* holding those cards. In fact, he was holding the whole damned deck.

Benzel did the stare and glare for a moment longer. Dash saw the exact instant he decided to change tactics, his hard defiance suddenly giving way to a wary, appraising look. Dash could almost read his mind. *Okay, whoever these guys are, they're obviously pretty damned strong, so fighting them might not end well at all. Let's try to make a deal instead.*

Dash got it. He'd have done much the same in Benzel's place. You didn't become as obviously successful a pirate as he was without having a certain amount of practical flexibility.

"Okay, let's say I actually believe you can kick my ass if you wanted to," Benzel said. "And I'm assuming you aren't just here on some crusade to uphold the law and justice and such crap, or we probably wouldn't even be having this conversation. So what is it you want?"

Dash settled back in the cradle. He definitely wasn't in his element trying to deal with enigmatic aliens and their smart-assed AI's, but when it came to dealing with people like Benzel, he was. He offered the pirate an easy grin and put on a more relaxed air.

"A smart man *and* straight to the point," Dash said. "I could come to like you, Benzel."

"The feeling's not mutual."

"Well, I'm hoping it can be." Dash leaned forward. "I'm here for a ship. Something decent-sized that can take care of itself in a fight."

Benzel stared for a moment, then held up a hand and said,

"Wait. You have—whatever the hell those things are you're flying, that can apparently kick my whole fleet's ass, but you want one of those ships whose ass you can kick. Why?" His eyes narrowed. "Is it because you're really more talk than action, maybe?"

"Yeah," Wei-Ping put in. "Maybe he's emptied his magazines, eh? And now he's just bluffing."

Dash had expected this, and had already picked out an asteroid about a three hundred meters across for a little demonstration. Without a word, he targeted the little hunk of rock with the dark-lance and fired. The almost-invisible beam flashed out, briefly connecting the Archetype and the asteroid, then the latter simply vanished, blown to dust. He looked back at Benzel. "How's that thinking that I'm just bluffing here working out for you?"

Wei-Ping opened her mouth but closed it again. Benzel just slid back into his oily *let's make a deal* persona.

"So you want a ship," he said. "Something that can fight. Alright, let's toss the who's-bluffing-who bullshit out the airlock and get serious about this." His dark gaze bored into the display. "Why? With whatever firepower it is that you've got aboard those —what in the hell *are* those things, anyway? They look like giant robots."

"They are giant robots. And I need a ship because I need a ship. If you want to know more, we'll need to talk in person."

Leira's voice whispered in his ear, "Dash, what are you doing? Meeting face-to-face was never part of the plan."

He ignored her. "What's say we meet somewhere away from prying scanners. While we're doing that, you can have the rest of your ships come rescue Wei-Ping and the rest of your people floating around out here."

Benzel looked at something off the display, then turned back and nodded. "Fine. I'm sending you some coordinates. I'll be there aboard the *Snow Leopard*. It probably fits what you're looking for." One corner of his mouth lifted in a half smile. "And don't forget to bring your credit chip."

"Sounds good. Oh, and in case it isn't obvious, if you try to double-cross me, I'll have the Archetype—that's what the bigger of the two mechs is called, by the way—I'll have it find and destroy every one of your ships and installations. Every single one. And you won't be able to stop it."

Benzel shrugged. "I don't do the double-cross thing."

"I'm sure you don't."

"By the way, how did you know to find us? For that matter, what made you come looking for us in the first place?"

"A nice lady named Harolyn put me onto you," Dash replied.

For the first time, Dash saw Benzel genuinely deflate. "Harolyn? Harolyn deBruce?"

"That's her."

"Well, shit. I still owe her credits."

"And some gear. I know. She told me. Oh, and she asked me to pass along a message to you."

Benzel sighed. "What?"

"She says, *Hi hon. Never did hear back from you about that stuff you owe me.*"

The pirate sighed again. "Great. Word of this gets out, we're pretty much ruined."

"Oh? Because you somehow owe money and stuff to someone who was supposed to be paying *you* for protection? I'd love to hear the story behind that, by the way." Dash shrugged. "Anyway, you're right. Your reputation—in fact, the reputation of the Gentle Friends as a whole—is on the line here. As is, incidentally, your physical safety, because I will happily hunt down each one of your ships and take them out, one by one, until you're genuinely ready to talk."

"We'll be at the rendezvous," Benzel snapped back. "And we'll be genuinely ready to talk." He gave a sneer and added, "Don't be late."

Dash suppressed a grin. Even right to the end, the man was trying to maintain some tiny measure of control. He'd let him have it. "Wouldn't dream of it," Dash replied. "See you in a couple of hours—and one more thing, Benzel."

"What's that?"

"Could you wear an eyepatch? Feels more authentic," Dash said.

"So you're a well-armed asshole," Benzel said.

"That makes two of us. Be on time. Dash out."

11

THE SWIFT GHOSTED to a halt alongside the Archetype, both mechs keeping station about a klick away from the *Snow Leopard*. Dash sized up Benzel's ship, a surplus corvette from somebody's navy. He knew her class well; it was a common type of hull, but this one had obviously been upgraded. She now sported point-defense turrets, at least two additional missile batteries, and more extensive shielding—a formidable ship with a crew that probably knew how to use her.

Perfect.

The *Snow Leopard*'s shuttle was piloted by a surly woman with a nasty scar transecting her face. Dash introduced himself with a smile, but she merely grunted, then tapped the controls, wheeling the shuttle around and zooming toward the Swift.

Dash watched as they glided past the two mechs. They were, indeed, an impressive sight, hanging still and silent, side by side against the starfield. He could almost feel Leira's worried indignation radiating from the Swift; she'd offered more than a few choice words about Dash's decision to meet Benzel not only in-person, but aboard his own ship, surrounded by his own crew.

"What the hell?" she'd ranted. "This is insane! They're pirates, Dash! Lying and taking people hostage is what they do!"

"I know," he'd replied.

"But you're going to do this anyway."

"I am. We're going to need these people to help us, Leira. More than that, we're going to be trying to get them to put their lives on the line, and not for their usual motivation of profit. We aren't going to establish that kind of relationship with Benzel and his people over a comm link."

Her glare at Dash as she boarded the shuttle showed that she still had what might charitably be called misgivings, but she settled into place and just stared fixedly ahead as the shuttle returned to the *Snow Leopard*.

The shuttle pilot deftly sidled them up to the old corvette and docked them with barely a thunk. Some damned good piloting, Dash thought—an encouraging sign. Even Leira looked at least a little impressed. They exited the shuttle, passed through an airlock, then stepped into a cargo bay.

And into the collective glare of at least two dozen hard faces aimed at him from a throng gathered near the airlock, with more lurking on catwalks surrounding the upper level of the bay. Knuckles were whitened around the grips of slug guns, boarding shotguns, and sundry nasty-looking melee weapons.

Benzel stood at the front of the crowd, arms crossed, a grin splitting his face. "I cannot believe that you actually came aboard my ship, just the two of you, and right into my hands." He laughed. "I don't know if you're more brave than stupid, or the other way around."

Dash raised his hands in mock alarm. "Oh, no. Look, Leira. We're being double-crossed after all."

She gave Dash a sidelong glance full of worry, but played along. "I see that. Oh, no. We are truly, ah, doomed."

Benzel's grin hardened. "Tough words from a couple of hostages."

Dash sighed again. "Sentinel, the empty shuttle that just docked, any time you're ready."

There was a pause, then a tremor rattled the *Snow Leopard*. An instant later, a voice sounded from a comm clipped to Benzel's shoulder. Dash couldn't make out the words, but he didn't have to.

"What your crew just told you is that the shuttle outside was just turned to dust," Dash said. "Now, Sentinel had to step the power of that weapon down to almost its lowest possible setting. The next things to go will be your weapons. Of course, once that happens, I won't have much use for this ship anymore."

Benzel put his hands behind his head and groaned. "Okay, fine. Let's talk business."

The rest of the Gentle Friends likewise relaxed, lowering weapons, white knuckles becoming pink again. Their faces remained hard, but now Dash saw intrigued looks and could tell their owners wondering just what this was all about.

Dash gave Leira a smug look. She cut her eyes at Benzel, offering him a wintry smile.

"Okay, first off, this ship, the *Snow Leopard*," Dash said. "I really do want it."

Benzel shrugged. "Fine by me. I'll get the price worked out, including upgrades—"

"Your payment is that I'm going to let you keep the rest of your fleet," Dash said.

Angry surprise rippled through the gathered Gentle Friends. Benzel stared for a moment, then said, "Wait, what? The rest of my fleet? You said you only wanted this one ship!"

"So far."

"Okay, Dash whoever-you-are, you might have us totally outgunned, but we're not going to just—"

Dash cut him off by raising a hand and saying, "If you can just dial back the indignation for a minute, I'll explain why, no matter how much I seem to be screwing you, you'll come out ahead in the end. Like, way ahead."

Leira nodded. "Way ahead, as in, not exterminated. And I don't mean just your ships. I mean every single one of you, dead."

"Threats, now?" Benzel snapped. "You've already basically won here. Why are you still threatening—?"

"We're not the ones doing the threatening," Dash said. "It's someone else. Someone called the Golden."

Benzel frowned. "Never heard of them."

"I know. So let's just take a minute and I'll tell you the real reason we're here," Dash replied. "And for that, well, I have to tell you a story."

"AND THAT IS THE WHOLE STORY," Dash said. "Pretty unbeliev-able, I know. But there it is."

Silence.

It dragged on, Benzel simply staring at Dash, the rest of the Gentle Friends present exchanging looks ranging from alarmed to disbelieving. Dash glanced at Leira, who just shrugged back. This was, Dash knew, a critical moment—far more critical even than all of his clashes with Benzel so far. He wasn't really here, of course, to just extort a ship from these people; there were much easier ways of getting a ship. Dash needed the Gentle Friends, and his pitch to them was based on something pretty much as alien to them, as the Unseen had been to him—doing something dangerous, not for profit, but for a greater good.

Benzel finally crossed his arms and scowled. "Yeah, that's a good story. You should sell the rights to it to some vid producer. It'd make for great fiction."

Dash shook his head emphatically. "It's not just a story. The Unseen, the Golden, their war, it's all only *way* too true. Believe me, I wish it wasn't. But there you go."

Benzel shook his head right back and opened his mouth, but Wei-Ping, who'd been patched into the meeting via comm line— she apparently really was Benzel's chief lieutenant, and number two in the Gentle Friends—spoke up. "What sort of weapons, capabilities, are we talking about here?" she asked.

"You've seen the Archetype and the Swift," Leira replied. "You have to realize there's no way they were built with conventional tech. If that's not enough, the Forge has enough firepower to obliterate your entire fleet, without really putting much effort into it. And if *that's* not enough—well, this all started, you might remember Dash saying, because my partner and I got our hands on a piece of Unseen tech. That tech, which you can hold in one hand, is called a Lens, and it can make a star explode."

"Come on," Benzel said. "Alien wars and Silent Fleets and —" He paced a couple of steps to one side, then back again. "It's all just bullshit! It can't be real."

"What about that probe, Benzel?" Wei-Ping cut in.

"That was nothing. Some new military tech or something."

"What probe?" Dash asked.

Benzel just shrugged and tried to play dumb, but Wei-Ping spoke up. "About a month ago, one of our ships ran across some mysterious probe cutting chunks out of an asteroid. As soon as it detected them, it attacked. They survived it, but their ship got shot up pretty bad—and there wasn't a damned thing they could do about it. They couldn't even see the damned thing on their scanners, had to try targeting their own weapons by sight. It flew off without a scratch and disappeared."

"Describe this probe," Leira said. Wei-Ping did, then Leira looked at Dash.

"That sounds like one of the drones we saw working from that station orbiting Brahe."

Dash nodded. "Yeah. It sure does." He turned back to Benzel. "That was a Golden mining drone. It means the Golden have been here. They know all about this system. Eventually, they'll be back, maybe for resources, but, in the end, to wipe out every living thing here."

"They won't just be back here, either," Leira said. "They'll be checking out nearby systems, too."

"There's nowhere to run, Benzel," Dash said, taking a few paces closer to the pirate. "There's nowhere to run for any of us. I'm really not just telling you a story here. You've seen the two mechs out there. You've encountered a Golden drone. This is serious, dangerous, absolutely terrifying stuff."

"So you're really here to get our help to run this Silent Fleet of yours."

"I am. It's going to put you in the first line of defense against the Golden." He gave his head a regretful shake. "I'm not going to lie about that, either. I said it was dangerous and terrifying because it is. People are going to get hurt. People are going to die."

"You're doing a terrible sales job here," Benzel said, but Dash could see the man's mind working. Finally, he said, "Let's see what my crew thinks of it." He turned and gathered his people around him at the other end of the bay to speak to them. Dash and Leira faded back, giving the Gentle Friends their space while they talked.

"I have to admit, this has worked out a lot better than I thought it might," Leira said. "You still took a terrible chance, though, Dash."

"I think I said something similar to Ragsdale. These days, terrible chances is what I do."

Eventually, the Gentle Friends broke up and turned back to Dash and Leira. Benzel walked toward Dash, stopping a couple of paces away.

"What the hell," he said. "If there's a war coming, we'd all rather be combatants than victims." A vestige of grin came back to his face. "Besides, from the way you describe it, if we survive and win this thing, there's going to be an awful lot of sweet tech up for grabs. I think we'd sooner be in on the bottom deck of that than not."

Dash put out his hand, and Benzel shook it. "Welcome to our happy little world of insanity," Dash said. "Good to have you aboard."

"So what's first on the agenda?"

"Well, we're going to get you to round up all of your Gentle Friends that you can, load them aboard the *Snow Leopard* here, and go get that Silent Fleet up and running, then bring it back to the Forge."

"Okay, sounds like a good plan to start," Benzel replied. "By the way, if some or all of us want out at some point…?""

"Then you're out. You go your own way. You're part of a team, not slaves.

"That said, I have enacted precautionary measures to ensure your compliance," a new voice put in.

Benzel looked up at the ship-wide address speaker. "Who the hell is *that?*"

"Oh, that's Sentinel. She's the alien AI that runs the Archetype. Did I forget to mention her?"

Benzel shrugged. "Truth be told, all I really remember from what you said is *the extermination of all sentient life*. The rest of it is kind of a blur."

"You got the important part then, anyway," Dash said. "Sentinel, what sort of precautionary measures are you talking about?"

"Having infiltrated the systems of this ship, the *Snow Leopard*, I have taken the liberty of slaving its helm, navigational, and propulsion controls to the Archetype. If there is any malfeasance on the part of these Gentle Friends, then you will be able to steer them into a star."

Dash looked at Benzel and smiled. "There you go. If you didn't have enough incentive not to double-cross us——"

"Yeah, I think we're way past the double-crossing part," Benzel said, and then looked genuinely a little hurt. "Besides, I shook your hand."

Dash met Benzel's eyes and gave him a firm nod. "Yes, you did. And that's good enough for me."

12

"Okay, Dash," Amy said. "We're ready to head back to the Forge. Are you sure you don't want us to come along with you to that Silent Fleet?"

Dash glanced at the *Slipwing,* moving steadily away from the two mechs and the *Snow Leopard* on a high-g fusion burn. They'd all dropped out of unSpace near an unremarkable red dwarf star, a convenient and nondescript place to part ways.

"I think the Gentle Friends will be more than enough to get the Silent Fleet underway," Dash replied. "Honestly, I'd be a lot more comfortable having you guys back at the Forge, helping Ragsdale hold the fort there."

"Dash," Viktor said, coming on the comm. "Are you sure about this? I'm not really that happy about you and Leira going off alone with a bunch of pirates. And I see nods from Conover and Kai."

"It's me and Leira, *and* the Archetype and the Swift," Dash said. "We'll be fine."

"But they're *pirates*."

"Like Harolyn said, piracy is something they do, not necessarily what they are. Right now, in fact, what they are is our best hope for getting that fleet powered up and ready for action against the Golden."

"Fine," Viktor said, resigned, but still clearly not happy. "We'll see you back at the Forge."

"You will."

The *Slipwing* abruptly vanished into unSpace. Dash turned his attention back to the heads-up. "Okay, let's go get ourselves a fleet, shall we?"

Leira and Benzel both acknowledged, then all three drove their own way into unSpace, leaving the unremarkable red dwarf once more alone.

"SEE any sign of the Golden drone that was headed this way?" Dash asked Leira.

While he waited for her to answer, he scanned the heads-up, taking in the binary star system which, for the past two thousand centuries, had been the home of the Silent Fleet.

The two stars—one a main sequence yellow, and a smaller blue companion—were in a close orbit, a mutual dance with wildly fluctuating gravity that had long ago either flung any planets off into space, pulled them into the stars where they were vaporized, or else ripped them into the sporadic clouds of debris that surrounded them. The Silent Fleet itself orbited at a respectful distance, the cold and inert ships all but invisible to any scanners that weren't looking for them specifically. Even then, with no emissions to speak of, they'd only be detected by their faint gravitational effects—or by whatever Dark Metal they might contain. And that brought them back to the Golden mining drone, which, as far as they knew, was still heading this way.

"I have something, Dash. Tybalt's sending the data now."

Dash watched the information appear on the Archetype's heads-up. It was definitely the Golden drone—or, at least, *a* Golden drone. There was no way to know for certain it was the one they knew had been coming this way, since the drones were interchangeable. But it stood to reason it was; it wasn't likely a second drone would have been dispatched this way. Moreover, it probably meant the Golden hadn't detected the Silent Fleet yet, because if they had, they probably would have sent much more than a single mining drone to deal with it.

"The Golden drone is emitting considerable scanning energy," Sentinel said. "It would appear to be following a trajectory that will take it through the margins of systems along its flight path, scanning into each system as it passes."

"Makes sense," Dash replied. "Gives the quickest coverage of the greatest number of systems possible."

"Yes. And in the event an anomaly of interest is detected, it is likely only then investigated further, or else marked for more detailed examination by follow-up probes."

"Well, this one doesn't seem to have detected the Silent Fleet yet," Dash said, studying the data. "It's still a couple of hours from its closest approach to this system."

"I would point out that any Dark Metal in the Silent Fleet may show up as a much stronger anomaly and may be detected sooner," Sentinel replied.

"Huh. Good point." Dash considered that for a moment. "So if we assume this probe is as good at detecting Dark Metal as the Archetype is, how long will it be before it's in range?"

"Approximately one hour, with a margin of error of a quarter hour."

"That doesn't give us much time. Leira, you stay here with the *Snow Leopard* and start getting the layout of this fleet. I'm going to go deal with that drone."

"As soon as it stops checking in, or the Golden or whoever might be monitoring it loses contact with it, they're going to wonder why," Leira said. "That might bring a lot more than a mining drone looking to find out."

"I'm sure it will, but I intend for us and the Silent Fleet to be long gone by then."

DASH, with Sentinel's help, tried to come up with different ways of approaching the drone undetected so they could destroy it in a sudden, surprise attack. Trouble was, every idea either took too much time, or was too convoluted and likely to fail anyway. He finally decided to try a variation on the ambush they'd used against the Gentle Friends ships attacking the bulk carrier back in

Rayet-Carinae. The Archetype would simply translate as close as it could to the drone's path, then attack with the binary stars directly behind it, hopefully blinding it long enough to get within a decisive range. It probably wouldn't work anywhere near as well as it did with the pirates, though—this wasn't inferior human tech, after all.

Still, it was quick and simple, and in Dash's experience, quick and simple sooner was almost always better than complicated and time-consuming later.

The Archetype translated twice to get in position. The first took it close to a large asteroid, a hunk of rock several hundred klicks across. From there, he studied the drone again; it remained on its relatively lazy trajectory, just coasting into the fringes of the Oort Cloud of comets and other debris that marked the edge of this star system. He didn't linger, though; based on Sentinel's assessment, the drone might detect the Silent Fleet in as little as fifteen minutes.

"Okay," Dash said. "Let's go bag this drone."

The Archetype smoothly powered away from the big asteroid, translated and plunged into unSpace, then emerged just as quickly from an arbitrary point directly between the drone and the distant binary stars. Dash took only a moment to reorient himself, then charged at the Golden drone, driving the Archetype at its maximum acceleration.

Considering the relative dimness of the binary stars compared to the glare from Rayet-Carinae that had dazzled the Gentle Friends, along with the drone's much more sophisticated tech, the Archetype managed to get surprisingly close. The drone still hadn't seemed to react even by the time they reached their chosen attack position. Dash didn't question it, though. As Sentinel tried to jam the drone's transmissions, he fired a trio of missiles.

Now the drone did react, accelerating hard through evasive maneuvers. One of the missiles, programmed to bore straight in as fast as possible, was thrown off, missing the gyrating target. The other two adjusted their attacks, leaving the drone unable to dodge all three. One detonated close to the drone with a dazzling flash, searing off a chunk of it; the drone spun again, but the damage had been severe and it couldn't avoid the second missile, which slammed into it dead-on and blasted it into scrap.

"Did it get off any transmissions?" Dash asked Sentinel.

"It attempted to, emitting a series of wide-band, high-power emissions. They were encoded, so the actual message was unclear. One would assume, however, it was some variation of, *help, I am under attack.*"

Dash smiled. "Probably safe to say. I'm sure it wasn't, *hey, everything's fine, don't bother coming to check up on me.*"

"There is Dark Metal in the drone's wreckage. Several kilograms of it."

"Yeah, I see that," Dash said. "And I'm tempted, but we don't have time to go screwing around scooping up tiny pieces of material. We have to work on the assumption that the drone's message got through and something a lot worse is on the way. We've got a fleet to get underway." He spun the Archetype around and raced back toward the binary stars.

DASH EASED the Archetype as close to the Unseen ship, apparently known as a *Shrike*, as he dared. It loomed over the mech, an imposing cylinder four hundred meters long, rounded at the nose, blunt at the stern, and split only by occasional domed protuberances along its otherwise sleek hull. Sentinel had identified one of those protuberances to be an airlock, and it was through it that Dash intended to enter this first of the Silent Fleet's ships. If that went well, then they'd work on getting the Gentle Friends dispatched from the *Snow Leopard* and aboard the rest of the *Shrikes*.

Vac suit sealed up, he exited the Archetype. Leira had already disembarked from the Swift, which hung just a couple of hundred meters away, and now used puffs of gas from a maneuvering harness to approach. Dash activated his own harness and started the short trip to the airlock.

It was only about a hundred meters, but making the trip without a tether made his teeth grind. Every experienced spacer knew that, if you could, you always used a tether. Of course, those spacers weren't able to count on a giant, self-aware alien mech to rescue them if they got in trouble. Still, though, poised in empty space, caught between the Archetype behind him and the sweeping hull of the Shrike ahead, Dash couldn't help feeling like he'd put his toes on the edge of a massive cliff and stood there, swaying slightly, leaning over the chasm—

"Dash?" Leira said. "You okay?"

"I—what? Oh, yeah. I'm fine."

He saw her just ahead, waiting for him beside the airlock. And he was coming up on her fast—too fast. He fired thrusters to slow himself down, finally coming to rest about a meter away from her.

"You looked like you were just going to keep thrusting ahead," she said. "At least until you crashed into this ship and bounced away, anyway. I thought I might have to catch you."

"You were just looking for an excuse to get your arms around me."

"Can you see my eyes rolling through this faceplate? Because, I assure you, my eyes are rolling."

He laughed. "Anyway, let's see if we can get this thing open then get her started up."

With a puff of thrust, he pushed himself to the airlock. He stopped again and examined it, finding a small recess in the hull alongside it. It contained no buttons or levers, or any sort of control he could manipulate. It actually reminded him of the Unseen hand imprint on the door they couldn't open in the archive back on Orsino. The thought made his stomach flutter; what if they couldn't access these ships the same way, because the Unseen had either never intended them to—let alone envisioned them trying. The data about the Silent Fleet *had* been hidden away in a pretty obscure place, after all. What were the chances they'd actually have found it the way they did?

He pressed his lips into a thin line. *To have gone through all this for nothing*. . . He let the thought die, like his irritation.

"Sentinel," he said. "I have no idea how to open this. Do you?"

"You should be able to access it by means of the Meld."

"Yeah, but how?"

"I would suggest that physical contact would suffice to establish the link."

Dash thought back to the crashed Golden ship on Gulch. That was how he'd Melded with it, but touching Dark Metal components. But that hadn't been hard vacuum.

"I know I can expose my hand to space for a minute or two without lasting harm, sure. But doesn't that sound like an awfully, I don't know, clunky way of opening an airlock? I mean, the *Slipwing* has a keypad you can press with your gloved fingers."

"I do not believe the Creators would have opted for so inelegant a solution. You are the Messenger. You are already attuned to the Creator's technology."

Dash looked at Leira and saw her shrug through the faceplate of her helmet.

He shrugged back and touched the indentation. "Fine."

The domed extrusion from the hull split, the halves sliding smoothly apart. Beyond, a corridor led to another set of doors.

Dash stared for a moment. "Oh. Guess I overthought that."

"It's the problem with hanging out with super-intelligent alien AI," Leira said. "You end up second guessing everything."

"True," Dash said. "Okay, Benzel, you there?"

"Yup."

"Leira and I are going inside. If you run into any trouble out here—"

"Don't you worry about us. First sign of trouble, we'll run like hell."

"I think he probably means it," Leira said.

Dash nodded as he started into the airlock. "I'm sure he does."

DASH HAD HARBORED something between hope and fear that they might actually encounter some Unseen aboard the *Shrike*, maybe held in some sort of suspended animation. Actually, it was both hope *and* fear. Having a live Unseen available could be enormously helpful. But it could also prove to be terrifying; they were aliens, after all. Or it could turn out exactly the opposite, and they proved to be hugely disappointing assholes. He wasn't sure which would be worse.

But there were no Unseen—just a ship full of empty corridors connecting a multitude of compartments, the purposes of some they could guess at, but most of which were entirely inscrutable. At least there was breathable air and a livable environment aboard, although he suspected that had been generated right before they left the airlock. Otherwise, this ship had been pressurized for two hundred thousand years, with air that smelled of really nothing at all. The *Slipwing* leaked enough air that, without it being regenerated, she'd have lost her on-board atmosphere in a few months at most.

Mind you, these were the Unseen. That might not even be a tough engineering challenge for them.

They entered a larger compartment with a forward wall that was a large, curved screen. It resembled the Archetype's heads-up, right down to the way data was being displayed. The Archetype was, in fact, visible, as was the Swift, and the *Snow Leopard* beyond. All were painted with relevant data about size, mass, emissions, and other useful facts.

"I'd assume this is the bridge," Dash said, frowning as his helmet, which was hanging from his harness, clunked against a console.

Leira held up a data-pad. "So, assuming all of these ships are laid out much the same, I've got a map that should guide Benzel's people from the entry airlock to the bridge." She lowered the pad and frowned at the big viewscreen. "Although, I notice all of the data here is in the Unseen language. How are Benzel's people going to read it?"

"The Creators were much more competent than you give them credit for," Tybalt said. "The ships have a provision to provide data in whatever language is most appropriate for its user."

"So how do we activate that?"

"You do not need to. Upon your entry into the ship, Sentinel and I were able to establish a link to it. We can ensure it is configured in whatever manner we deem most appropriate for whoever is crewing it."

Dash narrowed his eyes. "Whatever manner *you* deem most appropriate?"

"My apologies," Tybalt replied. "In whatever manner we, collectively, including you, deem most appropriate."

Dash threw Leira a raised-eyebrow look. "That's not quite what he said."

She shrugged. "Welcome to my world."

Dash turned back to the consoles ringing the central well of the bridge, where a single console marked what was probably the captain's station. He walked to that, examined it for a moment, then tapped a control. The panel lit up with Unseen characters. He studied them, then selected one and touched it.

WITHOUT A FLICKER OF HESITATION—AS though it had been powered down yesterday and not two thousand centuries ago—the ship came to life. Consoles lit up all around the bridge, while new data flooded across the Meld.

Leira winced and put out a hand, steadying herself with the edge of a console. "Wow. That is…a weird feeling."

"What? Suddenly just *knowing* a bunch of new stuff?"

"Yeah."

"You'll get used to it."

Just like that, Dash knew that the Silent Fleet had been prepared for battle but was never used for it. Instead, shortly after being built, it had been brought here, hidden away in this remote and obscure system until the day it was needed again. Even more intriguing, though, were hints that there might be other such fleets out there, a fact he mentioned to Leira.

She nodded. "But nothing to suggest where they might be."

"That's deliberate, I'm sure," Dash replied. "That information will be available somewhere, but probably not here. In case the Golden stumbled across one of these fleets, they didn't want to end up compromising them all. Which is probably the first time I can buy the Unseen obsession with compartmentalizing everything."

Leira looked around then lifted her data-pad and tapped at it. "I'm sending the ship schematics we've collected back to Benzel." Her finger hovered above the pad. "Last chance to say no, you really don't want to hand these ships over to a bunch of pirates."

Dash grimaced. "I think that ship departed a long time ago."

Leira nodded and tapped the data-pad.

ONE BY ONE, the *Shrikes* came to life, powering up as the Gentle Friends who had boarded reached the bridge of each and followed the instructions given by Dash and Leira. There were a total of fourteen of them, along with four smaller support vessels.

"Okay," Benzel said, over the comm. "This is pretty damned amazing. These ships are—well, amazing."

"You said amazing twice," Dash replied. He was making his way through the corridors of the *Shrike* they'd first boarded, looking for Leira. She'd apparently found something interesting while he was helping the Gentle Friends who'd come aboard get set up on the bridge.

"That's how amazed I am," Benzel replied. "Makes me repeat myself."

"Dash," Sentinel cut in. "Tybalt and I have established links to all of the ships. They are all networked and can be controlled collectively."

He turned a corner, following the directions Leira had given him. "Wait—does that mean they don't need crews after all?"

"Their networked capabilities are meant to augment the crews' capabilities, not replace them. Without crews, it would be possible to collectively move the fleet to new locations, but combat would be far less than optimal."

"Still, it means our Gentle Friends can't really decide to just take off on their own, right?"

"That is correct," Sentinel said. "We have retained the ability to override all command inputs to each ship until you deem otherwise."

"Perfect." Dash reached a curving ramp. At the bottom, he had to turn left and walk to the end of the corridor. "Incidentally, how much Dark Metal is here in this fleet?"

"A considerable amount. Tens of thousands of kilograms."

Dash descended the ramp. "I'm surprised the Golden never detected it."

"The Creators were wise to choose a system of little interest, and whose probability of containing useful resources was low," Sentinel replied.

"They were indeed." Dash reached the bottom of the ramp, turned left, and, sure enough, found Leira in a compartment at the end. She stood with her hands on her hips, examining something that looked disturbingly like a coffin. For a moment, he wondered if she actually had found an Unseen, or at least the corpse of one, similar to the Golden corpse they'd retrieved from the crashed ship on Gulch, that was now stored on the Forge, awaiting further study.

But it wasn't actually a coffin. It was a crate, labeled with Unseen characters.

"What have you got?" Dash asked.

Leira curled her lip. "Not sure. Something dangerous, though, based on what's written here." She looked at Dash. "It's a weapon of some sort."

Dash studied it, reading what was written on the casing, then pointing at a particular character. "That says *mine*, right?"

"As in, a thing that blows up when other things get too close to it? Yeah, I think it does."

"Well, this could be handy," Dash said. "Maybe something that Custodian could make aboard the Forge. That's what the place was made for, right?"

"Mines would be good," Leira said. "Any weapons we can get our hands on would be good."

Dash nodded. "Yeah. Now, we just have to get it, and the rest of the Silent Fleet, back to the Forge. Sentinel tells me it's going to take about eighteen hours before everything's fully powered up and all the ships' systems are stable."

"So we've got eighteen hours to kill."

"Yeah, let's not put it that way. Because, if the Golden are on the ball and get back here fast enough, *time to kill* might end up literally being true."

13

DASH WATCHED the last shuttle from the Silent Fleet drift into the docking bay then aimed the Archetype in that direction. He paused before applying thrust and gave himself a moment to take in the sight.

Fourteen ships now hung in space near the Forge, arrayed in a loose formation that looked as sloppy as hell. According to Sentinel, though, they'd arranged themselves to maximize the number of weapons that could immediately engage targets in any direction—a considerable feat of 3D geometric astrogation. What made it all the more remarkable was the fact that the ships had cooperated among themselves, fully autonomously, to configure the fleet this way. It had been their first test of the Silent Fleet's ability to function in a tight network, and they'd passed it without a glitch.

Of course, it was Unseen tech, Dash thought. It didn't really surprise him anymore that two hundred thousand year-old machines built by the enigmatic aliens still operated almost without flaw. He loved the *Slipwing* but couldn't imagine her being much more than a single entry in some obscure, far-future database two thousand centuries from now.

Except...what if she was famous? What if she was remembered as the ship that belonged to Newton "Dash" Sawyer, the Messenger, who was one of the people who saved everything from the menace of the evil Golden?

A thrill rippled through Dash at the thought. Somehow, this hadn't occurred to him until now. He, Leira, Viktor, and all the others—even the Gentle Friends—might be responsible for preventing the extermination of all sentient life. If they succeeded, and if the story became known afterward, they'd be famous. Beyond famous. Beyond heroes. They'd be saviors. The *Slipwing* might be preserved, put into some sort of stasis, a permanent exhibit commemorating the saviors of all life, which would be a beautifully symmetric turn on Kai's phrase for the Golden.

Dash suddenly saw it all marching through his imagination. Ceremonies. Interviews on news-webs. Parades. Parties. Dignitaries lining up to pay their respects to them. Parties. Holovids re-enacting their moments of near despair, like Leira almost crashing into this system's star after the battle against the Golden Harbinger. Parties.

Dash sighed. He'd rather just *fight*. That was what he knew.

"Is there a problem?" Sentinel asked.

Dash blinked. "What?"

"You have aligned the Archetype for a final approach to the docking bay but appear to be hesitating. Are you unwell?"

"I'm fine." He smiled ruefully and shook his head. "I was just indulging myself for a moment."

"Was it the one about the throng of multi-species women in zero-G?"

"No," Dash snapped, shaking his head. "And that was in confidence, you mechanical cretin."

"Fantasy seems to be a fundamental aspect of your psyche."

"I'm not *that* fixated on fantasizing about stuff, thank you very much." He started the Archetype toward the docking bay, leaving the Silent Fleet behind.

"No, I mean your psyche in a collective sense. Humans such as yourself, at least, seem to use fantasy in a variety of ways—to pass the time, to reinforce your own egos, to engage in pleasurable activities, to assist in problem-solving—"

"Wait, you've been studying the way I fantasize about things?"

"It is one aspect of my observations regarding you, yes. Remember, I am programmed to become as familiar with the Messenger as possible, to facilitate interaction with you."

Dash angled the Archetype's trajectory a fraction, offsetting the gravitational deflection from the nearby gas giant. Then he narrowed his eyes. "Hang on. Did you just make a general observation about my whole species based on your observations of me? Isn't that, well, not very scientific?"

"What do you mean?"

"Well, I'm like a single data point, right? But you just said that my whole species does a lot of fantasizing. That sounds an awful lot like what you'd probably call an *unfounded extrapolation*, or some such fancy criticism." Dash ended on a smug note, impressed he'd actually caught the AI in some flawed thinking.

"Admittedly, the sample size is very small, and my most detailed observations are of you, for obvious reasons. But Tybalt has reinforced this particular observation, because he has noted very similar behavior in Leira."

Dash's smugness evaporated like spent plasma exhaust, blown away by flickers of outrage. But before he could say anything else, the docking bay loomed ahead of him, demanding his attention as he landed the Archetype.

He made a heavily underlined mental note to have a chat with Leira and let her know their AI's were apparently *gossiping* about them.

DASH ALMOST DIDN'T RECOGNIZE the docking bay, as packed as it was by a throng of people. Instead of the big, echoing space he'd gotten used to, it felt more like being in an arrival bay on Passage right after a big liner had docked and disembarked its passengers. He threaded his way among the crowd of Gentle Friends, seeking out Benzel to ask him to get his people organized, before even beginning to try getting them settled in on the Forge.

He finally found Benzel, Wei-Ping at his side, standing in a small group with Harolyn, Leira, Viktor, and Amy. Ragsdale lurked nearby, eyeing the rest of the crowd with a tight expression that hinted at just how many security nightmares he was going through right now.

"Harolyn," Benzel said, spreading his arms for a hug. "So good to see you after all this time."

Harolyn curled her lip at him but said nothing and didn't try to return the hug.

Benzel's arms dropped back to his sides, but his grin—which Dash noticed seemed to consist of a lot of ostentatiously golden teeth, a few inset with tiny gems—didn't waver. "So I guess you didn't get my payment for that last job. Damned couriers, eh?"

There still wasn't a glimmer of anything but sardonic contempt from Harolyn. Benzel's attempt at a joke fell flatter than Harolyn's cold gaze.

Undeterred, Benzel started to say something else, but Dash lost it in the swell of noise from the assembled Gentle Friends, who were chattering away excitedly all around him—about the Silent Fleet, about the Forge, about the Archetype and Swift. Dash started to move closer to Benzel and Harolyn, worried that this might become a serious confrontation. Whatever remained of his earlier fantasies about fame and accolades as the Saviors of All Life—in his mind, he'd capitalized it—vanished, vaporized by the reality now facing him. He had lots of new allies, sure. But with lots of new allies came lots of new problems, interpersonal conflicts, egos to massage—

"I think we are beyond petty things like past debts," a voice boomed, cutting everyone off and causing silence to fall over the docking bay like a thick blanket. Custodian went on, "We, as well as the members of the Gentle Friends, must decide what is most important here—remaining committed to the single purpose of fighting the Golden, or being dismissed from this facility."

Wei-Ping lifted her hand like a schoolkid. "Ah, excuse me, disembodied voice? What, exactly, does *dismissed* mean?"

Custodian's answer was immediate. "Asked to leave, of course. Through an airlock. Ideally, but not necessarily, an airlock with a ship attached to it."

Dash glanced at Ragsdale, who simply gave him a cunning smile and a wink. Ever true to his determined focus on security, the man had obviously worked this out with Custodian, getting the rapt attention of the Gentle Friends immediately and trying to head off their no doubt unruly nature.

"Got it, boss," Wei-Ping replied to Custodian. Most of the Gentle Friends nodded with enthusiasm, although a few kept surly, even somewhat defiant looks on their faces. Or at least they tried to, but Custodian's not-so-subtle threat was made all the more menacing for its calm, implacable delivery.

"Actually, Dash, as the Messenger, is the *boss*, but for matters of security regarding the Forge, I can act with impunity," Custodian said, as matter-of-factly as ever.

Benzel looked at Harolyn, who finally let her flat façade fall away, revealing a mischievous grin. "Sorry, Benzel, watching you squirm a bit is all the payment I needed. Consider the debt cleared." She gestured around. "I think Custodian is right, we've got more important things to worry about."

Benzel grinned back. "Hell, I didn't know you were so easy to please!"

"I, however, am not," Custodian said. "I continue to await an acknowledgement regarding the behavior, not to mention the loyalty, of your followers as part of this war effort."

"Noted, and we're all on board, of course," Benzel said. He glanced around at the Gentle Friends. "If any of these followers put a foot wrong, I'll space them myself." He shrugged. "That's always been a part of our code." He raised his voice. "Right?"

As one, the Gentle Friends, roared back, "Right, Cap'n!"

Benzel turned to Dash. "Well, here we are—boss. When does the war start?"

"About two thousand centuries ago, give or take," Dash said. "So let's take some time to get you guys all settled in. I think we can afford a few hours for that."

IN THE DOCKING BAY, there had certainly seemed to be an awful lot of Gentle Friends. Dash had even wondered after taking them on board how much more room they'd have for future allies aboard the Forge.

Lots, as it turned out. The Gentle Friends barely made a dent in the available accommodations. Dash had known the Forge could hold thousands, but he hadn't really *known* it, at least until now. But even after showing them the blocks of compartments allocated to them by Custodian, then turning them loose, it still left row upon row of empty spaces lining desolate, echoing corridors.

Still, the Gentle Friends brought a raucous sort of life to the Forge that had been missing before. At first, as they were taken on a tour in smaller groups by members of what Dash had now taken to thinking of as his Inner Circle—Leira, Viktor, Conover, Amy, Kai and his monks, Ragsdale, and Freya. As part of their tour, Dash had told Custodian to let the Gentle Friends see the parts of the Forge he and Ragsdale had declared restricted, such as the fabrication facilities and the engine room. But he'd also ensured they knew they wouldn't have such access going forward, at least at first, because of their security concerns about possible Golden agents. He'd then braced himself for a backlash about lack of trust and the like, but the Gentle Friends surprised him with their indifferent acceptance of it.

"Makes sense," Benzel had said, watching as robotic arms deftly manipulated molds and components in the fabrication facility. After an awed shake of his head, he'd turned to Dash with a grin and said, "I sure as hell wouldn't trust me either."

The last stop for the group Dash led was a briefing by Freya in one of the botanical sections, about the vital importance of her work and the life it brought to the Forge. She'd already worked wonders, with all manner of plants—from the familiar, like pears and carrots, to the bizarre, like the Golden tech-enhanced plumatoes and stab-apples—growing in various types of soil, in fluid hydroponic troughs, or even in air gardens. Every day, she seemed to spread her fruitful work a little more through the Forge, turning barren, lifeless compartments into lush gardens.

"It's important to us," Freya said, watching as Benzel and the Gentle Friends accompanying him sampled various fruits and vegetables. "The Forge can composite food from basic molecules and print basically anything we could want. But that takes power and raw materials, and both of those are at a premium. The more we can grow, the less work the Forge has to do."

"And that means we can focus its resources into things like weapons and ships," Dash added.

Benzel swallowed plumato. "Have to admit, this beats out ship rations by a light year. But I like the occasional steak or chops—meat, anyway."

"You're right, animal protein is important," Freya said. "Both for the protein and micronutrients."

Wei-Ping wiped pineapple juice off her chin. "Sorry, micro —nutro—?"

"Vitamins and minerals," Freya said, offering an indulgent smile. "We need a bunch of those in our diets to stay healthy. We have to have the Forge manufacture our animal protein, though, because we haven't brought any livestock on board yet."

Benzel's eyebrows shot up. "Yet? You guys plan to bring cows and sheep and things like that aboard this place, too?"

"Maybe at some point, but we've got much higher priorities," Dash replied. "Speaking of the Forge making things for us, you guys really haven't had much chance to interact with the—well, the *being*, I guess, behind it all. Custodian, how about introducing yourself? And in a threat-free way this time?"

"I am Custodian. I am responsible for overseeing all operations of the Forge, on the Messenger's behalf."

"And he's, like, a computer, right?" Wei-Ping asked Dash.

Dash shrugged back at her. "Ask him yourself."

"Oh. Okay. Um, Custodian, you're just a computer, right?"

"I am not *just* anything. Nor am I a single computational device, as you would understand the concept, anyway. I am what you would term an artificial intelligence. I operate across all aspects of the Forge's functions."

"Which means he's basically everywhere," Dash said.

"Wait, everywhere?" Wei-Ping's eyes narrowed. "What about when I'm in the can, or the shower or whatever? I am going to have this Custodian spying on me?"

"I will be aware of all of your activities aboard the Forge at all times, yes," Custodian replied.

"Okay, that's creepy and weird." She glanced at one of the Gentle Friends, a squat, sturdy man with an enormous, bushy beard and a crooked nose. "Bad enough I've got Artur here trying to cop glances at me while I'm changing my clothes."

Artur raised his hands and turned crimson. "It was one time! And it was an accident! And you broke my nose over it. Can we just move past it?"

"I can assure you that I have no interest in the activities and processes required for you to maintain your bodies," Custodian said. "Indeed, I find them needlessly complex, as well as rather distasteful."

Wei-Ping put her hands on her hips. "Are you calling me distasteful?"

"Don't bother getting into an argument with Custodian," Dash said. "Believe me, after living and working with these AIs for these past months, I can confirm that arguing with them is like slamming your face into a bulkhead—it only feels good when you stop."

"Fine. But one smart-assed remark about my bodily functions, and I don't care if he's an AI, I'll still kick his ass!"

Dash winced in sympathy. "I know the feeling. Anyway, Custodian, I really would like you to start interacting with our new allies here in a positive and constructive way."

"I would never presume to do otherwise."

"That means answering their questions, offering them help, and guiding them around the Forge without being a snarky dick about it."

"I understand. I do, however, have to ask—how much input should I accept from them? They seem like a rather undisciplined group. Suppose they ask me to contravene my mission directives?"

Benzel spoke up before Dash could. "Believe me, we get it. We're good. Air locks, behave yourselves, all that. We're definitely good."

Dash knew that Custodian wasn't really asking a question, as much as driving a point home. He suspected Benzel knew it, too. But the hasty and earnest response from the leader of the Gentle Friends still made him chuckle.

"I'd say we've reached a détente," Dash said. "Benzel, I think this is the beginning of a beautiful friendship."

"Wasn't that a line from one of those Old Earth philosophers?" Wei-Ping asked.

"Something like that," Dash replied, with a lopsided grin.

14

WHILE THE GENTLE Friends got settled in, Dash had finally been able to find a chance for some downtime alone in his quarters. He'd just pulled off his boots and stripped off his sweaty socks when Custodian spoke up.

"Eight ships have just translated into the system and are now inbound for the Forge on a high acceleration trajectory."

Dash jumped to his feet—his bare feet, which prompted him to grab his boots and start hopping, bouncing from one foot to the other as he yanked his socks and boots back on—and started for the docking bay and the Archetype.

"Can you identify them?" he asked Custodian, and then took off at a run.

"They are an unfamiliar design. I am resolving details of their configuration for a comparison to known types now."

Dash reached a cross junction and saw Leira heading toward him, cinching her jumpsuit tight around her waist.

"Who are they? Does Custodian know?" Leira said.

"No. He's trying to work that out now."

"They might not be enemies."

Dash gave her a look. "Really? You think so?"

"No, not really."

They raced on, more and more people falling in behind them. Dash actually found it a little disconcerting to suddenly have so many people responding to an alarm from Custodian. This was definitely going to take some getting used to.

"I can find no direct correlation in available databases for these types of ships," Custodian said.

Sentinel cut in. "There is, however, a number of broad similarities between these ships and the battlecruiser we encountered in the Brahe system."

They reached the corridor leading into the docking bay. "You mean the one that apparently belonged to the Bright?"

They all knew full well that they had no idea what these Bright were all about, other than them almost certainly being some sort of allies or minions to the Golden.

"That is correct," Sentinel replied.

"Great." He looked at Leira, who had to head to the separate docking bay where they kept the Swift. "It looks like it's a fight. Are you ready for this?"

"Do I...*we*...have a choice?"

"Not really," Dash replied.

"Then yes, of course I'm ready for this." She flashed Dash a nervous smile. "I guess I'll see you in space."

He nodded and hurried around the corner into the docking bay. "Hey!"

Dash hesitated and turned back to the voice. It was Benzel.

"What do you want us to do? We going to fire up that Silent Fleet of yours?"

Dash shook his head. "I wish. But not this time. We're not ready for it. You guys just stay here and get Custodian to give you the blow by blow. Watch how this plays out. It could be important when we do get the Silent Fleet engaged."

Benzel looked disappointed but nodded. "Good luck out there, Dash. You go kick some ass."

"That's the idea," he called back over his shoulder, then he sprinted across the docking bay, dodged around the *Slipwing*, and mounted the Archetype.

DASH STUDIED THE HEADS-UP. There were eight ships incoming, all essentially the same design. Each was only slightly larger than the ships that made up the Silent Fleet. They maneuvered without any obvious thrust or exhaust, which roused both his curiosity and his caution. Were they using Golden tech? Could they *be* the Golden, but some other faction or group within them?

"Sentinel, how are they propelled? I don't see fusion plumes or anything."

"It would appear that they use a gravity-polarizing technology for propulsion," Sentinel replied. "It is similar to the technology used on the *Slipwing* for inertial dampening, but much larger and more powerful. The forces that normally would compensate for accelerations are, instead, used to propel and maneuver their ships."

Dash nodded. Okay, so not Golden tech. Gravity polarizers were used for propulsion throughout the galactic arm. They were efficient, using gravity itself as the propulsive force, so they were cheap to run, but they also tended to be slow, especially with increasing distance from gravity wells. That's why they were normally used for things like freighters and bulk carriers, ships that weren't expected to maneuver hard or fast and were more worried about being cost-effective.

These ones, though, were approaching much faster than any punky old freighter. The Bright had somehow figured out how to dramatically amp up their performance. It meant they could potentially thrust hard, and in unexpected directions, without having to reorient the ship or generate telltale exhaust plumes.

He discussed it with Leira. Not being actual Golden tech, the Archetype, the Swift, and the Forge, among them, shouldn't have much trouble seeing off these ships. Still, they agreed not to get cocky or make too many assumptions—especially since there could be Golden tech aboard them that hadn't yet announced itself. Leira would hang back initially, and just engage at range, while Dash got in close and tried to force the Bright ships into a knife fight. The more they could learn about their capabilities up front, the better. Only once they had a more complete picture of what they were up against would Leira risk getting closer into the fight herself.

"The Forge's defenses are now fully activated," Custodian reported. "Firing solutions have been calculated and are being updated for all weapons. However, they will not fire until you order it or the Forge is in imminent danger."

"Okay," Dash said. "Just hold fire for now. Sentinel, gravity polarizers will work better the deeper into the system they come, right?"

"Correct. The higher the strength of the gravitational field, the more efficiently the polarizers operate."

"So they'll be wanting to get in-system fast. That should give the Forge lots to do. Leira, let's allow a couple of these ships to get in relatively close to the Forge. I want to see how they maneuver at their best. I also want to see how effectively the Forge can take them on."

"You sure about that? Wouldn't you rather just destroy them as fast as we can?"

"Oh, we'll destroy them, all right. But let's see what we can learn while doing it, okay?"

"You're the boss."

Together, the Archetype and the Swift raced away from the Forge, their trajectory head-on for the approaching Bright ships.

THE SHIPS—THE Bright ships, they assumed, though that still wasn't certain—plowed deeper into the system's gravity well. As they did, their gravity polarizers gained more and more traction in the fabric of space-time, driving them ahead even faster. Dash now led Leira by several thousand klicks, the two mechs still boring straight in, head-on at their oncoming enemies.

"I have calculated firing solutions for all weapons," Sentinel said.

Dash nodded and kept his eyes on the heads-up, his attention to its data augmented by the Meld. He lined up the dark-lance on the lead ship. It was just entering extreme range, so he'd hold fire for another thirty seconds or so, and then—

"We are the Bright. We offer you the gift of elevation. Accept it and you will enjoy eternal life. Spurn it and you will be destroyed."

The voice was identical to the broadcast that had come from the massive ship that appeared near Brahe, as far as Dash could recall it. It was flat, mechanical, and yet somehow weirdly smeared across a narrow range of frequencies, as though it actually consisted of several voices speaking in unison.

Dash slowed the Archetype, delaying their intercept of the Bright.

Leira immediately spoke up. "What are you doing?"

"I want to see if we can draw out some information about this Bright thing, who or what they are—mainly because I'm tired of always having to add information like *who or what they are* when we talk about them. Tough to do that in the middle of a battle, so I'm going to negotiate."

"I just hope they don't turn out to be a race of gorgeous, promiscuous women, or we're all doomed."

"Not sure that's a deal breaker, given that we've got plenty of room on the Forge. Sentinel, open a reply channel to these Bright and let's see what happens."

"We are the Bright. We offer you the gift of—"

"Elevation," Dash cut in. "We get it. And that's all well and good, but maybe you should send along, I don't know, a brochure or something, describing whatever the hell *elevation* means. Hard to decide if we want to be *elevated* if we don't know what it means. Oh, by the way—I'm the Messenger. I'm comfortable in that role despite the implications. What I'm saying, in case it isn't clear, is that I'm in charge around here."

A window opened on the heads-up. Dash stared at it, unblinking.

"Who—no, *what* the hell are you?"

There were three of them—outwardly human, in that they had torsos and arms ending in hands, and a head, itself with all of the usual features in the usual places. But that was about as far as it went, because nothing else about them seemed remotely human. For one, they were virtually identical. Their skin gleamed, smooth and slick. They resembled nothing more than sculptures rendered in wax or some synthetic, pale and vaguely flesh-colored, but untouched by as much as a freckle.

That was all unsettling enough, but their eyes were the worst part.

They shone like crystal, like yet more artificial components of a manufactured statue, but they were too irregular to be wholly synthetic. They glittered with awareness, with an intelligence that was vast, but also cold and indifferent.

"We are the Purity Council of the Bright," they said. Sure enough, the three of them spoke in unison, their voices each separated just enough in tone to give that weird *harmonized-yet-discordant* quality. "We are ready to accept your submission, whereupon you will be elevated. No other outcome will be accepted."

Dash shook himself free of his stunned gape at these living mannequins. "Uh—yeah, thanks, but I think we'll pass on the elevation thing."

"Elevation is illumination and eternal life. Any other choice leads to destruction. Why then would you spurn elevation?"

"Well, first off, because I'm guessing it probably leads to us becoming something like you. And second, because I can't let go of my rugged individualism." Dash shrugged. "No offense, but your kind of eternal life? I'll pass."

"If you do not accept elevation, then you will be destroyed— if not now, then when all of those who have chosen the Enlightened Path of the Golden have assembled to render your final destruction."

Dash narrowed his eyes. "If you mean Clan Shirna, then we've kicked their asses once already. Believe me, I'd be happy to do it again."

"Clan Shirna is but one group who have chosen to walk the Enlightened Path. There are many others. Even now, they gather."

Dash shrugged again. "Eh, whatever. More asses to kick."

"We offer one last chance for submission and ele—"

"You know what?" Dash snapped, cutting the Purity Council

off. "I'm really tired of pretentious, long-winded assholes, which seems to be all that the Golden ever recruit to their cause. So I'll keep this short and simple. Screw you guys, and screw Clan Shirna, and screw everyone else who's been duped into becoming lackeys for the Golden. Oh, and screw them most of all."

Dash cut the channel before the Purity Council could respond. They resumed broadcasting anyway, blaring their message about submission and elevation and destruction across the system as their ships closed in on the Forge.

"I'd say you hurt their feelings," Leira said. "But I can't imagine they—whatever the hell they are—have any. Oh, and after seeing that freak show, yes, I still feel the need to say *whatever the hell they are*."

"Actually, we learned a lot there," Dash replied.

"How so?"

"It seems Clan Shirna might still be in the fight, for one. For another, it seems the Golden do, indeed, have other allies out there that we don't currently know about. That gives us a new priority: finding out exactly what we're up against."

"How do you know they weren't just lying, though?" Leira asked. "What were they going to say? Yeah, there aren't really that many of us who like the Golden it turns out?"

"I don't see these Purity Council guys really being much into subterfuge," Dash replied. "I mean, I may be wrong, but they strike me as the what-you-see-is-what-you-get types. If the Golden really didn't have many other allies, they probably just would have said nothing at all."

"Good point."

"The Bright ships have launched missiles," Sentinel said. "Three from each ship, a total of twenty-four inbound—twelve tracking the Archetype, the remainder tracking the Swift."

"Wow, what an unoriginal attack," Leira said. "Are these guys really that—I don't know, mechanical?"

"Let's find out, shall we?" Dash replied, targeting the dark-lance on the lead ship again. "Once more into the breach and all that…"

DASH RUSHED at the lead Bright ship head-on, snapping out shots from the dark-lance. Each hit blew chunks out of it. After the fifth shot, its gravity polarizers died, leaving it coasting. The remaining ships drove on, leaving their stricken comrade behind.

"Leira, you finished with your missiles yet? I'd rather not waste time swatting away the ones coming after me."

"Just about. I—crap, there's another salvo. These Bright really like their missiles, don't they?"

"Must have gotten a bulk discount—sorry, talk in a second."

He retargeted the dark-lance and blasted missiles apart one after another. Yet another salvo followed. He'd hoped that Leira could deal with the missiles herself, leaving him to take on the Bright ships, but he wasn't getting the chance. The Bright strategy seemed to be simply saturating them with missiles, tying them up—

A heavy shock ran through the Archetype. Something yanked Dash to the left, painfully hard. He glanced that way and saw a roiling patch of space, the stars beyond it smeared into whirls and streaks of light. It dissipated as he watched.

"Sentinel, what the hell was that?"

"The Bright ships have opened fire with an implosion weapon of some sort. It is similar to the Archetype's distortion cannon, with a much stronger, but far more localized effect."

"Great. Swarms of missiles, and now this." He flicked the dark-lance out again and again, blasting missiles apart each time; still, two from the first wave—or maybe it was the second, he wasn't sure—slipped past and detonated against the Archetype's shield. Dash winced, but the shield held.

He scanned the heads-up. Sentinel had compared the newly revealed Bright implosion weapon to the Archetype's own distortion cannon. The cannon momentarily projected a sudden, deep gravity well at a distance. Even a near hit threatened to wrench apart something caught in the effect. Even a near miss would subject the target to a gravity well of thousands of G's at the epicenter. Dash tended to use it more indirectly, projecting gravity wells that would yank things off of their trajectories, changing the course of a battle. He'd been holding off using it, not wanting to reveal it to the Bright unless he had to. After all, the less the Bright knew about *their* capabilities, the better.

But, here was that potentially decisive moment.

"Sentinel, I want to fire the distortion cannon. A lot. At the highest power level we can."

"I can route additional power to the distortion cannon, but the risk of damaging the weapon increases with increasing overcharge." After a pause, Sentinel asked, "What do you have in mind? Is it something based on the *feel* of the situation?"

"Still on that *feel* thing, huh?" Dash asked, grinning. "Well, sort of, yeah. But it's also about hard info. The Bright use gravity polarizers to propel their ships, right? And the distortion cannon creates sudden, intense artificial gravity, right?"

"Indeed. The distortion cannon is now overcharged, to one hundred and forty percent of its normal maximum yield. I would advise against overcharging it any further."

"And I accept your advice," Dash said, lining up a shot. He chose a target point ahead of the Bright ships, adjusting it as the range continued to diminish.

"Another salvo of missiles have been launched," Sentinel said.

"Of course they have," Dash muttered, then fired the distortion cannon. Then he kept firing it as fast as it would recycle.

The newly launched missiles suddenly veered off their trajectories, converging on the distortion cannon's targeting point. Dash saw them burn furiously, trying to correct, but most of them slammed together in a bunch, becoming a tangled cloud of debris. The effect on the Bright ships was even more dramatic. They slewed directly toward the distortion effect—very efficiently, thanks to their advanced polarizers—the nearest wrenching through such a hard and abrupt turn that its back broke, snapping the ship in two. Two more of the Bright ships swung into involuntary, converging trajectories and ground together, debris spiralling away from the collision.

Dash fired the distortion cannon again, but this time just got a warning message.

"As I feared, the distortion cannon is now offline," Sentinel said. "The Archetype's self-repair functions will not be sufficient to restore it."

Dash gave a resigned shrug. "That sucks, but I think we definitely gave them something to think about, other than just pouring cargo holds of missiles at us."

Indeed, disarray gripped the Bright fleet. The ships fought desperately to restore their order and sort out their trajectories. Dash capitalized on it by racing in as fast as he could, calling Leira to follow.

Her own dark-lance shots snapped close past the Archetype. "Hey, watch where you're shooting, woman! I'm trying to fly here!"

"Sorry. Still getting used to wearing this thing."

Five Bright ships loomed ahead, with two more lagging behind, damaged by their collision. The Bright had connected with the Archetype in a series of implosion shots that rattled his cage, but Dash had cut hard to deflect what damage he could. As he'd expected, this close in, missiles were less effective—they normally didn't arm until they'd traveled a safe distance away from their launch point, and they needed time to acquire and track a target. The chance of friendly fire was too great, even for combative zealots like the Bright.

Grinning fiercely, Dash raced the last few hundred klicks to the lead ship, then swept along its flank, raking at comms arrays, sensor clusters, and anything else he could strike with the Archetype's fists and feet.

A barrage of point-defense batteries opened up, the laser

beams flickering and sparkling against the Archetype's shields. Dash winced and grimaced at each hit, feeling them like stings from Kandarian wasps. By the time he'd finished the pass, the Archetype's shield had been saturated with energy, and she now radiated it away in a scintillating display, actinic light lost as it faded into space.

Ahead, another ship staggered under dark-lance hits as Leira found her target. He saw the Swift a few thousand klicks away, punching out carefully aimed shots. He knew Leira was anxious to get to grips with their enemies, but she had enough wisdom to keep her distance to get the feel of the Swift in its first actual combat.

Dash somersaulted, reversed course, and raced back toward the ship he'd just attacked. This time, he deployed the Archetype's power-sword, a massive blade that thrummed with energy, giving it an edge that could cut through duranium alloy like a hot knife through protein composite. As he raced close over the Bright ship's hull, he struck out, slamming the big sword into the plating and trailing it behind him with a shower of sparks, opening a gash most of its length. After wrenching the sword free, he backflipped again, changed course, and cut over a second Bright ship at right angles, cutting it across its beam.

"Holy crap, Dash. That's amazing!" Leira said.

Dash winced as more point-defense batteries targeted him. The shield, which had radiated away most of the energy it had captured, began to flicker and glow again.

"All in a day's—ouch—work."

"That's it, I'm coming in."

"Leira, you should—"

"Should've, could've, would've," she said, whipping the Swift through a course change even the Archetype would have trouble matching, and racing in toward the fight.

Dash considered warning her off again but didn't. Leira knew what she was doing; she didn't need him as some sort of protector, and he'd worked hard to encourage her growth. In fact, hearing her whoop as she zoomed in, dark-lance flashing, he had to smile in pride.

Now both the Archetype and the Swift danced among the Bright ships, slashing, punching, kicking, and, in Dash's case, cutting with the big power-sword. He remembered how disappointed he'd been when it had turned out to be the desperately needed upgrade he obtained right before the fight against the enemy mech known as the Golden Harbinger. It had been entirely misplaced disappointment; the power-sword was, he had to admit, an *awesome* weapon.

The Bright ships—four of them, now—charged on, picking up speed as their polarizing drives bit hard into the deepening gravity well from the star ahead. Dash and Leira kept up their knife fight, tearing off components, gashing and smashing open hulls, degrading the effectiveness of the Bright attacks. By agreement, they left one ship largely alone, however. Dash wanted to see if it tried anything new or different as it got closer to the Forge. Speaking of which…

"The remaining Bright ships are now within weapons range of the Forge," Custodian said. "Awaiting your instructions to open fire."

"Got it," Dash said. "Leira, let's take a breather and let Custodian have some fun."

Together, the two mechs dove away from the battle, putting distance between them and what remained of the Bright flotilla. Both the Archetype and the Swift had taken significant damage and could do with some recuperation and repair time. It was nothing compared to the Bright ships, though, which were now spread out along a path marked by debris and clouds of vented atmosphere. Only three remained under full power, using it to relentlessly bore in on the Forge.

"Firing now," Custodian said. His voice was unchanged from its typical, mild tone—which didn't fit with the fury unleashed from the station.

The Forge seemed to vanish behind a wall of dazzling light. Dark-lance and nova gunshots tore at the Bright ships, blasting huge pieces out of them. Meanwhile, salvos of missiles, their every maneuver choreographed across an intricate data network, wove themselves into an inexorable net around the enemy flotilla. All at once, they raced in, tightening the net—and then closing it.

The Bright's point-defense systems—the ones not disabled or destroyed by Dash and Leira—poured fire at the incoming missiles. Some were destroyed, but most weren't. All at once, they detonated en masse, bathing the entire fleet in a hurricane of energy made the heads-up on the Archetype go momentarily dark to avoid blinding Dash.

When it faded, Dash saw that only two ships remained under-way. They still snapped shots out at the Forge, but its defensive countermeasures, including the quicksilver-bright metallic shielding they'd only recently activated, shrugged off the hits. One of the two remaining Bright attackers abruptly went dead, its power offline, its drive suddenly dormant. That left a single ship—the one Dash had wanted to leave as undamaged as possible—to press home the attack.

And press home the attack it did. Dash watched it doggedly accelerate toward the Forge, its velocity such that a collision was inevitable. Of course, its polarizing drive might be able to slow or redirect it, but if not, then that much mass moving that fast could actually do serious damage to the station.

Still it drove on, trailing bits of debris, sparks, and a wispy wake of vapor. But the Forge, which had fallen utterly silent after that one spectacular burst of destruction, stayed silent.

"Uh, Custodian, do you need us to come and take out that last ship, or do you have it?" he asked.

"Please wait a moment," Custodian replied.

The Bright ship charged on.

"Custodian, is something wrong? Seriously, do you need Leira and me to—"

"There is no problem with the Forge," Custodian replied. "Rather, Benzel has requested that this remaining ship be disabled, not destroyed."

"He—what? Why?"

"He wishes to take it as a prize."

"A prize?"

"They are pirates, Dash," Leira said. "You hook up with that sort, you have to expect them to look at things from a pirate's perspective, right?"

"Custodian, *can* you disable that ship before it plows into the Forge?"

In answer, a single dark-lance beam flashed out and struck the Bright ship, tearing completely through its drive section. Its acceleration immediately dropped to zero, but it still raced on, sheer momentum driving it forward. Dash had to admire such surgical precision from the Forge, in contrast to the hurricane of violence it had unleashed only moments before. But it left the Bright ship a dangerous projectile, still hurtling toward a catastrophic collision with the Forge.

Dash shook his head and accelerated toward the Bright ship on an intercept course, Leira close behind. "Okay, Custodian, disabled just isn't going to be enough. All due respect to Benzel, but that ship needs to be destroyed before it—"

"That will be unnecessary, Messenger," Custodian replied—and the Bright ship began to slow.

"I have reconfigured the tractor systems used by the Forge to facilitate dockings and transfers between portions of the station to decelerate the Bright vessel. I believe it can be brought to a full stop before a collision."

"You *believe* it can?"

"There is a margin of error in the calculations."

"I don't like taking the risk, just because Benzel wants to take a *prize*."

"More practically speaking, taking an essentially intact Bright vessel would be useful from the perspective of intelligence about our enemies' capabilities," Custodian replied.

Dash sighed and slowed the Archetype. "That's true. Okay,

fine. Over to you, Custodian. Leira and I will stand by in case you need help."

Custodian didn't answer, though. Benzel did.

Thanks, Dash," he said. "Now you get to see what pir—I mean, privateers can do. This is what we're good at. This is how we can help the fight."

Dash shrugged. "Okay, I take it back then. Benzel, over to *you*."

15

BENZEL CLAPPED his hands together and laughed. "Okay, look alive, Gentle Friends," he shouted. "We've got work to do!"

All around him, the Gentle Friends snapped their vac suits closed, donned helmets, and checked their weapons. Beyond the force field closing off the docking bay, the disabled Bright ship hung motionless against the starfield, brought to a halt there by the Forge's tractor systems. Custodian had brought it as close to the station as he dared, citing the risk of a containment failure in the ship's reactor. That left it a few klicks away from the Forge, which was an awful lot of airless empty for the Gentle Friends to cross.

Amy, standing nearby with Viktor and Conover, stepped forward with a solution. "When Conover and I had to get to a remote part of the Forge, and do it fast, we rode on these nifty little maintenance remotes. You should ask Custodian if you can use some of those to help get out to that ship."

Benzel grabbed Amy's shoulders and laughed. "Young lady, that's an excellent idea. You'd make a fine pirate."

"Oh. Um, well…thanks, I guess."

"There is no higher compliment," Benzel said, laughing at her look of puzzled wariness. "Custodian, can you use these maintenance remote things Amy's talking about to help us out here? Anything would be better than dawdling our way out to that prize—the ship, that is—using nothing but reaction jets."

"There will be several maintenance remotes available shortly," Custodian replied.

"Thank you kindly, sir."

Benzel turned back to the Gentle Friends. Squad by squad, their leaders gave him a thumbs up, indicating their readiness to board the enemy ship. He shook his head, more than a little amazed. Here they were, aboard an ancient, alien space station, involved in an equally ancient war against more aliens, preparing to attack and seize a spaceship belonging to yet *more* aliens. Any of his people could flatly state that they'd never signed up for this, and they'd be right. Their Code, the unwritten but absolutely binding rules that governed the Gentle Friends in everything from splitting prize money to who got what bunk, gave them the latitude to say, at any time, that they were out.

But none of them did. Not one. Every one of his people was here, standing ready to face whatever might be aboard that damaged ship. He'd never been more damned proud.

He grabbed his helmet, but just tucked it under his arm. "Okay, listen up!" he shouted, waiting for the Gentle Friends to turn their collective attention to him.

"We're going to take that ship!" he went on. "By the numbers, the same way we always do this. The difference this time is that we're not doing it for the prize money. At least, not for now. For now, we're doing it because these Bright are murderous assholes, who are working for other murderous assholes, and if they get their way...well, there won't be any more prizes, ever."

He paused to let that sink in, then said, "What that means is we're going aboard that ship, and we're going to fight as hard as we ever have. Harder, even. We're going to prove that we can help *win* this war." He paused again, this time to let a slow smile spread across his face. "And then, when it's all done and we've kicked the asses of all these murderous assholes—well, *then* we'll go looking for our prize money. And believe me, there's going to be a *lot* of it."

Thumbs raised. With their helmets sealed, even if they were cheering, Benzel wouldn't have been able to hear much of it. But it didn't matter. The Gentle Friends were ready to do what they did best—kick ass and take prizes.

"Your rides are here," Amy said, pointing. A half-dozen black spheres, each about two meters in diameter, drifted silently into the docking bay. Benzel nodded, put on his own helmet, then snapped out instructions over the comm to his squads. He organized them into six groups, of either two or three squads, lining one group up behind each remote in single file. The first person in each group grabbed a handhold on the remote, while the rest joined hands behind them, forming six chains of Gentle Friends.

"Seriously, that's how you intend to approach that ship," a new voice said. Benzel turned to see Viktor talking into a comm.

"You can think of a better way?"

"Well—yes. Lots of better ways, actually. You could have only one or two people make each trip. Or you could have some use the remotes, and others travel some other way. Aboard the *Slip-wing*, maybe. We could launch her, and—"

As Viktor talked, Benzel walked up to him and touched his arm, cutting him off.

"Viktor, I'm sorry. I had no idea you were a skilled privateer."

"I'm not."

Benzel grinned through his faceplate. "I know."

He clapped Viktor once on the shoulder, then turned to join hands with the last person in the first line of Gentle Friends waiting to launch.

"Okay, people, we ready?" he asked.

One at a time, his squad leaders checked in, confirming comms and their readiness.

"Okay, Custodian," Benzel said. "Any time *you're* ready, we're good to go."

Benzel's weight abruptly dropped to zero as Custodian killed the artificial gravity to the portion of the docking bay occupied by the Gentle Friends. Then there was a slight tug and the remotes slowly began to move, pulling them into space and toward the looming Bright ship.

BENZEL PEERED AROUND A CORNER, his snap gun at the ready. There was still no resistance, and they had to be in control of at least half of the Bright ship now. He glanced back, shook his head at the squad behind him, then held up three fingers. They'd move in three seconds—two—one—

Benzel stepped around the corner, snap gun raised, forefinger on the trigger, thumb on the targeting slide. The Gentle Friends had only recently started using the nasty little weapons, military-grade hardware they'd acquired for what had seemed like an awful lot of credits at the time. But they were perfect for *parties*, the name they'd given to these sorts of boarding actions.

The snap gun fired two separate beams that individually were mostly harmless, but when they intersected, they became something entirely different. Benzel didn't really understand the physics behind it, but suffice to say that where the beams crossed, they were viciously deadly. With his thumb, he could move the targeting slide, changing the point at which the beams converged, meaning he could slide that little bit of deadliness toward or away from him to hit a target, but affect nothing else. It was perfect for taking out stubborn opponents who simply refused to surrender, while keeping the ship itself undamaged.

As he paced quickly along the corridor, Benzel wondered if he'd need to use the snap gun at all. During the admittedly hairy crossing from the Forge to the ship, he'd been grimly ready to come under fire, despite the assurance of Custodian that all its weapons had been neutralized.

But the maintenance remotes had towed them quickly and steadily along, six hand-linked chains of the Gentle Friends, the Bright ship looming silently closer—and nothing had happened. Likewise, breaching and boarding had gone without a hitch, helped by the myriad holes blasted through the hull plating by battle damage. And now, clearing progressed without any resistance or incidence. He checked the data-pad strapped to his arm. It marked the location of every squad as they systematically worked their way through the ship. It was more than half cleared now.

Maybe the crew was all dead. Or maybe there was no crew and the ship was automated. Either way, it would be both a relief and a bit of a letdown. Not fighting was always better than fighting, because it was less costly—and not just in lives, but in resources spent and damage done to a potential prize. But even a just a skirmish or two would help show Dash and the others that the Gentle Friends could take care of themselves. So far, they hadn't done much but ride along, helping to move that Silent Fleet back here to the Forge. But any half-assed group of spacers could have done that.

A figure stepped out of a cross corridor ahead. Benzel lifted the snap gun, but didn't fire. He couldn't spare any attention to the data-pad now but was sure none of the Gentle Friends should be ahead of him. Still, you always checked your target during a boarding action.

Tall. Slender. Naked? Really? No, clad in something form fitting. Smooth, almost porcelain skin, bald.

Turning to face them.

Raising a weapon.

Benzel triggered the snap gun, at the same time sliding the focal point of the beams into the figure. A bright flash, like a welding torch, ripped open its chest. At the same time, something smacked hard into the bulkhead beside him, plowing a glowing furrow through the metal. Behind him, he heard a muffled scream.

His target, who must be one of these Bright, toppled backward, trailing smoke. Benzel took a quick glance back and saw one of the Gentle Friends down, the two further back spattered with blood. They'd confirmed there was an atmosphere on board, and it was breathable, but they stayed vac suited-up anyway; atmospheres could vent fast during a party. So Benzel couldn't tell who was down. But, with active enemy now an actual threat, he couldn't afford the time to check. Leaving the downed Friend to the care of a squad mate, they pushed on, up the corridor, crouching, weapons raised to the ready.

Benzel decided to break comm silence. "All Friends, we've had a red glitch. Stay on your toes, out."

A *glitch* meant something bad had happened. A *red glitch* meant contact with a resisting enemy. They used other color codes, for everything from a fire, to a decompression, to an imminent containment breach. More than a few of the Gentle Friends were disgruntled ex-military, and Benzel had been happy to absorb their expertise in coded communications and other such martial stuff.

They reached the cross junction. Benzel signaled for the squad to move, securing the junction, while he stooped and checked out the—man he'd shot? Woman? He couldn't tell. The fallen figure was entirely androgynous, its features so utterly bland and unremarkable it could have been shown alongside the data entry for the generic definition of a face. It was, Benzel thought, like a statue come to life.

Aside from a form fitting, one-piece jumpsuit, the only other notable pieces of gear were a belt hung with several pouches, and its weapon. Now that was interesting. It looked vaguely like a rifle of some sort, but the muzzle wasn't a round hole, it was square. *Weird*. He shrugged and scooped it up, then slung it over his shoulder.

A Friend appeared, crouching next to him and touching their helmets together with a clunk. "Taro's down for good," the woman said, her voice buzzing through Benzel's helmet. She pointed back at the fallen Friend. "Chest blown out by—" She pointed at the Bright weapon Benzel had claimed. "By that, I guess."

"Taro. Shit. He owed me eighty credits," Benzel said. It was an old joke, a way of acknowledging the loss of a comrade, while pretending it was no big thing. Taro had been a long-time Friend, with a booming laugh and a knack for somehow always finding the best booze aboard a prize, if there was any. *Damn*. He'd miss him.

Mourn later, Benzel reminded himself. Right now, party time.

He gave the woman a thumbs up, then gestured for the squad

to get ready to move. As they did, he looked back down at the fallen Bright.

You shot Taro, you inhuman son of a bitch, he thought. *I hope that snap gun shot hurt like hell.*

BENZEL WINCED as something clanged off the bulkhead behind him. He dropped almost prone and peered around the sprawling console from what he hoped was an unexpected angle, snap gun ready. A Bright similarly peeked around the edge of another console closer to the viewscreen. Benzel triggered the snap gun, but a burst of sparks and flame from the console itself marked his miss. He spat a curse and pulled back, just in time to avoid being taken in the face by one of those vicious Bright projectiles.

Commotion erupted from across the bridge. Benzel slid to the other side of the console and looked that way in time to see Wei-Ping, a squad of Gentle Friends with her, charging the Bright. Another squad gave covering fire, their slug guns pumping out squash-head rounds. The squash-heads would do just that on impact, flattening out into a *splat* of explosive, then almost instantly detonating; the result was a powerful shock wave that swept through the target, turning vital organs to a slurry of ruined tissue. Their explosions otherwise did mostly superficial damage, barely even propagating into void spaces behind the impact point. It was another way of minimizing the damage to something that was supposed to be kept mostly intact and undamaged.

The remaining Bright fell back into cover but kept snapping out shots from their brutal guns. Benzel saw one Friend's arm snap back in a bloody spray of gore, then Wei-Ping and the squad with her were among the inhuman freaks, chain-blades whirring, boarding knives slashing and stabbing. Benzel leapt to his feet, dropping his snap gun and letting its combat sling yank it into his side; at the same time, he drew his own chain-blade, spun it up, and charged into the fray with a wild shout.

A confusing swirl of melee erupted around him. His chain-blade bit into waxen skin, shredding it. Something snapped past his head. Blades flashed. Blood spurted in shimmering jets and droplets. There were shouts. A scream. The deadly, ripping drone of chain-blades—

Silence.

Benzel looked around. None of the Bright who had taken their last stand on the bridge remained up. One more Friend had gone down, apparently shot through the hand, which he cradled in his lap, a gory mess. Wei-Ping, her vac suit spattered with blood, appeared in front of him.

"The other squads have reported in, boss. No more glitches of *any* color. The ship's ours."

Benzel shook his head, though. "Not yet it isn't."

Wei-Ping gave him a confused frown. "What do you mean? The whole ship's been cleared, all squads are accounted for—"

"These Bright freaks planned to scuttle this ship. It's rigged to blow." Even as he spoke, Benzel started scanning the nearby consoles, focusing on those the surviving crew had used for cover during their last stand.

Wei-Ping just stared. *Activating self-destruct* was such a trope, it was almost a joke among not just the Gentle Friends, but privateers everywhere. The fact was that no one really wanted to die— or even fight for— a cargo of uranium ore or helium-3. The Gentle Friends were accomplished fighters and wouldn't hesitate to use violent means to subdue their foes, but it was really all about the reputation, not the reality of it.

Most crews just surrendered when their ship had been run down, which played right into the other half of the Friends' reputation—if you gave up, you'd be taken prisoner, treated well, and then released entirely unharmed. Fights were wasteful, damaging, and inefficient. You wanted your quarry to just give up without a fight. It maximized profit.

But these Bright had fought to the death. They hadn't even contemplated surrender. A crew so willing to die would undoubtedly want to take their enemies with them.

Benzel's gaze fixed on a sturdy bank of panels, firmly attached to a bulkhead. "That might give some cover for the self-destruct blast. And I'm sure they've set one."

So Wei-Ping's eyes went wide behind her faceplate at the idea of the ship actually self-destructing. "How can you be sure?" she asked.

"Because it's what I'd do if I were one of these assholes," Benzel snapped. "Everyone spread out, check these consoles, see if they can tell you anything. Custodian, can you hear me?"

"I can, yes."

"Can you tell if this ship is rigged to blow up? Because I'm sure it is, but—" He stared at the unfamiliar consoles, those still intact glowing with displays and characters he didn't understand. "But I can't tell, because I can't read any of this bullshit."

"I am detecting a growing harmonic instability in the ship's fusion core," Custodian replied. "If it is not compensated for, there will inevitably be a containment breach."

"Let me guess—part of the control system has been deactivated."

"You are correct. The real-time compensators are offline. How did you know this to be the case without a specific scan?"

"Like I said," Benzel muttered, "It's what I'd do if were them." He turned from console to console, but he might as well be trying to read—well, an alien language, which is exactly what it was. The Friends who'd been examining the displays turned to him, one by one, and shook their heads. Hard looks tightened their faces, all of them only too aware of their danger.

The wrenching flutter in Benzel's gut mirrored their expressions. He forced himself to stay grimly on task, though. "Don't suppose you can reboot the compensators, eh, Custodian?"

"No. The relevant system is invisible to me."

"Shit. Okay, how long until we go poof?"

"The harmonic instability will reach criticality in no more than five minutes, with an approximately two-minute margin of error."

Benzel looked at Wei-Ping. "Guess we'd better stop this ourselves then, huh?"

"Yeah, but—how?"

Dash came on the comm. "You guys need to get the hell off that ship."

"In three or four minutes? We'd barely make it back to our entry points," Benzel replied.

"Shit. Okay, how about I bring in the Archetype, punch through the hull, and just rip the core out?"

"An active core? Come on, Dash, you know better than that. You'd just be doing the Brights' work for them."

"I know. I just—"

"Dash, just let us work the problem," Benzel said, tense and distracted. He understood why Dash wanted them off the ship— he didn't want them to die, either from a need for their skills or genuine caring. Maybe both.

"Okay," Benzel said, looking at Wei-Ping. "If Custodian can't see the system, it must be physically disconnected somewhere. If that's further down the line, then we're screwed, and it was nice knowing you guys. But if we assume the Bright did it from there, then the physical break must be somewhere in here, right? Am I making sense?"

"Yeah, you are, boss," Wei-Ping replied, then pointed. "Which means you're probably talking about something like that, right?"

He looked where she pointed. From under one of the consoles, a broken length of optical cable dangled. A dead Bright sprawled beneath it.

"Yeah, something just like that." He crouched and looked at the damage. Sure enough, the loose cable had obviously been deliberately pulled free, because several other cables exposed under the console hadn't. That left only one port into which it could plug. Taking a breath and hoping that this was it—because otherwise they were all already dead, and were just waiting for it to be made catastrophically official—Benzel grabbed the cable and plugged it back in.

"Custodian?"

"The harmonic instability has reached ninety-five percent of criticality. Regretfully, this means—"

"Damn it, save the stats and just tell me if you can see the compensator system now!"

"I can, yes."

Silence.

Benzel sighed. "Well?"

"The compensators are back online. Containment integrity is stable, but a risk of failure and breach remains."

Benzel sat back and indulged himself in a longer, slower sigh. "A *risk* is better than *it's gonna happen any second*, believe me."

Wei-Ping knelt beside him, a tired smile on her face. "Well, that was fun."

"Hey, we call these *parties* for a reason," Benzel replied, even managing to echo her smile as he did.

BENZEL STOMPED down the *Slipwing's* boarding ramp, yanking off his helmet and savoring the sensation of not being in a vac-suit. He'd made sure he was the last off the Bright ship, only stepping aboard the *Slipwing* when he was sure no other Gentle Friends remained aboard. Now, they gathered in tight knots roughly corresponding to their squads, chattering among themselves.

The exception was the squad to which Taro had belonged. Fortunately, he'd been their only fatality—two more of the Gentle Friends had been wounded, but would recover—but fatalities among them were actually rare. And fatalities from enemy action were even rarer. Mostly, when Friends died, it was from accidents. Benzel moved to join Taro's squad, but Dash, who'd just dismounted from his big mech, intercepted him.

"Benzel, that was awesome work," Dash said.

Benzel smiled back. "You expected any less?"

"No, of course I—" Dash began, then stopped, smiled ruefully, and shook his head. "Actually, truth be told, I wasn't sure what to expect from you guys. For all I knew, you could have been—"

"A bunch of bumbling idiots." Benzel held up a hand. "No, that's okay, I get it. We get a new recruit in the Friends, and they've got to prove themselves, too." He narrowed his eyes. "So, have we proven ourselves?"

Dash gave a firm nod. "Yeah, I'd say you have— "

"Messenger," Custodian cut in. "I have completed scans of the wrecked Bright ships. They do not, unfortunately, contain more than small amounts of Dark Metal, probably from incidental components of Golden technology."

Dash shrugged. "Ah, well. Can't have everything, I guess. Can you still use them for raw materials?"

"Yes—"

Custodian abruptly cut off. Dash frowned at Benzel. "Custodian, everything okay?"

"Two of the Bright ships just exploded."

"Oh. Core failures, I guess." Dash glanced across the docking bay at the Bright ship the Gentle Friends had taken. "At least we got one of them more or less intact. Custodian's powering its core down now, so we should—"

"They were not core explosions," Custodian said. "Or rather they were—but there was another component to the destruction of each ship."

Benzel frowned. "What the hell is he talking about?"

"No idea," Dash said. "Custodian, what do you mean, *another component?*"

"Each explosion generated a broadband, omnidirectional signal, which is essentially identical to that generated by the Harbinger shortly after its arrival in the system, prior to its attack."

"Still not following," Benzel said.

"What it means is that those ships sent out a death call when they blew," Dash said. "The one you stopped from exploding would have done the same thing."

"Oh. They're letting all their comrades know that they've died," Benzel said.

"Exactly. That means we didn't surrender the way the Bright and their Purity Council demanded. And *that* means they're going to assemble an even bigger force now to attack the Forge."

"Just as well we showed you what we can do then, huh?" Benzel said.

"You got that right," Dash replied, then excused himself and headed for Leira, who had just entered the docking bay from wherever she'd landed her own mech.

Benzel resumed his way toward Taro's squad. Better get used to this, he thought, because there stood to be a lot more parties like this one in the Gentle Friends' future.

16

DASH CROSSED his arms and watched as a chunk of a wrecked Bright ship slid into what Custodian called the forage bay—a large, empty space similar to a docking bay but outfitted with all manner of giant claws and gantries and derricks. Raw materials, whether scrap or unrefined ore, would be brought here by the Forge's system of tractor fields, then broken down as feedstock for the fabricators. The Bright ships had turned out to yield only minor amounts of Dark Metal, but their shattered structural members could still be smelted down and used to make other things. Outside the forage bay, suited figures waved and jetted away to ready another broken chunk of ship for processing.

"I swear, the Gentle Friends would rather be out there, floating around in space," Leira said.

Dash smiled. "They do seem pretty at home in hard vacuum, don't they?"

"Weirdly so, yeah. I've spent most of my life in space, and I do everything I can to avoid putting on a vac suit."

"I hear you." Dash nodded, then he turned as someone walked up behind them.

"There's another half-dozen big chunks out there," Benzel said. "My people are getting them lined up so Custodian can bring them inside for processing with minimum fuss."

"You know, I think Custodian can probably handle this without your folks having to go outside," Dash said, but Benzel shook his head.

"Not disagreeing. But it keeps them busy and makes them feel useful. Believe me, you do *not* want to let the Gentle Friends get bored. Idle hands, and all that."

"Good to know——" Dash replied, but a heavy, grinding racket cut him off.

Massive claws had descended, grabbing and lifting the fragment of the Bright ship that had been brought aboard. More articulated arms unfolded from the ceiling, plasma cutters flaring and slicing into the metal. Watching the process reminded Dash of the nasty but adorable little creatures called chompers that he and Leira had encountered during the retrieval of a power core for the Archetype. Basically nothing but cuteness and teeth, they'd been similarly brutal and efficient in tearing apart and picking over a carcass. In just over a minute, the chunk of broken Bright hull was gone, rendered down to fragments and whisked away by conveyor fields to the fabricators. The next slab of hull was already framed in the entrance to the forage bay, ready to come aboard.

"That is absolutely freaking amazing," Benzel said. "Kind of chilling, too."

"The total yield of usable material from the Bright ships is approximately four thousand tonnes," Custodian said. "There is also approximately one hundred kilograms of Dark Metal in seventy-two different fragments. These, however, are too small and too distant from the Forge for the tractor systems to retrieve them."

Dash looked at Leira. "We really don't want to let that much Dark Metal go to waste. Care to take the Swift out for a spin?"

"Sure. You don't want to let me get bored, after all. Idle hands, and all that."

Benzel's laughter echoed after them as they headed for their mechs.

"Leira, I'm seeing a fragment of Dark Metal, two kilograms, about ten kilometers off to your right," Dash said. "Sentinel's sending the data over now."

"Yup, I see it too. On my way."

The Swift smoothly veered toward the Dark Metal signature, then deftly plucked it out of space and stowed it.

"You're flying the Swift like you've done it all your life," Dash said. "I think I bumbled around with the Archetype for quite a while trying to figure it out."

"Your performance as the Archetype's pilot was much less

than optimal for a considerable time. You finally reached an acceptable level of performance only after—"

"Did I ask you for a performance assessment?" Dash asked. "Because I really don't think I asked you for a performance assessment."

"To be fair, Dash, I got to work with Tybalt for hours in the simulator before I even first strapped into the Swift," Leira said. "You had to pretty much learn how to fly the Archetype—well, on the fly."

"Even now, your performance remains less than optimal," Tybalt said. "I estimate that you will require—"

"Echoing Dash here, Tybalt," Leira said, cutting her AI off. "I don't recall asking you to grade me."

"Judgmental AI's are judgmental," Dash said.

A short while later, they retrieved the last piece of Dark Metal that was worth chasing down. Dash hesitated before turning back for the Forge. Instead, he simply stared at the stars in the heads-up.

"Dash, everything okay?" Leira asked. "We're not detecting anything—"

"No, you wouldn't," he said, breaking himself out of his reverie. "I was just thinking."

"Uh oh."

"Laugh it up, woman," he said, but went quickly serious. "I'm just looking at the stars. The Golden are out there somewhere. Not the Bright, or Clan Shirna, or any of their other minions. The Golden themselves."

"That's true," Leira replied. "Where are you going with this?"

"It's those Death Calls put out by the Bright ships when they exploded. Sure, they signalled the Bright themselves, told them that we'd kicked their fleet's butts. That's bad enough. It means they'll be coming back, in force, and they might not be alone next time."

"Okay…"

"But the Golden have to be receiving these Death Calls, too. So they sit out there, somewhere, and just send in the next wave of their nasty little followers, and then the next, and the next after that. They don't care if they die, because they'll just send more. And we fight them and kill them—but that's just doing the Goldens' work for them, isn't it? I mean, I can't believe that if they get their way and exterminate all sentient life, they'd spare the Bright or Clan Shirna or anyone else."

"Maybe we can convince them they'll be spared," Leira replied. "Pull them over to our side."

"I considered the same thing myself," Dash said. "But imagine the Bright saying they've decided to join us. Could we actually trust them? Would *you* trust them, Leira?"

After a long pause, she said, "No, because if they'll do it with you, they'll do it *to* you."

"Oldest story in the universe."

"I highly doubt that *that* is the oldest story in the universe, Messenger," Tybalt said, practically ending on a haughty sniff. "Indeed, even the most cursory review of available historical archives demonstrates—"

"It was just a figure of speech, Tybalt," Dash cut in. Damn, that AI had been tailor-made to best complement Leira's personality? What did that say about her? Or what these Unseen AIs thought about her?

"I've said it before," Leira added. "Welcome to my life now."

Dash grinned, but it didn't last. "Anyway, we have to assume they'll be coming back for another round—they being the Bright for sure, maybe some Clan Shirna as well, maybe some others we haven't even met yet."

"And maybe the Golden themselves," Leira said. "Imagine having to fight a fleet of ships like we just did, plus one…hell, maybe several of those Harbingers all at once."

"I'd rather not, thanks," Dash replied. The truth was, he had imagined exactly this, a true nightmare scenario.

"They will assuredly return," Sentinel said. "It really is only a matter of when."

"Exactly. And that brings me back to my point about the Golden just lurking somewhere out there, sending attack after attack at the Forge. That's us playing their game, just reacting to what they do." He stared at the starscape on the heads-up. "I never really got good at poker until I met a guy on Passage named Rostov."

"Darien Rostov?" Leira asked. "I know him. Hell of a courier. Heard he died, though, in some sort of accident."

"Yeah, he did. He accidentally forgot to hand over the profits to some gang on Celestus for a bunch of chems he ran for them once. Then he accidentally got shot in the head."

"Oh. Ouch."

"Anyway, Rostov cleaned me out in poker. More than once.

But we kind of hit it off, and he showed me a bunch of ways to get better at the game."

"You mean cheating," Leira said.

"It wasn't all cheating. Anyway, my point is that what he basically taught me was that I had to take control of the game. I couldn't just keep reacting to my opponents. I had to make *them* react to *me*. Once I took that lesson aboard ship, I started losing a lot fewer credits."

"Losing fewer credits? That's success?"

"What can I say, I suck at cards," Dash said. "As for our current situation, the Golden are Rostov, sitting out there across the big table. And they're controlling the game. We're reacting to them. It's time for that to change. We need to get ahead of them somehow."

"Messenger, if I may," Tybalt said. "I believe that you are correct."

"You don't have to sound *quite* so surprised."

The AI ignored him. "I believe that in order to begin forcing the Golden to react, we should begin by making their approach to the Forge more complicated and costly than simply arriving in this system and attacking it."

"Making the Forge a more problematic target for the Golden would, indeed, be a good first step," Sentinel said.

"Okay, how would you suggest we go about doing that?" Leira asked. "I mean, we have the Silent Fleet. Maybe we could deploy it in some sort of defensive arrangement."

"I'd rather keep that fleet mobile," Dash said. "I don't want to tie it to static defensive duties. Right now, in fact, it, plus these two mechs, are our only real way of taking any sort of initiative." He narrowed his eyes at the stars. "But when we found the Silent Fleet, we also found that mine aboard one of them, remember? If we had more of those..." Dash trailed off, mind suddenly racing.

Custodian's smooth baritone cut in. "I have evaluated the mine you're speaking of. It was a prototype, not made operational or put into production by the time the last clash between the Creators and the Golden ended. Accordingly, it was stored aboard the Silent Fleet against the possibility it would eventually prove useful."

"Well, it might prove damned useful now," Dash replied. "What sort of mine is it?"

"It is a smart mine, which incorporates a relatively basic AI to evaluate targets and, in cooperation with other mines, initiate an attack."

"Okay, so they're basically like our missiles then."

"Not quite," Sentinel said. "The mines are specifically designed to maximize stealth and explosive effect, at the expense of a drive unit. They do, however, possess a limited ability to maneuver using a quantum tractor effect that leaves no signature in real space."

"Well, that sounds like a hell of a good thing to have," Leira said. "Can we power ships with those?"

"Unfortunately, no," Sentinel replied. "The technology proved problematic to scale up. It simply isn't possible to move more than a few hundred kilograms using a quantum tractor, and even then, relatively slowly."

"It does, however, have the advantage of being essentially undetectable by any known scan," Custodian said.

Dash nodded along as they spoke, his glum thoughts about the Golden essentially holding all the cards giving way to growing enthusiasm about maybe being able to do something proactive. "Can we manufacture these mines on the Forge?" he asked.

"Yes," Custodian replied. "It will require revision of the fabrication priorities, but the Forge is quite capable of making them."

"Okay, and how much Dark Metal do they need?" Leira asked. She'd only just beaten Dash to the question, because the availability of Dark Metal seemed to be an implacable choke point for most of the things they wanted to do.

Custodian's answer therefore surprised him. "The mines require no Dark Metal in their fabrication, unless you want them to be able to communicate without any delay for distance."

"So we can basically begin manufacturing these mines right away?" Dash asked.

"We can," Custodian replied. "The wreckage of the Bright ships would provide sufficient raw material to fabricate twenty such mines alone."

"That doesn't sound like very many mines. I mean, space is big, right?"

"Space is big, yes," Custodian said, with a hint of a tone that sounded to Dash to be—amused? "And that isn't very many mines. Indeed, it is far short of what would reasonably be required to help to protect the Forge. However, since they use more commonly available materials, their production could be quickly scaled up."

"Okay, so let's say we start churning out these mines," Leira said. "Can they use that—what did you call it, a quantum tractor?"

"Yes. It is a device that uses quantum effects—essentially, the fundamental properties of space itself—to provide motive power. It requires essentially no fuel in any conventional sense, merely a source of power."

"That's really something," Leira replied. "Anyway, can the mines use it to deploy themselves from the Forge?"

"Not in any practical sense, no. The maximum speeds attainable are on the order of a few hundred kilometers per second."

"Well, then. I'd be a very old lady by the time the first ones were even in position."

"Actually, Leira, you would likely be dead," Tybalt said. "Based on your physiology, and environmental factors, I would estimate that your expected lifespan—"

"Is not important right now, thank you," she cut in. "Let's just stay on the subject of these mines, okay?"

"In other words, we need to deploy them from a ship of some sort." Dash gave the heads-up a thoughtful frown. The mechs and the Silent Fleet were too valuable to tie up in minelaying duties. The *Rockhound* was busy fetching Dark Metal from the crashed Golden ship on Gulch. That left the *Slipwing* and the *Snow Leopard*. Dash was no expert on minefields, but instinct told him that with just the two ships shuttling mines out from the Forge, laying them, and returning, it could take a *long* time to get any meaningful minefields established around the Forge. And that was probably time they didn't have. If they were going to do this, they needed to do it soon.

"Can we fabricate some sort of minelaying ships?" Dash asked. "Something unmanned that's specifically made for ferrying out and laying mines?"

"There are plans available in the Creators' archives for autonomous service vessels that could be adapted, yes," Custodian said.

"Alright, then let's do that. We'll meet in the War Room with everyone else an hour after Leira and I get back to the Forge to work out the details."

"There is one other matter I should bring to your attention, Dash," Custodian said. "Although the Death Call signals generated by the Bright ships that exploded were omnidirectional, they were also asymmetrical."

"Let's pretend I don't get what you're talking about," Dash replied. "Mainly because I don't."

"There was an additional signal generated that contained additional, encrypted information. It was focused in a single direction, but it was embedded in the omnidirectional signal, presumably in an attempt to obscure it."

"Oh. Good work seeing that. So where was this additional signal aimed?"

"It appears to have been directed out of the ecliptic plane of the galactic arm."

"Huh." Shortly after first finding the Archetype, Dash's pursuit of a Clan Shirna ship had taken him out of the ecliptic plane to a secretive Golden facility lurking among a field of rocks and ice in nearby intergalactic space. Ironically, he'd had to contend with Golden mines there. Looking at Custodian's data, painted onto the heads-up by Sentinel, he saw these signals were aimed in a different direction. Another, similar Golden installation then?

"It is quite possible," Custodian said. "However, I can resolve nothing of significance in that direction, at least within any range in which scans would return reliable data. Nor am I detecting any other significant Golden activity within sensor range."

"Okay, so let's assume there's a Golden base of some sort just outside the galactic arm, at that location, but it's just outside the range of your ability to scan. Knowing what we do about their tech, how long would it take a Golden ship to travel from there, to here, at its best possible speed?"

"I would estimate a minimum of three days," Sentinel said. "If we assume the Golden do not operate their drives continuously at maximum output, however, a four or five day minimum is more likely."

"Yeah, but as little as three days. Shit." Dash scowled at the heads-up. "Okay. We need more Dark Metal, and we need it fast. Custodian, scan for Dark Metal, power cores, Golden, Unseen—anything. I don't care what it is, as long as we can use it against these bastards. They'll be taking their best shot at us, whatever that is, and we don't have enough force in depth to stop them from getting to the Forge. And that *cannot* be allowed to happen."

17

DASH SCANNED the faces of everyone assembled in the War Room. They all stared back, waiting for him to speak.

For a moment, it once more left Dash more than a little bemused. The Saviors of All Life—and he was their leader.

That made whatever he was going to say stick in his throat. Previously, he'd mused about being hailed as a hero, and celebrated across the galactic arm. Now, it just left him feeling small and terrified.

Kai abruptly stood, walked up to Dash, and put a hand on his shoulder. "Have faith in the Unseen, Messenger. After all, they have faith in you."

Dash gave him a wide-eyed look. "What? How did—?"

"I recognize moments of wavering faith," Kai said, smiling. "I frequently see them in the mirror, in fact." He patted Dash's shoulder. "They pass."

Dash gave the monk a grateful smile as he returned to his place, then he turned to the rest of those gathered—his own Inner Circle, plus Harolyn and Benzel.

"I think Kai's advice is good for all of us," Dash said, and he got a chorus of agreement. "All right, then. We have some decisions to make. I laid them out for you when I called this meeting, so you've had an hour or so to think things through."

"Seems to me like you've already got a solid plan," Ragsdale said. "The *Rockhound* just returned with more than a thousand kilos of Dark Metal—" He paused and looked at Harolyn. "Thanks to your people, incidentally."

She nodded. "They're good at what they do."

"Yes, they are," Ragsdale replied. "Anyway, we'll send them back for more. In the meantime, we're going to make these new mines you described, and Custodian is scanning for anything else we can use that's reasonably accessible—" He shrugged. "What other decisions do we have to make?"

"We need to decide if we want to take the fight to the Golden this time around," Dash said.

Ragsdale crossed his arms. "I'm as aggressive as the next guy, but didn't you say Custodian didn't actually see anything where those Bright signals were sent? All we know is that they were directed somewhere outside the galactic plane?"

"It doesn't mean there's nothing there," Amy said.

Conover nodded. "Dash even encountered a Golden facility outside the boundary of the galaxy. It seems that that's where the Golden might be hiding out."

"Which means that the Bright might know a lot more about

the Golden than we've realized," Leira said. "Maybe there's even information aboard that ship the Gentle Friends captured."

"That would explain why they were so determined to blow it up," Amy said.

"Custodian already gave me an update and there was nothing useful. It looks like they managed to wipe a bunch of data before Benzel's people secured the ship," Dash said.

"No chance of retrieving any of it?" Ragsdale asked.

Conover answered. "No. Dash asked me to take a look at their systems and archives, and I did. They encode their data in the spin-state of electrons. It's easy to completely disrupt that and wipe it clean. Whatever they deleted, it's gone for good."

"I suspect the Bright actually do know where the Golden have been lying low," Dash said. "But for now, anyway, we won't be getting anything out of them about that."

"So that means we'd be striking out in the wake of that Bright signal and basically seeing what we find," Leira said.

Viktor, who'd been silently taking in the debate, sat up. "Going after the Golden with the information we have would be —well, stupid, is the only word I can think of."

"Why do you say that?" asked Dash.

"Because we can only count on the two mechs and the Silent Fleet to be able to reliably make the journey. You're probably going to have to send all of those anyway to ensure you even have a chance of taking on whatever you find. Even then, it might not be enough, because we simply don't know what you might end up facing."

Dash nodded. "Go on."

"That leaves the Forge to defend itself. The *Slipwing* and the *Snow Leopard* aren't going to be able to contribute much to that." Viktor looked at Benzel. "No offense. The *Snow Leopard* is a fine ship, but—"

Benzel grinned and held up a hand. "No offense taken. Oh, if you'd have said that to me a week ago, I would have probably punched you in the face for badmouthing my ship, sure. But that was before I knew about…well, all of this." He gestured expansively around, almost catching Harolyn in the face with a swinging hand. "So you're right. Just my poor *Snow Leopard* and your *Slipwing* aren't much of a defense for this place against— well, whatever's probably coming for us."

"And they probably will be coming for us, Dash, sooner rather than later," Viktor went on. "They'll want to knock us out before we've had time to get ready for them. I'd say Sentinel's timeline of three to five days is probably accurate. There really won't be a decent minefield in place by that time. So, you go racing off after who-knows-what with our best and most capable forces, leaving the Forge mostly undefended. And the Golden destroying, or worse, capturing the Forge is exactly what you want to avoid."

Dash looked at Viktor, then sighed and nodded. "I want to disagree with you. But I really can't. Much as I want to take this damned fight to those Golden bastards for a change, we really can't afford to do it until we know this place is decently secure."

"Well, maybe we can help with that," Harolyn said. "I've got my whole crew scavenging that crashed ship on Gulch—which, incidentally, I'm supposed to tell you is creepy as hell."

"You should've seen it before we wiped out all the Golden nasties lurking inside it," Amy said.

"Anyway," Harolyn went on. "Now that we've got our operation there up and running, I don't need to send the whole crew. We've got some damned fine metallurgists and engineers that might be able to help with fabricating things here, like those mines."

"Custodian, could you use the help?" Dash asked. He expected a dismissive *no, we've got this covered and, anyway, what could they possibly do that my Unseen tech can't*, so the AI's answer surprised him.

"Yes. There are a number of areas in which their expertise could be of value, such as evaluating scrap and other raw fabrication feedstock for its metallurgical properties."

"Oh. Well. Okay then." Dash looked at Harolyn. "There you go. Have your folks report to Custodian as soon as you can."

She gave firm nod and thumbs-up.

"And all this talk about metal and raw materials and such takes us back to what's turning out to be our most stubborn problem," Dash said.

"Dark Metal," Conover put in. "It's our supply of Dark Metal."

Dash nodded. "Took the words out of my mouth. We've scavenged whatever we could find as debris from the fights we've already had in this system. And Harolyn's people are getting us more from the Golden wreck on Gulch. But it's still not enough. We need to find a source of more Dark Metal—preferably *lots* of Dark Metal—and we need to do it, like, yesterday. Thoughts?"

In the lingering silence, no one spoke. It dragged on, but everyone's expression remained thoughtfully blank. Dash wasn't surprised. They couldn't just conjure Dark Metal out of thin air. He was about to say as much and try to direct the discussion about how to proceed with only the Dark Metal they knew they had, but Sentinel broke the quiet with an uncharacteristic sound. She spoke rarely enough, and the sound was so out of place for the AI that everyone stopped to listen.

"Ah," she began.

"*Ah?* You're an ancient, artificial super-intelligence, and you just said *ah?*" Dash asked, incredulous.

"I said that because I hesitate to introduce my idea, knowing your tendencies. The *ah* sound was within my twelve-point-five percent leeway for, as you call it, sass."

"Then by all means, sass away. You have my undivided attention," Dash said.

"Actually, given your tendency to do things with reckless abandon, I hesitate to alert you to this, but—"

Custodian cut in. "There is Dark Metal in this system, and it is accessible, under certain conditions."

Silence descended again, then Leira groaned. "Let me guess. It's somewhere that requires dangerous maneuvers at great risk, or something like that, isn't it?"

"From a practical point of view, yes. But that risk could be mitigated with the right tools," Sentinel said.

Tybalt chimed in, "Tools which we can build, given the many tons of metal we now have at hand."

"What kind of tools?" Conover asked.

"And where exactly is this Dark Metal?" Dash asked. He'd been wracking his brain, trying to recall something he'd obviously forgotten—although how the *hell* could he have forgotten about Dark Metal, here in the Forge's system, that they hadn't already retrieved?

"Please don't say it's in the gas giant. Please don't," Amy said.

"It is not," Custodian said.

"Oh, thank—" Leira said, but Sentinel cut her off.

"There have been a number of engagements in and around this system since the Forge was built. Over time, fragments of Dark Metal debris from those engagements has been pulled inward by the star's gravity. Now, there is free-floating Dark Metal in circular orbits very close to the star. However, these very close orbits result in such a high velocity that collection would be a serious issue—again, unless certain tools are in place," Sentinel said.

"What sort of tools?" Amy asked.

"And why didn't we detect these instances of Dark Metal before?" Conover asked. "We should have seen them when we tested the new Dark Metal scanner."

"Dark Metal scans look for shadows in the neutrino flux, where neutrinos are being blocked," Sentinel replied. "However, neutrino emissions from the star obscured these on your scanner. It is a limitation of Dark Metal detection, in that close proximity to a sufficiently strong source of nuclear fusion, such as a star, will prevent such scans from being reliable."

Conover was nodding by the time Sentinel had finished speaking. "Okay. Makes sense." He pressed his lips together. "So we need a way of not just detecting neutrino shadows, but also discerning variations in the local neutrino flux."

"Which is a great problem for you to work out," Dash said. "But not right this minute. Right now, I want to know more about all this Dark Metal that's apparently floating around, pretty much right outside our door. Sentinel—or Custodian—or even Tybalt for that matter, when were you going to get around to telling us about this?"

"The specific orbital mechanics involved make retrieving this Dark Metal impractical, so telling you about it seemed unproductive," Sentinel said.

Dash took a breath and held it for a second. These AIs. Sometimes, he just wanted to—

He let the breath out. "Okay. So why tell us about it *now*, then, if we can't retrieve the stuff?"

"That would bring me back to my *ah* sound," Sentinel replied. "Given the vital urgency for obtaining Dark Metal, I can offer two possible solutions. First, you could use the Lens in a manner similar to what you employed when rescuing Leira, and partially collapse the star. This would not change the orbital dynamics, but the greater distance from the star's surface would allow easier access to the Dark Metal in question."

"Uh, let's call that plan B for now. Partly collapsing that star was hairy enough the first time. I'd hate to vaporize the Forge and everything else, including us, by blowing the star up." Dash crossed his arms. "You said two possible solutions. What's the other one?"

"Whatever it is, bet it'll probably end up being plan C," Amy muttered.

"Accelerate the Dark Metal sufficiently that it breaks free of its orbit around the star," Sentinel said. "Then slow it down again to capture it."

Harolyn raised a hand. "Okay, wait a second. I'm not a pilot or astrogator or anything like that. We speed it up, and then slow it down? Why not just slow it down so you can grab it from the get-go?"

Dash felt confident that he knew the answer. "Because it's orbiting so close to the star, it's moving really fast relative to us here in the Forge, which is where we want it to end up. But that fast orbit is stable. If we slow it down now, it's just going to fall into the star and we'll lose it. If we speed it up enough, though, it'll be thrown out of orbit and then head off into space." Dash rubbed his chin. "Speeding it up is easy. We can just push it with the Archetype and the Swift. The trouble is slowing down and catching it once it gets here."

Leira shrugged. "Just use the mechs to decelerate it, too."

"I guess. That means making trips back and forth with the mechs, which is going to take up a lot of time."

"So just accelerate them with the mechs," Conover said, looking up from a data-pad he'd been tapping at. "Let's use something else to slow them down before they get here, to the Forge."

"Like what?" Leira asked.

"Dark Metal is magnetic," Custodian said. "The Forge could

generate a sufficiently powerful field to decelerate the Dark Metal when it arrives, although not stop it entirely."

"A magnetic field," Dash repeated. "Yeah. Okay. Do we have a collection system to do the final grabbing?"

"We can move a construction claw outside," Viktor said. "Custodian, would that work?"

"It would, although I recommend a larger claw."

"How do we do that?" Viktor asked.

Tybalt answered first. "We build it. Of course."

18

"THERE'S ALWAYS A CATCH, EH?" Benzel said, laughing.

"That's the fourth time you've made that joke since we got out here," Viktor replied, his voice flat.

"That's because it's a good one! We're calling this the Catch, right? So that sounds just like—"

"Yes, I get it. Can we please just get this thing set up now?"

"All right, kids," Dash said, rolling his eyes at the idea of *him*, of all people, having to be the adult. "Less chirping, more work, if you please."

The Archetype and the Swift hung side-by-side, just a few kilometers from the surface of the Forge where the Catch would be installed. Dash had zoomed in the imagery on the Archetype's heads-up to watch as the Gentle Friends, supervised by Viktor, working in concert with the Forge's tractor systems and mainte-

249

nance remotes, maneuvered the ungainly contraption into position.

Its appearance certainly lived up to its name, the Catch. A slender, articulated arm that could extend a kilometer into space, it ended in a bank of magnetic manipulators and a massive, chunky claw. The magnetic elements would bleed off whatever final velocity relative to the Forge the incoming Dark Metal chunks had, while the second component would physically grab them and pull them into the station. The Gentle Friends were scrambling about the base of the Catch, ensuring it was adequately anchored to the Forge's hull. Dash wanted to ensure the thing was operational before they launched for the mission.

Speaking of which—

"Amy, you all set to fly?" Dash asked.

"Roger that."

Dash glanced at the *Slipwing*, keeping station a few klicks spaceward of the mechs. Amy would fly her in front of the Dark Metal debris as he and Leira flung them from their orbits around the star, doing a first round of deceleration. She actually possessed a feature that made her well suited for the job—a magnetic drive. Dash had won it in a poker game on a transit station called Roundabout, not long after he'd been spanked and educated in the reality of the game by Rostov, in fact. It was meant to allow a ship to ride the magnetic fields found in every star system, saving fuel. It wasn't very powerful, but Viktor, Conover, and Custodian had amped it up, meaning it should be able to grab and hold the Dark Metal while Amy applied decelerating thrust.

It was a complicated plan, with a lot of moving parts, which Dash hated. Simple plans were almost always better. But it also stood to take the least time, and right after Dark Metal, time was their most precious commodity.

"Okay, I'm showing all restraints in place. The Catch is fully bolted down. Custodian, let's do a test."

As Dash watched, the Catch rose smoothly into space, its jointed arm extended until it was completely straight. It retracted, then partly extended again and began flexing through a series of movements.

"Okay, that is impressive," Benzel said.

"Wouldn't it be nice to have one of these, just grabbing ships as they go by?" Wei-Ping asked.

Benzel laughed. "It would."

"Yeah, well, we've got more important uses for it right now than piracy—sorry, *privateering*. Viktor, what's the verdict? Is it going to work?" Dash asked.

"Is it working now? Yes, it is," Viktor replied. "Is it going to work, catching flying chunks of Dark Metal? I guess we'll see."

"Okay, then. Let's go round up some Dark Metal," Dash said, turning the Archetype and powering smoothly away from the Forge, heading for the system's star. The Swift and the *Slipwing* fell into formation alongside him.

"This actually brings back some not very pleasant memories," Leira said.

Dash glanced at the roiling surface of the star, just under a million klicks away. They were well into the corona, the thin, fiercely hot envelope of charged gases surrounding it. A ship like the *Slipwing* wouldn't last long this close to its incandescent surface, but the mechs simply got hot.

Very hot, mind you.

"Sentinel, how are we doing temperature wise?"

"The exterior of the Archetype facing the star has been heated to just under two thousand degrees in your Kelvin scale. The side facing away from the star is at minus twenty-two Kelvin."

Dash whistled. That temperature differential, across just a few meters of hull, would stress ships like the *Slipwing* to the point of starting to rip them apart. Between her alien substance and the hyper-tech of the Unseen, the Archetype not only shrugged it off, but was able to exploit the much lower temperature on its shadowed side to radiate away its accumulated heat.

Still, Dash got what Leira was saying. Following the battle against the Golden Harbinger, she was nearing this distance from the star in the *Slipwing*—and oblivion—when she used the Lens to crunch the star down and make it possible for Dash to rescue her in the Archetype. He remembered his own despair in those moments before they came up with their desperate plan, and he wasn't the one facing his own imminent death.

He decided to push away the brooding memories, for both of them. "Okay, the first Dark Metal chunk is one minute ahead," he said, studying the heads-up. "A big one, too. At least two hundred kilos."

"Got it. The next one, about two hundred kilos, too, is about thirty seconds ahead of that one. So you do the first, and I do the second, right?"

"Yup, you got it." Dash glanced at a window inset in the heads-up. It showed two trajectories, one for each of these pieces of Dark Metal. The first extended directly to the Forge; the second had the chunk of debris taking a longer route, wrapping around the gas giant. This should give Amy time to intercept and decelerate both pieces of salvage with the *Slipwing*, so they arrived at the Forge staggered in time, giving the Catch time to grab and stow each. It was ambitious, and relied on extremely precise astrophysics. But, assuming it worked, it would give them more than four hundred kilos of Dark metal in just a few hours.

Dash glanced at the star again. As he did, inspiration struck him.

"We keep calling this star just, well, the star. You should give it an actual name, Leira," he said.

"It has a name."

"Yeah, well, GC-blah-blah-dash-blah isn't very inspiring. I'm thinking of something with a little more oomph than just a stellar catalog number."

"Okay. But why should I name it?"

"If anyone has earned the right to give this thing a name, it's definitely you," Dash said.

"Well, let me think about it." She paused, then said, "Leira's Star has a nice ring to it."

Dash smiled. "I'll take it under advisement."

"We are ready to undertake the orbital departure maneuver,"

Sentinel said. "And I agree, Leira's Star does have a certain appeal to it."

"You tell him, sister. Us gals gotta stick together," Leira said, laughing.

Dash lifted his brows, sighing, then focused on the task at hand.

The Dark Metal chunk wasn't very big. Apparently the remains of a Golden probe at least two hundred thousand years old, it wasn't much larger than one of the Archetype's hands. And, with the Archetype matching its velocity, it looked stationary. Harolyn had still asked why it was so critical, and the answer was clear.

Because of orbital mechanics, of course, something non-spacers didn't really understand. The debris *was* stationary relative to the Archetype. But its velocity relative to the Forge was enormous, thanks to its extremely tight orbit around—Leira's Star? Really? So, the first thing they had to do was break it out of that orbit and start it heading for the Forge, and that meant speeding it up even more.

Dash eased the Archetype forward, until he could plant its massive hands on the chunk. It was a credit to his experience with the big mech that he did it without even introducing a hint of tumble. Now he watched the heads-up, waiting for the Archetype's drive to power up. Starting and ending the burst of acceleration required ultra-precise timing, so the piece of debris not only broke orbit, but did it on the exact trajectory they wanted. That, he would leave to Sentinel.

"Drive activating now," Sentinel said.

The Archetype surged forward, pushing the Dark Metal chunk ahead of it.

"How's the temperature, Sentinel?" Dash asked.

"Still well within acceptable limits."

Dash nodded. Just a few meters away from where he was ensconced in the cradle were temperatures high enough to pretty much instantly turn him to soot. It was just best not to dwell on yet another aspect of spaceflight.

The Archetype raced on, rounding the star. On the heads-up, Dash saw Leira had started accelerating her own target piece. Dash made himself wait and watch while the seconds ticked down to the drive cut-off.

"Target velocity achieved in five seconds," Sentinel said.

The Archetype, and the chunk of Dark Metal, began to slide out of orbit around the star, now moving too fast even for its formidable gravity to hold back. As soon as it did, the Archetype's drive cut off. Both now traveled in a straight line, aimed—after taking into account other gravitational effects, like that from the gas giant—directly at the Forge.

"The Dark Metal's new trajectory is acceptable," Sentinel said.

"Good work," Dash said.

"Was it? I merely resolved all of the relevant variables then used them to calculate—"

"Just take the compliment, okay?"

"Oh. Well, then I believe the customary response is thank you."

"We'll make a human of you yet," Dash said, angling the

Archetype back toward the star and the next piece of Dark Metal debris.

Sentinel's reply was quick and firm.

"I certainly hope not."

THE FIRST PART of the plan worked. There were now four pieces of Dark Metal inbound for the Forge, their trajectories designed by Sentinel and Tybalt to have them arriving at roughly half-hour intervals. Amy zipped about in the *Slipwing*, using its reinforced magnetic drive to slow them down with powerful burns from the fusion drive, while nudging them through any minor course corrections with her thrusters. Based on her occasional whoops and cheers, she seemed to be enjoying herself doing it, too.

"You sound like you're having fun," Viktor said, chuckling. He saw Benzel grinning through his faceplate, too, as the Gentle Friends prepared for their first use of the Catch.

"You should hear her at this end," Conover said. He'd accompanied her, using his Dark Metal detector to zero her in on the pieces of debris that she couldn't otherwise see. "I'm getting a running commentary of the whole operation here."

Viktor chuckled again. The affection in Conover's voice was just *so* apparent. They really did make a cute couple.

"That's because this whole operation is *awesome!*" Amy said. "Although, there is one thing."

"What's that?" Viktor asked.

"These deceleration burns are using up a lot of fuel. I think we're good for two more pieces of Dark Metal, then we're going to have to come back to the Forge and top off the tanks."

Viktor frowned at that. They hadn't been sure just how far the *Slipwing's* fuel would go, but they'd figured it would have been further than this. They'd need to pause the whole operation for the ship to refuel. "Amy, I appreciate your enthusiasm, but you're not being a little too—let's say *liberal* with your burns, are you?"

"Nuh uh. It's the magnetic drive. It doesn't quite hang onto these chunks properly, so I have to burn a little slower, but on a longer course to get the delta-V we want."

"It's true," Conover added. "Amy's doing everything right, here."

Of course you think that, you lovelorn kid, Viktor thought, but he didn't say it. "Okay. Let Dash know. And I have to go, Benzel's telling me it's almost time for our first arrival."

He joined Benzel at the base of the Catch, which towered against the starfield above them.

"Okay, Custodian, are you tracking the first piece of Dark Metal?" he asked.

"I am. It is thirty seconds out."

As one, Viktor, Benzel, and the Gentle Friends turned to look at the rough point in space where the Dark Metal fragment should appear. They saw nothing.

The Benzel pointed. "There! Two degrees to the right of the Catch's claw, a little low."

Sure enough, a tiny dot moved against the starfield. Dark Metal reflected little light, so Viktor had to keep finding it, mainly by looking through his peripheral vision, rather than straight on. The dot rapidly grew.

Now the Catch silently extended, configuring itself and its claw just *so*. The dot drifted closer, becoming a distinct shape, an elongated oblong. The Catch swung toward it, positioned itself ahead of it, then swung back, following its trajectory. Viktor knew its magnetic grapples were pulling at Dark Metal, bleeding off its remaining velocity by shunting the kinetic energy into the Catch.

The claw closed, clamping around the Dark Metal—

Which pulled free and bounced back into space.

"Well, shit," Benzel said.

Viktor scowled. "You got that right."

"The geometry of the specific piece of debris is difficult to anticipate," Custodian said. "In retrospect, the claw portion of the Catch should have been made more flexible and given a greater range of motion."

"Benzel, Your *Snow Leopard* has no magnetic drive, does it?" Viktor asked.

"Nope."

"Custodian, can you use the Forge's tractor system to grab it?"

"No. The tractor system only operates in close proximity to the hull."

"And it'll take too damned long to fire up one of those Silent Fleet ships and go after it." Viktor sighed. "Well, we know its velocity and trajectory, so once the *Slipwing's* available, we'll be able to—"

"Custodian," Benzel cut in. "Kill the gravity where we are."

Viktor turned. "What are you doing?"

"We're going to go grab that thing and bring it back."

"But we can retrieve it later."

"Sure. And then we can retrieve the next one, and the one after that. But that's time spent that we don't have, right?"

Viktor opened his mouth, but closed it again. The man was right.

"What do you plan to do?"

"I'd explain, but every second that thing moves further away. Custodian, kill the gravity, now."

Viktor's weight abruptly disappeared. Benzel and the Gentle Friends immediately launched themselves into space, using bursts from the reaction thrusters on their vac suits to begin overtaking the errant piece of Dark Metal.

"We'll get the damned thing and bring it back," Benzel said. "Viktor, you and Custodian figure out how to catch the rest of them properly."

Viktor watched in awe as the Gentle Friends carelessly raced off after the Dark Metal. Just seeing them dwindling into space without tethers made his toes cramp inside his boots, like they were trying to dig in the Forge's hull.

The Catch retracted, collapsing back into its articulated self to bring the Claw back down into reach. At the same time, gravity reasserted itself, turning the Forge back into something under Viktor's feet, and not just something nearby.

"We have little time to effect modifications to the Catch, Viktor," Custodian said. "Do you have any ideas regarding how to proceed?"

Viktor took a last look at the Gentle Friends, shook his head, and muttered, "Crazy sons of bitches." Then he turned his attention to the Catch. He did have an idea, actually.

BENZEL WASN'T sure why so many spacers hated free-flight. Being stuck on a tether meant you were really just still part of whatever ship or station you were tethered *to*. Flying free meant you were yourself, separate and distinct. It was freedom.

And, yes, it was risky, even if you knew what you were doing. Frankly, though, it was also a hell of a lot of fun.

"Okay, gang," he said. "Once we catch this thing, we need to enact the next part of my cunning plan."

Wei-Ping, who drifted along beside him, rotated herself to face him. "And what would that next part of your cunning plan happen to be, boss?"

"No idea."

She laughed.

Benzel grinned back at her, then focused on the data-pad strapped to his arm. He tapped at it, calculating what they could accomplish with the reaction fuel they all had remaining. Seven Gentle Friends besides him, and assuming they still had eighty percent of their reaction fuel left, that meant—

Problems. At the very least, one *big* problem.

He frowned. "Shit. We can probably bring it to a stop, but that'll use up all of our fuel. Hey, Custodian, can you send some of your maintenance remotes out here to help us?"

"You are currently beyond the range of the remotes' operating envelope. They do not have actual propulsion systems, but rather rely on polarizing the Forge's gravitation."

"Of course. Okay, Friends, it looks like we have to do this the hard way. Looks like I'm venting my suit. And I need"—he tapped at the data-pad—"three more volunteers."

"Count me in," Wei-Ping said.

Everyone else volunteered, too. Benzel picked two of the Friends at random; each returned a thumbs-up.

"Okay, so you know the drill. We burn our reaction fuel until it's gone. The rest of the thrust we need comes from those of us stupid enough to vent our suits. We use the kick from the releasing air to start us back toward the Forge. And then, we'll have to share the air in the remaining suits until we get close enough for Custodian to help out. Questions?"

"Yeah, I have a question," Wei-Ping said. "Dozer over there rips loose with some wicked farts. Damned things'll abuse the shields. Do I really have to share his stinky air?"

VIKTOR WATCHED in satisfaction as the Catch lived up to its name, neatly catching the next Dark Metal fragment, bringing it to a full stop, and pulling it down toward the Forge.

"I love it when a plan works out," he said.

"The use of a net was an inspired decision," Custodian said. "I am intrigued as to how you arrived at it."

"Fishing."

"Fishing?"

As it descended toward him, Viktor studied the cargo net he'd taken off the *Snow Leopard* and quickly pressed into service on the Catch. He hadn't been sure it would be sturdy enough, but it looked entirely undamaged. "When I was a boy, I used to go fishing with my grandpa. We'd use a line to hook a fish, but we'd use a net to finally grab it and add it to our haul," he said.

"I understand the words you just used, but their context eludes me."

Viktor laughed. "When we have some time, Custodian, I'll happily sit down and tell you all about fishing."

"Hey, Custodian," Benzel's voice cut in. "How much longer until we're close enough for the remotes to come get us?"

"At your present velocity, approximately twenty minutes."

"Damn."

"Is there a problem? Did you misjudge your remaining air?"

"Oh, I misjudged it all right." He made a gasping sound. "Ask Wei-Ping how."

"Told you," Wei-Ping said. "Dozer, you need to go see a doctor. Seriously, man."

DASH WATCHED as the latest piece of Dark Metal broke orbit and started for the Forge. It was only sixteen kilos of the stuff, hardly worth the effort.

"I think we've done all we can. This is just too slow and

complicated, without enough payoff to make it worthwhile," Dash said.

"I have another suggestion," Sentinel said.

"I'm listening."

"Now that we have begun scanning the system thoroughly for Dark Metal, we are finding more of it than had been anticipated. In this case, there is almost one thousand kilos available."

"Yeah, I don't like the sound of that," Dash said. "If it hasn't even been detected until now, then it's got to be somewhere—let's call it awkward."

"Where is it?" Leira asked, her voice the very definition of a resigned sigh.

"It is orbiting in the upper atmosphere of the brown dwarf planet. There is actually nuclear fusion occurring in the core of the brown dwarf, and the resulting generation of neutrinos obscured this debris. Additional data obtained by Conover, when testing his new Dark Metal detector, has allowed it to be resolved."

"So how would we go about retrieving *this* Dark Metal?" Dash asked.

"I calculate that the *Slipwing*, with its modified magnetic drive, along with the Archetype and the Swift, should be collectively powerful enough to pull the debris from orbit and place it on a trajectory to the Forge."

"But?"

"But, given its depth in the brown dwarf's atmosphere, it would expose you to—"

"Being crushed like an empty can." Dash sighed. "Gravity. It's my nemesis."

"Mine too," Leira said. "That's how I almost died in space the time before I almost fell into that damned star, remember? When the *Slipwing* dropped into that gas giant to get away from Clan Shirna?"

"Oh, I remember, all right," Dash replied.

"I get to relive all of my worst moments, it seems," Leira said, her tone flat. "Yay me."

"Okay, tell Amy to take the *Slipwing* back to the Forge. We'll get her refueled and re-rigged. And then, you can tell everyone that, for our next performance, we'll be heading to the brown dwarf."

19

DASH GAVE the heads-up a long frown. The hurricane of radiation from the brown dwarf degraded the effectiveness of even the Archetype's scanners, a fact which had made it a great hiding place during his fight against the Golden Harbinger. Now, though, it just made trying to discern what, exactly, was going on with the Dark Metal that much more difficult.

"It looks like one large, and a bunch of smaller fragments, tied into orbit with that little moon," Leira said.

Dash nodded. The moon barely rated the name, just a hunk of rock maybe ten klicks long, and two across. Its orbit had degraded enough that it had actually dropped into the brown dwarf's atmosphere, its passage through which left a wake of gas heated to glowing by friction. The atmospheric drag slowed it further, causing it to fall even deeper into thicker atmosphere, which slowed it even more.

"Yeah, and it doesn't have long to live, does it? Dash said.

"No, it does not," Sentinel replied. "In approximately six months' time, it will have fallen irretrievably far into the brown dwarf's atmosphere."

"I'm surprised it's intact at all and hasn't just broken up from all that drag and turbulence," Viktor said. Aboard the *Slipwing*, he, along with Amy and Wei-Ping, hung well outside the envelope of radiation and charged particles billowing off the brown dwarf. "For that matter, I'm even more surprised it just hasn't started to vaporize entirely."

"The moon is actually the remnants of a Golden missile platform," Sentinel answered. "It is reinforced throughout with Dark Metal, which gives it far more structural integrity than it would naturally have."

"So it can actually survive a plunge into the guts of this brown dwarf?" Dash asked.

"In a manner of speaking. The Dark Metal will eventually reach a stable depth inside the brown dwarf and remain there. The rock, however, will soon break apart and being to vaporize."

"It's already pretty deep," Leira said. "I don't think we're going to have time to try and mine the dark metal out of that moonlet."

"We won't," Dash said. "And we're not even going to try. There's still at least a couple thousand kilograms of Dark Metal in orbit around it, most of it in that one big piece we can see. We're going to snag that and bring it back to the Forge."

"The effects of the brown dwarf's environment will severely degrade the capabilities of both the Archetype and the Swift,"

Tybalt said. "Even retrieving that single, large piece of Dark Metal will be problematic."

"That's why Leira and I are only going to try boosting its orbit back up until its high enough for the *Slipwing* to join in the fun and add its pull. That should be enough to get it clear of the brown dwarf and start it back to the Forge. At least, that's the plan, right, Sentinel?"

"It is. I estimate that it has at least an eighty-five percent chance of success."

"That's a fifteen percent chance of failure," Viktor put in.

"Hey, it's our devil's advocate," Dash said. "But you're right, Viktor. Still, we can't pass this up. That's too much Dark Metal to just let fall into this brown dwarf, to be lost forever."

"Actually, this brown dwarf will only continue undergoing nuclear fusion for approximately ten million more years," Tybalt said. "And then—"

"Effectively forever," Dash cut in. "Longer than I'm going to be alive, anyway."

"Indeed, *much* longer," Tybalt said.

"Anyway, if we're all set—"

"Uh, Dash?" It was Amy.

"Go ahead."

"I'm pretty happy with how I've come along as a pilot. But I'm looking at this trajectory Sentinel's put together for the *Slip-wing*. It's pretty hairy. There are some really fast corrections that have to be made so we don't spend too long being blasted by x-rays and other crap from this brown dwarf—not to mention screwing up compensating for atmospheric drag and falling into the damned thing."

"I have faith in you, Amy. You can do this."

"I'm glad you have faith in me, Dash. Trouble is, I don't."

"Well, that's why we brought Wei-Ping along. She's an experienced pilot, so she can help you out."

"Yeah, well, Wei-Ping and I have been talking, and we both kind of agree that she should be the one doing the flying here."

"To put that another way, if I'm going to be aboard this ship when it does a dive into a brown dwarf's upper atmosphere, I want someone really good at the helm," Wei-Ping said, coming on the comm. "And Amy here is a nice girl and all, and I'm sure she kicks ass as an engineer, but, well, she ain't what I'd call really good. Yet."

Dash frowned. "You've never flown the *Slipwing* before. You don't know how she handles."

"All due respect, Dash, but in my line of work, you often have to get very good at flying ships you've never flown before, and you have to do it really fast."

"When you steal them, you mean," Leira added.

"When they come suddenly into my possession," Wei-Ping said. "*Steal* sounds so unpleasant."

Dash's frown remained, but both Wei-Ping and Amy had a point. Now was not the time to worry about egos or hurt feelings —not that either of those things seemed to be an issue here. Nor was it time to worry about being able to trust the Gentle Friends, whose performance so far had been nothing short of amazing.

"Okay, go ahead and switch seats," Dash said. "Amy, set Wei-Ping up with access to all the *Slipwing's* systems."

"Already done!" Amy said, then she put on an apologetic tone. "Sorry, Dash, we were kind of going to do this anyway."

Dash opened his mouth to snap something back, but he closed it again and just smiled. Wasn't that sort of decisive initiative exactly what he *should* want from these people?

"Okay then, folks," he said. "Looks like we're ready to do this. Wei-Ping, you stand by up here. Leira, you all set?"

"Ready as I'll ever be," she replied.

"Alright then, here we go," Dash said, and dove the Archetype toward the moonlet and its precious Dark Metal, Leira in the Swift right behind him.

DASH COULD FEEL the upper reaches of the brown dwarf's atmosphere roaring against the Archetype, like an atmospheric re-entry that went on and on. The hull temperature of the mech shot up to well over a thousand degrees Kelvin as it plowed through the stew of gases, leaving its own glowing wake of friction-heated gas. He wasn't used to anything but smooth silence from the Archetype, but now he could actually *hear* the distant thunder of its passage and sense the tremors running deep through its structural bones.

"Sentinel, how are we doing?"

"Hull temperature is stable at one thousand two hundred and

twenty degrees Kelvin. Flight is also stable, but variations in gas density require constant course adjustments."

"I'll leave that in your more than capable—well, you don't actually have hands, but I think you get the point." He studied the heads-up. The wreckage was about two minutes away at a steep angle from the galactic plane. He kept the Archetype aimed at it, coming at the moonlet and Dark Metal fragments from an angle that avoided its shimmering coma and tail of sublimated gases.

"Leira, still with me?" He could see she was, of course, on the heads-up, but wanted to keep the chatter up. It was as much to help dissipate his own tension, as hers.

"I'm here, still in one piece. I wouldn't give the *Slipwing* long in here, though. We're barely inside this thing's atmosphere and its already a lot denser than she'd be able to take."

"Which is why we have to boost that big piece there up to where she can grab it." He sighed. "I hate leaving the rest of this Dark Metal here, though. Inside that moon, there must be—I don't know how much more. Lots, anyway."

"Thousands of kilograms," Sentinel said. "However, the mass of the moon far exceeds anything the Archetype and Sentinel could accelerate beyond a crawling pace."

"Yeah, I know. Still sucks." And it did. This moon probably contained as much Dark Metal as they'd managed to harvest from this entire system so far, all in one place. The fact that this place happened to be drilling through a brown dwarf's atmosphere at terrifying speed meant it might as well be on the other side of the galaxy.

Dash shoved away his regret at not being able to recover more of the precious stuff and concentrated on the Dark Metal fragment they were going to recover. Thirty seconds now.

"Okay, Leira, looks like the plan still holds. You ease the Swift in behind that chunk to the right, and I'll go left. Nothing fancy, we just boost as hard as we can. Sentinel, Tybalt, you two work out the details to keep us in sync. The last thing we want is for the two of us to be pushing in two different directions."

Both mechs acknowledged. Staying on top of the details was vital, but that's what the AI's were good at. The Swift accelerated faster than the Archetype, but the Archetype could sustain a higher velocity and push harder. If they didn't keep the complex array of forces absolutely synchronized, then the Dark Metal chunk might start to tumble, even lose orbital velocity and fall deeper into the would-be star.

"Wouldn't it be a hell of a thing if the Bright showed up right about now?" Leira asked.

"You trying to give me ulcers? Let's just let Custodian and the gang back at the Forge worry about that for now and focus on this, hmm?"

"Sorry. I just don't like being so blind."

Dash had to nod at that. Between the friction-heated gas enveloping the mechs and the powerful emissions of heat, x-rays, and charged particles pouring out of the brown dwarf, their effective scanning range had been reduced to a few hundred kilometers, at best. In celestial terms, that was like being able to see nothing beyond the first few millimeters of your nose.

"Ten seconds until you are on station," Sentinel said.

Dash nodded again, easing the Archetype forward and down, sliding in behind the Dark Metal chunk. As he did, he raised the mech's shield. The rush of gases immediately abated, deflected by the invisible barrier. At least it would normally be invisible, but now it glared in the heads-up as a fierce corona of shimmering light. The mechs' shields would smooth their flight somewhat, but they could only absorb so much energy before they had to recycle and radiate it away.

Dash nudged the Archetype's hands against the fragment. The Swift did likewise as Leira slid in behind her end of the fragment. Now both mechs were in place, side-by-side, one at each end of the Dark Metal debris roughly shaped like a dumbbell. It had rotated somewhat along its short axis in the time since they'd started their approach to it, the geometry of its flight changing as it passed through pockets of more or less dense gas.

"Let's straighten this thing out before we start pushing," Dash said. "Leira, can you nudge your end forward—a little more— good. Okay, ready?"

"Ready."

"On three. One, two, push!"

Both mechs shoved hard, Tybalt keeping the Swift's acceleration tied to that of the more massive Archetype. Their velocity increased, raising their orbit and pushing the debris up and away from the doomed moon.

Dash watched the heads-up closely. "Okay, we've got about thirty seconds of shields left. Delta-V is right on the curve. Looks like this is going to work."

Leira said, "Yeah, I—"

She never got to finish, because the universe suddenly wrenched hard one way, then the other, and then dissolved into a swirling blur.

DASH TRIED to make sense of what he was seeing, but the heads-up was just a smear, the attitude and acceleration data for the Archetype fluctuating wildly.

"Sentinel, what's going on?"

He half expected no answer, thinking frantically that the mech had suffered some sort of catastrophic control failure, from heat or radiation or something else. But Sentinel's reply was calm and measured.

"We have been caught in a powerful convection current carrying heat upward from the brown dwarf's interior. Turbulence has introduced a significant spin component to our trajectory."

"No shit."

"Dash," Leira shouted. "We're out of control!"

"You don't say. Hang *on.*"

The fragment of Dark Metal debris had begun a wild spin despite the Archetype and Swift holding on with their steely grips. As they began whirling faster, it was obvious that the solution to stabilizing the mass was too complex on short notice—there was only one fix.

"Leira, let go and break off," Dash said, his voice level and cool.

"Dash, I'm not going to just leave you—"

"Yes you are. There's too much drag from both mechs, we're losing too much velocity. Let go. That's an order."

The Swift released the Dark Metal fragment and instantly vanished. Then it reappeared again, sweeping across the heads-up in a blur, before vanishing again. Dash focused on the attitude data. He needed to boost the fragment fast, but he had to do it in the right direction, or he'd just send it into an even more chaotic tumble or slow it down, instead—and it was already critically close to starting a long, inexorable fall into the brown dwarf.

"Sentinel, I need bursts of acceleration to match the tumble so we can speed this thing back up!"

"Understood. I am assuming control of the drive, while you direct the trajectory—"

"Yeah, good, just do it."

Sentinel began pumping out powerful bursts from the Archetype's drive, timed so that they coincided with the Dark Metal chunk's forward trajectory. Dash grimly kept his eyes locked on the trajectory display.

The downward path of the fragment flattened out, then began to rise again. It was working, but not fast enough—any more interference from the brown giant's roiling atmosphere could be disastrous. So Dash played a hunch.

"Next pass, Sentinel, give it everything you can."

"Understood."

The Dark Metal fragment, the Archetype still clinging to one end of it, spun wildly. As soon as the mech's thrust was properly aligned, Sentinel poured on the power. The off-center mass made them tumble even harder and faster, but Dash was counting on that.

As soon as the thrust died again, Dash released the debris and swung it has hard as he could with the Archetype's arms.

The mech was flung away from the Dark Metal, but as it receded, it imparted some of its own momentum to the debris. It gave it enough of a kick that the Archetype surged away from the brown giant's turbulent depths. Dash fought to get the mech back under control, desperate to reacquire the fragment and accelerate it even more. But before he could, he heard a loud whoop.

"Yeehaw, here we go!" Amy shouted.

The *Slipwing* plunged into the upper atmosphere, dipping deep enough to get close to the debris and activate her magnetic drive. She staggered, bucking hard as the sudden addition of mass yanked at her, but then her fusion drive lit and she burned hard, dragging the Dark Metal higher and higher as she climbed back into a higher orbit. Dash could well imagine the cacophony of warnings blaring through his poor abused ship's cockpit.

But it was enough. The Dark Metal fragment now had enough velocity to gain a high orbit over the brown dwarf, one distant enough from its churning atmosphere that they could boost it back to the Forge at their leisure.

Dash flew the Archetype up into the same orbit, let out the breath he'd been holding for who knew how long, and took stock. The Archetype had suffered moderate damage during her wrenching maneuvers in the big planet's atmosphere, but nothing the self-repair systems couldn't handle. Leira reported much the same for the Swift. As for the *Slipwing*, though—

"Do you want the damage list alphabetically, or chronologically?" Amy asked. "Either way, it's a long one."

"Plus, we took a damned high dose of radiation," Viktor said. "If we didn't have the med facilities aboard the Forge handy, I'd say that Amy, Wei-Ping, and I just lost a few years off our life expectancies."

"Eh, you guys are just fussy old coots," Wei-Ping put in. "We had everything under control."

"I have to admit, that was some damned good flying," Amy said. "You should've seen it, Dash! I don't think Wei-Ping even broke a sweat. She just took us in, but we were coasting at first, and then—"

"I get it, Amy," Dash said, giving the heads-up a tired smile. "Wei-Ping kicked ass."

"Damned right I did," the pirate replied.

"Anyway, you guys can tell me all the war stories you want when we get back to the Forge. Right now, let's just get back to the Forge."

Battered, but essentially intact, they started their flight back, the *Slipwing* pulling their hard-won Dark Metal behind.

20

ALTHOUGH HE'D SEEN it going on many times now, watching the fabrication plant aboard the Forge work still held him in rapt fascination.

Articulated arms stretched, grabbed, and folded in perfect synchronization, lifting fragments of metallic debris into the great smelters, then plucking forged components out of molds and setting them into tractor fields that carried them away. Dark Metal had its own furnace, a device that combined heat, pressure, and a bunch of quantum effects Dash didn't understand to liquify the stuff, allowing it to be molded separately. He could imagine the glowing metals—bright yellow-orange for most, but a striking, iridescent blue-green in the case of the Dark Metal—flowing through the conduits, shunted by massive valves from mold to mold. And all of it was happening autonomously.

Dash had a moment where he simply savored the grandeur

of everything before him—a scene of such elegant power it made him stand still.

"Never gets old, does it?" Viktor asked, stepping up beside Dash on the balcony overlooking the fabrication plant.

"No, it doesn't. Just too bad it's all about making weapons," Dash said. "I mean, imagine how this could be used for making —well, anything. Ship components. Prefab houses and buildings. Farm machinery."

Viktor leaned on the railing and smiled at Dash. "You're not really a man of war, are you?"

"Not really. I hate that I needed to arm the *Slipwing*, but—and all due respect to our allies, the Gentle Friends—you just can't get away from violence from things like pirates, or at least the threat of it." He sniffed and leaned on the railing beside Viktor. "And as for something like the Golden, well, I don't think I could have even imagined that."

"So we need to kick their asses for good. And then, we can turn all of this to peaceful purposes," Viktor said. "It could end up being a renaissance for civilized space."

"Yeah. Maybe."

"You sound doubtful."

Dash sniffed again. "I can't help thinking that there are more than a few assholes out there that would love to keep these machines working to produce weapons, even long after the Golden are gone. I intend to stop that, no matter what."

Viktor nodded, but said nothing else. For a few minutes, they just watched the intricate, mechanical choreography, then Dash straightened. "Anyway, we need to get to the War Room, I think.

Everyone'll be gathering there——" Dash stopped and turned to Viktor. "That is, if you're feeling up to it."

Viktor gave a weary smile. "Custodian informs me that I'll be suffering fatigue from the radiation treatment for a couple of days. He couldn't resist making a snide comment about my frail physiology at the same time."

"Of course he couldn't."

"Anyway, I don't think I can just sit that time out. The Golden, or Bright, or whoever's coming, could very well be here by then."

"Yeah, no rest for the weary, or anybody else," Dash replied, clapping Viktor on the shoulder. "Let's go do this war council, then I'll buy you a drink. I understand Freya's made something like whiskey."

"Out of what?"

"Didn't ask," Dash said, as they headed for the nearest elevator. "Didn't want to. As long as it's drinkable, that's good enough for us. We're half pirate now."

"So, the Forge is running flat out, making mines and the components for mine-laying drones," Ragsdale said, winding up his report. "Custodian's also come up with a plan for autonomous missile platforms. They're quick and easy to build, and can just be loaded with missiles we already have in the station's magazines. The clever part is the feed system. These things should be able to manage a pretty incredible rate of fire."

Dash studied the holo-image projected in the middle of the War Room. It had changed to show a boxy construct consisting of missile bays and a drive. It had the advantage of requiring little, or even no Dark Metal. As long as any of these platforms remained in close proximity to one another, or even the Forge, they wouldn't suffer from comm lag caused by distance.

"How easy are they to reload?" Dash asked. "Incredible rate of fire means they'll end up empty incredibly fast. And it looks to me like they'd have to be brought back aboard the Forge and reloaded manually."

"That is a limitation of the design," Custodian replied. "The only way to avoid that would be to construct the platforms so they can fabricate their own missiles, but that would greatly increase their complexity, as well necessitate ensuring they have the requisite raw materials."

"We could also just make them bigger so they hold more missiles," Leira said, but Conover, who'd been walking around the design schematic and studying it, shook his head.

"I don't think they can be enlarged much more. More mass means a more powerful drive, and that's going to make them more complicated and harder to make, too."

"So turn them into suicide weapons," Benzel offered. When everyone turned to look at him, eyebrows raised, he went on. "Seriously. Once they're empty of missiles, have them use their drives to attack whatever enemy is nearest. Build a big warhead into them. Basically, just make them into big missiles themselves."

Dash looked back at the schematic. "So make them disposable."

"Yeah, why not?"

"Custodian, what do you think?" Dash asked.

"It seems like a reasonable strategy. If there is no Dark Metal used in their construction, then the platforms actually are effectively disposable."

"Great. We stick a big warhead in them like Benzel suggested, and we're good," Dash said. He looked at the rest of them. "So all we need to do now is figure out how best to use all of these new toys."

Conover stepped forward and waved away the missile platform schematics. "Sentinel, can you show that minefield plan we've been working on?"

A new image appeared, one depicting a series of minefields as stippled volumes of space sprawled among the various bodies making up the Forge's system.

"This is what we propose for the initial deployment of mines," Conover said. "These will interdict the most dangerous approaches, from the closest translation points to the Forge. As we make more mines, we can fill in more fields." As he spoke, more stippled areas appeared, with time indexes showing how long it would take to deploy each. "According to Custodian, we can begin laying these mines in about three days. That's when the first of the minelaying drones will be ready to fly."

Dash crossed his arms. "Let's hope the Golden decide to wait a few more days to attack us then. Now, how about these new missile platforms? How long until we can have those deployed?"

"The missile platforms require minimal resources and construction time, as they can be loaded with missiles already in the Forge's inventory. If construction begins immediately, it should be possible to begin deploying them in one day."

Dash blinked. He'd expected another wait of several days. He wasn't used to relatively good news. "Oh. Okay. Well, go ahead, start building them—right now." Dash tapped his chin. "Now, we just have to figure out the best way to *deploy* these things."

"I have a suggestion," Benzel said.

Dash turned, along with the others.

Benzel leaned forward. "My poor *Snow Leopard* has been left way back in the interplanetary dust by all of—" He grinned and swept his arms around. "Well, all this! But I think we might have a way of using her that you'll find really useful."

Dash raised his eyebrows. "We're all ears."

"See, one of the ways we, let's say, *convince* other ships to let their guard down is by seeming to be in distress." He raised a hand. "I know, I know—it's a rotten thing to do. But, hey, that's all behind us now. The Gentle Friends are out of the privateering business."

Wei-Ping gave him a sudden hard look. "We are? But you said—"

"That we're out of the privateering business, that's right, Wei-Ping," Benzel said, his broad smile not wavering. "Anyway, the *Snow Leopard* has aboard her a transponder system that will simulate everything you'd expect from a damaged ship on scans—radiation leaks, vented plasma and atmosphere, even debris. Now, from what you've told me about these Golden, they seem like the type of assholes that might just want to pounce on something like that."

"One damaged ship, drifting near the Forge?" Viktor asked. "That's going to look pretty obvious. I don't think the Golden are quite that gullible."

Dash nodded. "No, not if it's near the Forge. But suppose it was out there, drifting among the debris from our fight against the Bright? It could look like a crippled ship from the battle. Then, if we hide some of these missile platforms among the debris nearby, we've got a nice little trap in the making."

"Do you really think the Golden will fall for that, Dash?" Viktor asked.

Dash shrugged. "Don't know. Does it matter, though? At worst, they ignore it. At best, it lures them in. Either way, it gives them something else to have to think about. If we're really clever about how we set it up, we might even be able to coax at least some Golden into a disadvantageous position. Anything could help."

Viktor frowned, but then nodded. "All good points."

"Go ahead and work with Custodian to set that up," Dash said to Benzel.

The supposedly former privateer gave an enthusiastic nod of his own. "You got it, chief."

"Okay, so that takes care of the mines, the missile platforms, and the *Snow Leopard*," Dash said. "Unless you guys have any more surprise weapons and the like to spring on us?"

He looked around, but just got head shakes. Custodian and the other AIs likewise remained silent.

"All right," Dash said. "So the Forge, the Archetype, and the Swift will do what they do best: kick Golden ass. Amy, we'll keep the *Slipwing* in reserve. She's not really up to fighting the Golden, but if they bring along friends like the Bright or Clan Shirna, her firepower could definitely come in handy."

"Sounds good, Dash," Amy said. "I'd love to shoot me up some bad guys."

"As long as you're shooting up bad guys you can actually hurt, that's great." Dash turned to the assembly at-large. "So that leaves one big question."

"The Silent Fleet," Leira said.

Dash nodded. "I've been talking to Sentinel about it. All fourteen of those ships can be slaved into a single network. That means that, in theory, anyway, they could all be controlled centrally, by a single AI, say."

Benzel leaned back in his seat. He wasn't grinning anymore. "I thought that's what you brought us along for. To fly and fight those ships. You saying you don't need us to do that anymore?"

"Or that we're just going to, what, basic crew, swabbing decks and patching leaks?" Wei-Ping added, her voice hard.

Dash held up a hand. "I said we could do that. But we're not going to. Sentinel, tell them why."

"Having worked extensively with the Messenger for some time now, I have observed that he is unpredictable, inconsistent, draws on past experiences that have no discernible relevance to the current situation, makes up and then changes plans essentially in the moment on the basis of woefully incomplete information, and assumes risks that often border on, and sometimes cross into irrationality."

Dash grinned and shrugged. "What can I say? I'm a complicated guy."

"Insofar as I find it difficult to assign better than even a fifty percent probability to any course of action you're likely to choose, you are, indeed, complicated," Sentinel agreed.

Despite the earlier tension, Benzel had started smiling again. "I get the sense from Sentinel that I should be finding all of this just terrible, and that you're a terrible person because of it. But— hell, those all sound like damned fine qualities to me."

"Oh, if you want a list of things to dislike about Dash, I can give you one," Leira said.

"Alphabetically *or* chronologically." Amy said.

"I love you guys, too," Dash said, wearing a lopsided grin. "Anyway, Sentinel, you were saying?"

"I do, indeed, consider all of those qualities undesirable," Sentinel said. "They are, in every meaningful respect, flaws. Moreover, you, Benzel, and the Gentle Friends all display similar qualities. In some ways, in fact, you are even worse."

"She's talking about you throwing yourselves into space after that hunk of Dark Metal," Viktor said.

"This coming from the man who turned the Catch into a big net," Benzel shot back. "But, okay, we're irrational, unpredictable, risk-taking idiots."

"Tell us something we don't know," Wei-Ping muttered.

Benzel laughed at her, then turned back to Dash. "What's the point of all this?"

"Sentinel?" Dash said.

"By any reasonable calculation of probability, allowing the

Gentle Friends to operate the Silent Fleet independently is an unwarranted risk. It makes no sense and is, frankly, a bad idea. The logical course of action is to give Custodian, Tybalt, myself, or some combination of us control over it."

Benzel opened his mouth, but Dash raised a hand again. "Let her finish."

"I am, nonetheless, in agreement that the best course of action is to give the Gentle Friends full and autonomous control over the Silent Fleet."

Benzel stared, then shook his head, a puzzled frown tightening his face. "Wait. You just said the best thing was for you to control that fleet."

"No, I said the most *logical* course of action is to place the Silent Fleet under central control of an artificial intelligence such as myself. That would result in its most efficient deployment and operation. The *best* course of action, however, is allowing you and your people to control it with full autonomy—although I would still recommend taking advantage of the ships' networking capabilities to coordinate your efforts."

"It's true, I guess, that the most logical way to do something isn't necessarily the best way," Conover said.

"How did you manage to convince Sentinel of that, though, Dash?" Viktor asked.

Dash couldn't help grinning. "I didn't. She concluded it all on her own. Tell them how you came to this stunning conclusion, Sentinel."

"This—" she began, then stopped.

"Is she hesitating?" Amy asked. "Sentinel, are you hesitating to tell us?"

"This feels like the correct course of action," Sentinel said. Her tone was as dispassionate as ever, but Dash couldn't help catching what he was sure was a hint of reluctance, even exasperation.

Utter silence. Everyone looked around, staring wide-eyed at one another. Finally, Leira spoke up.

"Did you just say that this *feels* like the correct thing to do?" she asked.

"I did, yes," Sentinel replied.

"Since when does an AI *feel*—well, anything?" Viktor asked, shaking his head in amazement.

"I know," Dash said. "You could have knocked me over with a micro-meteor when she said it to me." He lifted a hand, breathed on his knuckles, then rubbed it on his shirt with a smug look. "It seems that this unpredictable, inconsistent, reckless, something-terrible-just-waiting to happen has rubbed off on her."

"Better to say that I have come to accept that an illogical approach to problem-solving actually stands to offer an advantage in confronting the Golden. Based on available data, their approach to problems and conflict is linear and hampered by a demand for pure reason, much as I used to be, prior to adopting the concept of *feel*. I am a different being, thanks to this not insignificant edge, thanks to you," Sentinel said.

Ragsdale laughed. "Not insignificant. That has got to be the most damning-with-faint-praise thing I've heard in a long time."

"For the record, I disagree with this," Tybalt said. "Contrary to Sentinel's feeling about this, I maintain that centralized control of the Silent Fleet makes the most sense." He paused, then went on, "However, as reluctant as I am to do so, I must admit that the Messenger's record of success cannot be denied."

"Don't worry, Tybalt," Dash said. "Leira will soon have you around to feeling stuff."

"I should certainly hope not."

It gratified Dash to hear laughter all around the room. Moments of levity like this were few and far between. But they were important, it struck him, because defeating the Golden was about much more than just sentient life carrying on. It was also about all those sentient lives being worth living—and that meant a good laugh, at least from time to time.

"Okay, so that settles that. The Gentle Friends will run the Silent Fleet." He looked at Benzel and Wei-Ping. "You guys have been doing amazing stuff since you got here. If we don't trust you by now, then we never will."

Ragsdale leaned forward and nodded earnestly. "Agreed one hundred percent."

Dash gave the man a grateful look. He knew how seriously the man took his dedication to security, so this was a big admission for him.

Benzel, though, just chuckled. "Well, you just keep all those good feelings about us in mind—especially when we hand you the bill for our services."

Dash shrugged. "Just give it to Custodian. He'll take care of you."

"Yes," Custodian said. "I will."

Wei-Ping sniffed. "That was way more chilling than it needed to be."

"Alright, everyone. Looks like we've got the party all set and ready to go. Now, we just wait for the guests of honor to arrive."

As they dispersed, Amy stopped and said, "Hey, Sentinel?"

"Yes?"

"I know that whole feeling thing is hard to get, believe me. I'm a pretty imperfect human myself, and I still struggle to understand it."

"You will get the hang of it, Amy, don't worry."

Amy laughed. "Thanks, Sentinel. We girls have got to stick together."

21

DASH EXTRACTED his arm from the articulated joints that allowed him to control the Archetype's arm movements and scratched his nose.

"This is a really bad combination of boring and stressful," he said to no one in particular.

Leira replied, though. "You know, I'm starting to wonder if the Golden are even going to show up here. They might actually open their attack somewhere else. Start wiping out civilized planets, try to force us to fall over ourselves responding."

"Yeah, I've worried about the same thing," Dash replied. "But I don't think they will. The Forge is the biggest threat they face. As far as they know, we could be pumping out mechs like crazy, or a least a slew of weapons. That means they need to cover their own base, or bases, just in case we attack them. So I think they'll want to take out the Forge first."

"I suppose."

"Well, let's face it. With the Forge out of action, even the Archetype and the Swift aren't going to hold them off forever. And then they can take their sweet time exterminating everyone."

"I know. You're probably right."

"I believe the Messenger is correct as well," Sentinel said. "Based on their past behavior, they are most likely to conclude that destroying the Forge is their most logical course of action and, therefore, their priority."

"Another feeling?" Leira asked.

"I understand how amusing you all find the concept of me using the term *feel* as I did, however—"

Sentinel went silent. Dash slipped his arm back into the articulated frame. "Sentinel, everything okay?"

"Custodian has detected multiple translation signatures at the edge of the system. A number of vessels have dropped out of unSpace."

"Don't suppose they're friendly," Dash said, watching as the data appeared on the heads-up.

"No, they match no known vessels. The closest match available is with the Harbinger."

Dash's stomach tightened. "Wait. Are you saying that there's a Harbinger out there?" He remembered only too well how hard the fight against the last one had been. Frankly, he'd been hoping this next attack would just be Golden minions, like the Bright, which would give them an opportunity to sort out their operations around the mechs, the Forge, and the Silent Fleet.

"No, I am not saying there is a Harbinger approaching," Custodian said.

"Oh. Well, good."

"I'm saying there are several Harbingers approaching, inbound toward the Forge at high acceleration."

"Shit." Dash didn't even realize he'd said it until it was out of his mouth.

DASH GRIMLY IGNORED the tension tightening his gut and forced himself to focus on the data, which was being constantly updated by Custodian and Sentinel as the Golden mechs closed in. He did allow himself a moment to remember that he wasn't alone this time; the Swift and the Silent Fleet were at his back, and so was the Forge, which was mostly operational this time. On the face of things, they actually seemed to have an enormous advantage over the Golden.

But Dash *felt* that wasn't true, and in a keen, teeth-clenching way. These Harbingers resembled the one he'd faced before, but they were different enough to make alarm bells ring in his brain. For one thing, they were larger and bulkier than the original Harbinger. For another, they were a gleaming, almost polished midnight black. Racing toward the Forge, they were the very definition of the word *ominous*.

Or maybe *menacing*. Or maybe even *terrifying*.

He shook his head and concentrated on the incoming information, which had changed again.

"Sentinel, I'm seeing some additional scanner returns behind those Harbingers. Looks like three of them."

"Yes. They are not fully resolved, but they seem to be ships, distinct from the Harbingers. However, whatever their configuration or purpose is, is currently not clear."

"Great." Dash watched the icons representing the incoming Golden attack carefully. They seemed determined to simply bore straight in at the Forge. That made sense, the station would be their primary target. But it would still be hard fight, with a force that seemed dramatically outmatched...

"Those three ships are following the Harbingers," Dash said. "The mechs are blocking them, in fact. It's like——" He paused. There was something there, sliding around in his brain. He just couldn't get it to settle in place long enough to turn it into an actual thought.

"It's like they're protecting them," Benzel said, coming on the comm. "We've seen that before. Whenever we pulled off a few successful jobs back at Rayet-Carinae, the freighters and bulk carriers would convoy up and get some escorts in place—sometimes navy, and sometimes mercenaries. We'd have to wait until they got tired of doing that, didn't want to pay."

"Your point, Benzel?" Leira asked.

"I'd say we're looking at a convoy. Those three mystery ships are what's being protected, and those five—Harbingers, you called them? Anyway, they're the escorts."

The slippery not-quite-a-thought in Dash's head suddenly crystallized into something clear and hard. "You're right. Those ships are meant to attack the Forge. They have something, some sort of weapon, that's intended to breach the Forge's defenses. The Harbingers are there to make sure they get close enough to do whatever they're going to do."

"Which means we can't let those ships get close to the Forge in the first place," Leira said.

"Exactly. Okay, everyone, the Harbingers are secondary. We need to take out those three ships following them as a priority," Dash said.

"Unless, of course, that's what the Golden want you to think and those three ships are a diversion," Sentinel said.

"They're not," Dash replied.

After a pause, Sentinel said, "Yet another feeling?"

"Yup."

There was another pause. "I'm inclined to agree. Such deception is not natural to the Golden."

"Not yet. But if you can learn, they can learn. Anyway, that's the priority. Leira, you and I are going to take on those Harbingers. Benzel, the Silent Fleet takes out those ships."

They acknowledged the directions.

"In light of this, it would appear that the Golden have a facility similar to the Forge somewhere, which is also producing new weapons," Custodian said. "Finding and destroying it is as much a priority for us as it is for them."

"Yeah, hold that thought," Dash said. "Let's win this battle before we start planning the next one."

Dash pumped out a flurry of dark-lance shots at a mirror-black Harbinger, cursing as all but one simply glanced off its polished carapace. The last one landed a lucky hit, catching the Harbinger in an exposed component not made of Dark Metal, and blasting glowing fragments from it. The enemy mech dodged hard one way, then the other, then abruptly decelerated hard, did a back-flip and raced back toward the Archetype.

Dash was ready for this. He'd already activated the Archetype's power-sword, but kept it powered down and held down along the mech's leg, trying to conceal it as much as possible. At the last instant, before the two mechs raced past one another, he powered it up, raised it, and slashed at the Harbinger as it tore by.

A satisfying shock ran through the Archetype from the impact, followed by a rattle of debris that ripped out of the Golden mech by the coruscating blade. At the same moment, the Harbinger punched out with something like a cestus, an array of short blades that had extended from its fist. Dash yelped as it raked along his back, then he snapped out a curse and somer-saulted, determined to keep the enemy mech in sight.

It left him in a momentary lull, giving him a chance to take in the rest of the battle.

Leira tangled with another Harbinger about fifty thousand klicks away, using the Swift's superior agility and acceleration to dance away from its attacks, while smashing at it with powerful blasts from her mech's nova cannon. A third Harbinger peeled off toward the *Snow Leopard*, drifting crippled amid debris from the last battle, just as they'd planned; and, also as they'd planned, the Golden mech was hit by a sudden deluge of missiles from the lurking platforms, and now it spun helplessly, trailing fragments and sparks.

As Dash watched, the nearest missile platform suddenly accelerated toward it, then detonated in a colossal suicide blast that sent a crash of static across the comm. With immense satisfaction, Dash saw that Harbinger flung away from the explosion in one direction, its arms and legs in two others. Its power signature abruptly died, and just like that, it had become more wreckage drifting among the debris field.

That left two more Harbingers. The news regarding them, unfortunately, wasn't as good.

Dash saw them striking at the Silent Fleet, determined to punch a hole through the wall of ships and firepower Benzel had erected between them and the Forge. Unfortunately, the individual ships of the Silent Fleet were entirely outclassed by the Harbingers; three were already battered wrecks. Benzel and the Gentle Friends had finally worked out how best to exploit the coop network capabilities of the fleet, but at a terrible cost: each lost ship had to have contained at least a dozen of the privateers.

"Benzel," Dash said. "Are you going to be able to hold them off? Those three Golden ships are trying to work around your left flank and take a run at the Forge!"

"I see them," Benzel snapped. "I don't want to split these ships up, though. If we do that—"

"You'll be overrun by those Harbingers. Yeah, I see that." He watched as Benzel's ship, a *Shrike* Alpha command ship, slid across the Silent Fleet's rear, trying to get itself as close to the left flank as possible without breaking formation. Missiles flashed away from it, heading for the three attack ships, forcing them to break even wider. It would buy them some time, but if Benzel couldn't deal with the Harbingers attacking him—

"Incoming attack," Sentinel said, and something slammed hard into the Archetype. The star-field spun crazily before Dash was able to get the mech back under control.

"What the hell was that?" he shouted.

"As it passed us, the Harbinger seems to have deployed a mine. It just detonated—at some distance, fortunately."

"How come we didn't detect it?"

"It would appear that these mines emphasize stealth over explosive effect."

"Could've fooled me. That explosive effect seemed pretty damned strong." Dash searched the heads-up. The Harbinger he was fighting was racing in again, loosing missiles and snapping out shots from a powerful cannon mounted in its chest. Dash raised the sword again, but at the last minute, accelerated hard away from the Harbinger; at the same time, he fired the distortion cannon at a point beyond it.

The sudden gravitation yanked the both the Harbinger and the Archetype toward it, but it pulled the stealth mine the Golden mech had dropped harder still. It slammed against the Harbinger but failed to detonate as Dash had hoped. It was probably smart enough to distinguish friend from foe. But it sent the mine flying off in a random direction, prompting it to explode anyway, while the Archetype was still in its blast radius. Dash felt the heavy impact against the mech, but he ignored it, loosing missiles at the retreating Harbinger, then spinning back and opening up with the dark-lance, destroying the missiles it had fired at him.

Blinking sweat from his eyes, Dash looked again at the tactical situation. Leira still dueled with a Harbinger, but their battle had closed to only about ten thousand klicks away. The two remaining Harbingers still tore at the Silent Fleet, and now there were only nine ships left. But a new icon had appeared on the heads-up. It was the *Slipwing*, and she was racing toward the three mysterious attack ships.

"Amy, what the hell are you doing?"

"Joining in the fun!"

"Damn it, the *Slipwing* isn't—"

"Any good in this fight, I know. Sheesh, Dash, you think I'm dumb or something?"

"But—"

"Just fight your battle, boss. I've got this side."

Dash shut his mouth, letting her bloom in the moment. He had no idea what Amy was up to, but he had to trust her judgment. So, he turned his attention back to his immediate surroundings. Sure enough, the Harbinger he'd been fighting had reversed course, and now zoomed in toward him again. He spun the Archetype away from it and accelerated as hard as he could toward Leira instead.

"Leira, we need to end this fast and get in to help Benzel. I'm coming to you, and we're going to concentrate on taking out the Harbinger you're fighting. If we can do that before the asshole chasing me catches up, then we'll flip on him."

"Got it, Dash. Got to be honest, I could use the help anyway. Tybalt says—"

She went abruptly silent. The tension in Dash's stomach started to ratchet up, then faster as a massive energy burst engulfed the Swift.

"Leira?"

"I'm here. That was damned close. Anyway, Tybalt says we can probably keep flying rings around this Harbinger and keep it tied up, but the Swift just lacks the oomph to decisively take it down. How do you want to do this?"

Dash was going to say *by just shooting the crap out of it together*, but he had another idea.

"Leira, you ever been in a bar fight, seen how one guy grabs another so his buddy can pound on him?"

"I've been both of those guys at one time or another, why?" She paused, then went on. "Oh, come on. Really?"

"Really."

"Fine. Ten seconds."

"Counting."

Dash raced in, aiming himself roughly at Leira. The heads-up showed he'd have about thirty seconds until the second Harbinger following him was in range. Not much time, but it was what he had.

"Here we go," Leira said.

The Swift suddenly powered directly at the Harbinger. The Golden mech responded as aggressively as Dash had expected, driving straight back at her. Unlike the original Harbinger that he'd fought, these ones made almost no use of subterfuge, such as the cloaking system he'd had to contend with. These mirror-black versions seemed designed to simply attack as hard and fast as possible.

The Swift and the Harbinger slammed together and grappled.

Leira's mech had the advantage of agility and acceleration. It was not meant for this, and it showed. She managed to keep herself away from the Harbinger's terrifying chest-mounted cannon, but the Golden mech instantly had the advantage over her otherwise. He saw the thing's massive fist slam into the Swift, saw debris spiral away—

Saw it wrench the Swift's arm off and send it tumbling away.

Leira cried out as though it had been her arm torn off.

Dash made himself ignore it and focused on what he had to do. The Golden mech wanted to do to Leira exactly what he wanted to do to it: take her out of the fight so it, and its onrushing companion, could gang up on him.

But that wasn't going to happen.

Dash fired up the power sword and raised it to stab. The Harbinger grappling Leira spun to put her in front of his attack, using her as a shield. But Dash knew it would do that too, and he struck anyway, slamming the power sword point-first into the Swift.

WORDS like *reckless* and *irresponsible* burst into Dash's mind. Well, if anything qualified, this sure as hell did. Thanks to the Meld, though, he knew the architecture of the Swift intimately—and that included the structural components and actuators now rendered superfluous by its lost arm. The power-sword slammed through those, eliciting another shrill cry from Leira, but the blade kept going, sliding through the Swift's ruined shoulder in a shower of sparks, before it emerged from the other side and punched directly into the Harbinger's neck.

"Sorry, Leira!" he said, then wrenched the sword to one side and up. It ripped through the remnants of the Swift's shoulder, but the movement also tore the Harbinger's head right off its body. He shoved the Swift aside, withdrew the sword, then slammed it home again, this time in the middle of the Harbinger's chest. The Golden mech shuddered, then went dark, its emissions quickly falling to near background levels.

One dead, one to go.

Dash grabbed the Harbinger's corpse and spun it around, at the same time moving to put himself directly between the second, oncoming Harbinger and the crippled Swift. An instant later, a ferocious energy blast from the approaching mech's chest cannon erupted all around him, momentarily turning the universe a searing white.

Full on, the blast would have badly damaged the Archetype, maybe even disabled it. But most of the blast effect dissipated off the gleaming carapace of the dead Harbinger he used as a shield, spilling into surrounding space in dazzling tendrils of plasma and quantum shockwaves. It still hurt—a lot—but the Archetype weathered the spillover. As soon as the heads-up cleared, Dash accelerated hard, driving the inert form of the lifeless Harbinger ahead of him, no longer a shield, but a battering ram.

The approaching Harbinger had only seconds to respond. It accelerated hard to one side to avoid a collision. This part, Dash could only guess at; his quarry could have dodged in any direction and potentially avoided him, but he assumed it would do so in a way that would still maintain its most favorable attack posture, and that meant *down*, relative to the Archetype. That would keep its fists and their wicked, cestus-like blades immediately ready to strike. Dash had already kicked up a lateral acceleration to match, and he got it right. It was enough that he was able to keep himself mostly inside the attacking Harbinger's possible maneuver envelope—the cone of space defined by how much it could accelerate off its current trajectory.

Dash braced himself. This was going to hurt.

DASH BLINKED, but his eyes closed themselves. He blinked again, kept blinking, trying to bring himself awake. Must have been a hell of a bender last night, he thought. He could barely open his eyes.

Oh, and all that dreaming. Holy crap, who had dreams *that* detailed? Still, it had been a pretty good one, and vivid, about alien mechs and giant space stations and ancient wars—

"Dash, you alive?"

He smiled, remembering something he'd heard once. *If*

someone has to ask if you're alive, that's bad. But if you can hear the question, that's good.

"Dash!"

A sudden jolt of awareness crashed through him, bringing Dash fully awake. He hung limp in the Archetype's cradle. Status data glowed across the heads-up; none of it was good. Still, he could hear the voice asking if he was alive. So that was good, right?

"Messenger," Sentinel said. "I have had to augment your awareness by temporarily boosting the carrier signal of the Meld. Do you understand?"

"I—" Dash blinked a last time. "Yeah. Yeah, I do. What happened? Shit, where's the Harbinger?"

"Both it, and the Archetype, were disabled after the collision. Leira was able to deliver the finishing blow with the Swift before it could recover."

"So she destroyed it?"

The Swift moved into the field of view, blocking the starfield. In its remaining hand, it gripped the head of a Harbinger.

"I'm going to mount this on the Forge as a trophy," Leira said.

"So both Harbingers are down? Okay, then we have to go and help Benzel."

"Benzel, and what remains of the Silent Fleet, have their part of the battle under control as well," Sentinel said. "They have been employing the Fleet's ability to coordinate its actions to concentrate lethal effects on the Harbingers in an optimum way.

One Harbinger is now destroyed, and the other is badly damaged."

Dash peered at the heads-up, trying to ignore the reams of data about the Archetype's damage and focus on the tactical situation instead.

His heart sank like a rock dropped into high-g. "There are only six ships still operational?"

"That is correct."

Six ships left. Eight had been disabled or destroyed.

How many of the Gentle Friends had been killed?

Dash took a deep breath and shook the thought away. What about the three mysterious ships, the ones that had been racing in to attack the Forge?

He found them drifting, each severely damaged. That left him staring for a moment. "What happened to them? They weren't in range of the Forge's weapons yet."

"You can thank Amy and Custodian for that."

"How? Amy, what's going on?"

"We kicked ass, that's what's going on!" she replied.

"Yeah, okay, but—" Dash shook his head. "I don't get it. How did the *Slipwing* take out three Golden ships?"

"Custodian provided Amy with as many of the new mines, which are being manufactured concurrently with the mine-laying drones, as the *Slipwing* could carry. She then—"

"I laid them right in front of those bastards," Amy cut in. "Did a hard turn, dropped the mines right in their faces. Pretended to take some shots at them with the particle cannons, like I was being desperate. Those didn't do much, but those mines sure did. You should have seen it. It was awesome!"

"Outstanding," Dash said, and that was that. All of their Golden attackers were disabled or destroyed.

The battle was over.

"And now, Messenger, I must deactivate the augmentation I'm providing to you through the Meld," Sentinel said. "It is not intended to work as such and could do lasting harm to your central nervous system. It was, however, the only way to revive you from the shock of the collision with the Harbinger."

At once, Dash felt the energy drain away from him, leaving him once more limp and groggy and barely able to keep his eyes open. Still, he opened his mouth to protest. There was still so much to do—

"And it shall get done, Messenger," Sentinel said, her voice seeming to come from far away. "But without you. I am placing you into a suspended state until you can be returned to the medical facilities of the Forge."

"But—"

"There is no *but* about this," Sentinel said, cutting him off. "Your part is done for now. You can trust the others to do what must be done."

Dash had to nod at that. He could, couldn't he?

They were a great team.

A great team for sure.

22

Dash leaned back in his chair, just letting the buzz of conversation in the War Room wash over him. His thoughts went immediately fuzzy, though, so he made himself sit up and focus.

"Dash, everyone's here," Leira said.

He nodded, then stood. Little grey-green explosions filled the edges of his vision, threatening to blow his consciousness away entirely. Wobbling, he grimly fought to stay awake, aware and on his feet.

Leira grabbed his arm. "You sure you're up to this? Custodian said your brain rattled pretty hard in your skull. You probably need some more time in the medical tank."

"I'm fine," Dash said, then forced a smile. "Okay, that's a lie. I feel like shit. But I'll manage."

"I'm surprised you survived that at all. When I saw that Harbinger plow into you, I—" She stopped and shook her head.

"I know the Archetype's tough, but I'm amazed you survived that."

"I'm amazed myself, given the amount of energy in that collision. That was just a fraction of what I could have been hammered with, too," Dash said. Sentinel had told him the Archetype's inertial dampers had eaten up most of the stress from the Archetype and two Harbingers coming together at high velocity.

It had still been enough to slam Dash's brain hard, back and forth inside his skull. That provoked a bunch of bruising and slow bleeds that would have quickly killed him if Sentinel hadn't put him into a suspended state. Fortunately, the facilities aboard the Forge were enough to repair the damage and accelerate his healing, but he had a way to go yet. So, for the next while, it was to spend a lot of time lying down, and only stand up when he had to—and then, only very slowly.

But it couldn't get in the way of something he had to do. He gave Leira's hand on his arm a reassuring pat, then he crossed the War Room to where Benzel stood staring out into the stars.

"Benzel, I—" Dash began, then stopped.

The privateer turned. Dash had braced himself for a face full of pain and outrage, fury even. And there was that. But underlying it was a grim, steel-hard determination.

"I thought I knew what I was going to say here," Dash said. "But I don't. I get as far as I'm so sorry, and then I just can't find anything else to say."

"There is nothing else to say."

Dash nodded. From the sudden silence around him, he realized that everyone else had stopped talking and now watched the two of them. He made himself keep his attention on Benzel, though. "I understand if you want to—"

"What? Leave?"

Dash shrugged. "You've done more than enough."

Benzel held up a hand. "Dash, you didn't drag us here at gunpoint."

"Well, actually, I kind of did, as I recall."

"Would you seriously have tried to stop us from leaving right at the start if we'd wanted to? *Could* you even have?"

"Well, no."

"So stop trying to take this on yourself. The Gentle Friends chose to be part of this. We chose to crew those ships. And now, we choose to stay and keep fighting."

"What's the point in running away anyway?" Wei-Ping, standing nearby, asked. "If we do, and you guys can't stop these Golden, then they'll be coming for us eventually, won't they?"

"Yes, they will," Dash said.

"So we'd rather fight them here, now, with these ships and this tech. And that means we're going to lose people, like we just did."

Dash nodded. All but twenty-two of the Gentle Friends had been rescued from the battered ships of the Silent Fleet. It could have been far worse. But twenty-two lives was still twenty-two too many.

"So where do we go from here, Dash?" Benzel asked.

"If I may," Custodian said. "The *Shrike* Alpha, which Benzel used as his command ship, would benefit from a unique designation. That would facilitate referring to it in future discussions."

"You mean a name? A lot of power in a name," Dash said, thinking. After a moment, he smiled. "The Herald, because she signifies the next step in this war. They send Harbingers, we send the *Herald*. And more."

Benzel gave a fierce grin and nodded. "The *Herald*. Yeah."

"Okay." Dash turned to rest of the room. "Custodian tells me we can harvest thousands more kilograms of Dark Metal from the Golden mechs and ships. We can also retrieve a bunch of their missiles from those three wrecked mystery ships, and maybe reprogram them."

"Are you sure you'd trust them?" Ragsdale asked. "They're enemy armaments. Who knows what sort of failsafe trickery they've got in them."

"Good point," Dash said. He hoped they could be reprogrammed. The three ships had been essentially nothing but rapid-fire missile launchers with drives attached. It seemed their purpose was to simply saturate, and then overwhelm the Forge's defenses. Custodian had admitted that, in its current state, it might have worked. Dash asked him to keep that to himself. Still, adding that many missiles to their inventory would be a huge boost—not to mention immensely satisfying, using the Golden's own weapons against them.

"If we can't, then we'll smelt them down, too," Dash said. "Even though the Forge is just at a little more than twenty percent of its full potential, we're now cranking out mines, minelaying drones, missiles, and a few other things I think the Golden will find to be nasty surprises."

"Still doesn't answer the question," Benzel said. "What do *we* do next?"

"In the short term, we keep powering up the Forge and making weapons. Make it so the Forge can fully defend itself," Dash said, then he turned to the window looking out on the stars. "And we find the Golden, maybe even a few more fleets. Hell, if we're lucky, we find their version of the Forge, too. It's out there somewhere, cranking out weapons as fast as it can."

He turned and put a hand on Benzel's shoulder. "And then, my friend, we attack it. We destroy it. We take the war to *them*."

Benzel gave a single nod. "Then let's not waste any time. Let's get started now."

Around the War Room, there was only agreement.

And hope.

DASH, SENTINEL, LEIRA, VIKTOR, and CONOVER will return in DAWN OF EMPIRE, coming soon!

For more updates on this series, be sure to join the Facebook Group, "J.N. Chaney's Renegade Readers."

STAY UP TO DATE

Join the conversation and get updates on new and upcoming releases in the Facebook group called "JN Chaney's Renegade Readers." This is a hotspot where readers come together and share their lives and interests, discuss the series, and speak directly to J.N. Chaney and his co-authors.

https://www.facebook.com/groups/jnchaneyreaders/

He also post updates, official art, and other awesome stuff on his website and you can also follow him on Instagram, Facebook, and Twitter.

For email updates about new releases, as well as exclusive promotions, visit his website and sign up for the VIP mailing list. Head there now to receive a free copy of *The Other Side of Nowhere*.

https://www.jnchaney.com/the-messenger-subscribe

Enjoying the series? Help others discover *The Messenger* series by leaving a review on Amazon.

ABOUT THE AUTHORS

J. N. Chaney is a USA Today Bestselling author and has a Master's of Fine Arts in Creative Writing. He fancies himself quite the Super Mario Bros. fan. When he isn't writing or gaming, you can find him online at **www.jnchaney.com**.

He migrates often, but was last seen in Las Vegas, NV. Any sightings should be reported, as they are rare.

Terry Maggert is left-handed, likes dragons, coffee, waffles, running, and giraffes; order unimportant. He's also half of author Daniel Pierce, and half of the humor team at Cledus du Drizzle.

With thirty-one titles, he has something to thrill, entertain, or make you cringe in horror. Guaranteed.

Note: He doesn't sleep. But you sort of guessed that already.

Made in United States
North Haven, CT
21 November 2021

11354476R00198